STONEWALL INN EDITIONS
Michael Denney, General Editor

Books by Peter McGehee

Novels
Boys Like Us
Sweetheart

Stories
Beyond Happiness
The I.Q. Zoo

SWEETHEART

Peter McGehee

St. Martin's Press
New York

SWEETHEART. Copyright © 1992 by the Estate of Peter McGehee. All rights reserved. Printed in the United States of America. No part of this book may be used or reproduced in any manner whatsoever without written permission except in the case of brief quotations embodied in critical articles or reviews. For information, address St. Martin's Press, 175 Fifth Avenue, New York, N.Y. 10010.

Library of Congress Cataloging-in-Publication Data

McGehee, Peter.
    Sweetheart / Peter McGehee.
      p.   cm.
    ISBN 0-312-07863-3 (hc)
    ISBN 0-312-09399-3 (pbk.)
    I. Title.
    PS3563.C36374S93   1992
    813'.54—dc20   92-4032
                                                      CIP

First Edition: June 1992
First Paperback Edition: June 1993

10 9 8 7 6 5 4 3 2

For my prince, Doug Wilson

AUTHOR'S NOTE

Sweetheart continues the stories of the characters introduced in *Boys Like Us*. The novels may be read independently, in sequence, or out of sequence.

Special thanks to Doug Wilson and Gail van Varseveld, the first readers of the work.

Thanks also to the Saskatchewan Writers' Colony, the Banff Centre, and Yaddo for retreat time.

CONTENTS

SWEETHEART

TIME AND OTHER BOMBS

November 1989

"Randy's ashes came today."

"They did?"

"Alan sent them from Vancouver. By courier. They're in the box on the table."

Searcy looks at it. Picks it up. Gives it a rattle.

"Any ideas about what we ought to do with them?"

"Oh, the traditional thing," Searcy says. "A tasteful scattering."

"We can't just scatter them."

"We can't?"

"No. We might need them someday."

"Need them? Need them for what?"

"I read recently about these cloning experiments where they take something like a chicken bone, put it through a process, and the next day have a real live chicken. If they can do it with chickens, surely it's just a matter of time before they'll be able to do it with humans."

"Zero, you don't really think you're gonna clone Randy back from these ashes, do you?"

"They're not just ashes. There're pieces of him in there. Good solid bone."

"Hon, Randall is dead!"

TIME AND OTHER BOMBS

I take the box from him and pace the length of the living room. "I know he's dead. But I just don't want to scatter them. Not yet. I'll get a couple of urns, nice urns. Use 'em as bookends."

"Lovely," Searcy says, ever dubious of my taste. "May we go now?"

"Of course. I was ready before you even got here."

He snorts.

I herd him out of the apartment, locking the door behind me. We pound down the staircase. His footfalls are thunderous. The entire structure shakes under his weight.

My ex-lover, David, lives on the ground floor.

Searcy raps on his door and calls, "Hurry up, hon. We're late enough as it is."

David appears an instant later, carrying a bag of fliers.

"What are those for?" asks Searcy.

"A demo I'm helping organize for the release of ddI. It's a drug for people who can't tolerate AZT."

"I *know* what it is, darling. I also know about that mother who's been sitting in front of the Bristol-Myers' offices for weeks, trying to get it for her son. Who's dying."

"*Very* good." David hands him a flier. "Perhaps I can count on you to come lend your strong voice to the protest?"

Searcy scans the information while turning up Church Street. His mere presence is enough to part the sea of pedestrians.

"Of course I'll be there," he says, folding the flier carefully and putting it into the pocket of his pantaloons. "I'd do almost anything, considering the gains we've made of late."

"Gains?" David asks sarcastically.

"Yes, gains," replies Searcy. "This is an historic day. We're about to witness the opening of Canada's first legal puff parlor. If that's not a major victory, I don't know what is."

"This pentamidine clinic is long overdue," mutters David. "And you know as well as I do it wouldn't be opening at all if it weren't for the screaming and yelling we activists have done."

"It didn't hurt matters when the medical community finally jumped on the bandwagon," I say. "Things seemed to move pretty quickly from there."

David shoots me a fiery look.

4

Searcy sighs. "Well, I just hope they haven't eaten all the hors d'oeuvres. I'm starved!"

"You're always starved."

"I have to consume a great amount of food to keep up my glorious figure."

"Has that ever been a problem?" David asks.

"You're not gonna start hounding me about my size at this point in our friendship, are you?"

"No, of course not."

A gang of young men greets Searcy enthusiastically, asking who's headlining his Gong Show this week.

"Boys," Searcy says with pride. "I've booked a cross-dresser from Sudbury. He twirls a baton, sets off firecrackers, and sings the national anthem, all at once. Thursday night. Nine-thirty. Be there or die!"

"We'll be there." They twitter off down the street, imagining the excitement of it all.

"Oh," says Searcy, rubbing his hands together. "Aren't new fans wonderful? I'm telling you, taking over that Gong Show was the smartest thing I ever could've done. Talk about staging a successful comeback!"

"Searcy, you've had more comebacks than Judy Garland, Craig Russell, and Pierre Trudeau combined," says David.

"I have not! And don't say that so loudly."

"Curious," I throw in, "that the original Gong Show host would fall down the staircase at your birthday party and break his neck."

"We don't call that curious, hon. We call that a bloody miracle! And while we're on the subject, isn't it about time for the two of you to come see it again?"

"We've seen it," says David.

"Three times," I add.

"Well, my dears, when you have a friend who is the star of a show, you simply can't see it enough."

The pentamidine clinic is located in an old house kitty-corner from the hospice. Various guests and members of the press mill about the lawn. The Celebrity AIDS Person stands on the front porch, clutching a pair of scissors. Stretched in front of him is a blue ribbon,

5

held on one side by the clinic's fund-raiser and on the other by Dr. Susan Fieldstone.

"Do you realize he's lived with this disease since before it even had a name?" David comments.

"Yes," I say. "He was a friend of Randy's."

"He works much too hard," says David, who serves on several committees with him. "Though that's probably what keeps him going."

"He's an absolute saint!" declares Searcy.

"He's a pain in the ass," says David, laughing.

The Celebrity lifts the scissors. He waves them at the crowd, then snips the ribbon with the assurance of a Ladies' Auxiliary volunteer. As the two halves float lazily to the ground, he gears up for his words. He speaks with a slow, steady cadence, each phrase carefully measured to suit his breathing capacity, which is somewhat limited thanks to five bouts of PCP.

"The purpose of this clinic," he says, "is to dispense aerosolized pentamidine, a drug that has proved extremely effective in treating, as well as preventing, PCP. Pneumocystis carini pneumonia has been the major killer of people with AIDS."

He takes a few shallow breaths, then continues. "We've fought a lot of battles. To get the government to release the drug. To put a stop to the unethical placebo trials so that all patients who need the treatment can get it. And to open this clinic today. Thanks to the work of AIDS Action Now! we've seen remarkable changes in some of our most vocal opponents, often, though not exclusively, in the medical profession itself."

I look over at Dr. Susan Fieldstone, who's staring thoughtfully at her sensible shoes.

"The bottom line is simple," continues the Celebrity. "As opportunistic infections become preventable, our hope is that Acquired Immune Deficiency Syndrome will begin to change from a terminal disease to a manageable, albeit chronic, illness. But we cannot manage AIDS without the cooperation of the government, the doctors, and the drug companies."

Big round of applause.

"It is with great pleasure that I invite you to come into the clinic and have a look around. Coffee, juice, and cookies will be served. And please make a donation. I needn't remind you there are lives at stake."

More applause.

"Brava!" shouts Searcy. "Brava, darling! Brava!"

Inside the clinic's rooms, people demonstrate how to use the nebulizers, which deliver the drug mist to the lungs. Doctors discuss dosage and the various body positions you should be in to maximize the drug's effect.

Dr. Susan Fieldstone spots me and comes over to say hello. She was Randy's doctor when he was still in Toronto, and regardless of what anyone says, she took care of him, good care.

"I suppose you've heard the news?" I ask.

She nods and smiles sympathetically.

"It was amazingly quick," I tell her. "Not at all like the usual horror story. He lost a whole bunch of weight from cryptosporidium, then got this weird brain infection. A week later, he was gone."

"Were you there?" she asks.

"Not that he knew."

"How's his friend?"

"You mean the Widow Alan? Oh, he seems to be coping. He sent me Randy's ashes. I just got them this afternoon. Say, do you know anything about cloning?"

"Some."

"Is it true each cell contains a blueprint of the entire person?"

"We call that DNA."

"Do you think they'll ever be able to clone humans?"

"I think they're doing it already." She laughs, looking around at the crowd. Then she asks, "Will there be a service of any kind?"

"We haven't decided yet. Randy didn't want one. He hated those kinds of things."

"Well if there is, let me know. I'd like to come." She squeezes my arm and moves on.

David comes up behind me, whispering, "Hypocritical bitch."

"She was just asking about Randy."

"Yeah, and if it were up to her, this clinic wouldn't even be here."

"It would, too."

"She was in charge of the trials, Zero."

"She's changed."

"She's still the doctor who gave sick people a placebo and watched them die in the name of science and research."

"Don't you think that's a little dramatic? Besides, you don't have to preach at me. I'm on your side, remember?"

"Look at her. Buddying up to everyone, so full of care and concern."

"She *does* care."

"Yeah, like a mother who feeds off her young. I don't trust her."

"You don't trust any doctor. You better hope you never get sick. When your time comes, it better be spontaneous combustion."

"Amen."

Dr. Susan Fieldstone moves in on the Celebrity AIDS Person.

David nudges me in that direction. "Come on. I'm just dying to know what she has to say to him."

"I understand," she's saying, "that during the course of your long illness you've refused all anti-viral medication, including AZT."

"So? What's it to you?" asks the Celebrity.

"Well," she continues, "your survival."

"That I attribute to luck and devil worship."

"Luck and devil worship," she mouths, wondering how this intriguing complementary therapy could have evaded her until now.

Searcy comes running up, positively bubbling. "Do you girls see that gorgeous creature over by the cookies?"

"I see several."

"The one in the middle. Just look at him! The skin on his arms is absolutely hairless. I bet his whole body is hairless. A drag queen's dream! Who *is* he? I need some information. Name, occupation, dimensions."

"He's one of the new HIV specialists," says David. "Just moved here from Edmonton."

"A doctor!" gasps Searcy. "Oh my! Oh my my my! I'm in love, l-u-v, and I want an appointment. Now!"

"Well, go over and introduce yourself."

"I can't just walk up and introduce myself!"

"Since when did you become shy?"

"Since the moment I laid eyes on him! Desire does strange things to me, puts me in a terrible state."

Searcy grabs Dr. Susan Fieldstone. "Susan, honey, would you do me a favor?"

"It depends," she says, looking at him suspiciously.

"Introduce me to your new colleague from Edmonton."

"You mean Garth? Sure, I see no harm in that."

"Garth," Searcy repeats, swooning. "What a beautiful name. Have you ever heard a more beautiful name?" He waltzes off with Susan Fieldstone, confiding, "I have achieved many dreams in this life, but the one I've yet to realize is marriage to a doctor."

"Shameless," says David. "I'm getting another juice. You want one?"

"Sure."

David heads for the refreshment table and I mosey over to the Celebrity AIDS Person to offer my congratulations. "Great ribbon cutting," I say.

"Thanks."

"So how you doin'?"

"Fabulous," he says wryly. "Any minute I'm gonna run a marathon."

"I don't know why I keep forgetting you don't like to be asked that."

"Yeah, well, you needn't waste any time being polite, either. Say what you've got to say and be done with it."

"I just thought I'd tell you, in case you hadn't heard, that Randy died."

He considers the news. He takes an index card from his shirt pocket. The card is covered with marks, messy little pencil scratches. He adds one.

"That a tally of all your dead friends?" I ask.

"Yes," he replies.

"Must be a hundred marks on that thing. You know that many people?"

"That many and more. How many have you known?"

"Just a few dozen." I say it with a choke in my throat, as if I'm about to cry.

The Celebrity says, "I haven't shed a tear since 1987." He puts the index card away. "Being on a first-name basis with the dead helps."

"I'll remember that."

It is not the Celebrity's habit to say good-bye, to say see you later, or to conclude any conversation whatsoever. He simply prefers to let one moment drift into the next, so I move back into the crowd without pretense.

I notice a guy looking at me, smiling.

It takes me a minute, then I smile back.

Eventually, he walks over and introduces himself. "I'm Jeff Lake," he says, extending his hand. He's got big hands and long, sexy fingers.

"Zero MacNoo."

"I know." He grins. "I follow your column in *City Magazine*. I just wanted to tell you how much I enjoy it."

"Thanks. I somehow never tire of hearing that." Is he flirting with me?

"So," he says, surveying the crowd. "Good place to gather material, huh?"

"Well, you never know where inspiration may strike." Pause. "And what keeps you busy?"

"Actually," he says, "I'm sort of retired. I used to be an accountant, if you can believe it. I can't."

"You look a little young to be retired. How'd you ever manage that?"

"Well, when I found out I was seropositive I did a lot of reevaluating," he says bluntly. "I figured I might as well start doing some of the things I'd always wanted to."

"Like what?"

"Help get this clinic open, for one. And the usual things: books I want to read, music I want to learn, places I want to visit, people I want to meet. Like you." He smiles again. So he is flirting with me.

David walks by and hands me a glass of juice. He takes in the sight of Jeff, grins to himself, and keeps right on going.

"Who's that?" Jeff asks. "Not your lover?"

"My ex-lover."

"But you're not still together?"

"We're friends."

"That's nice."

"Yes, it took some doing, but it is."

10

November 1989

He shifts his weight from one leg to the other. "So," he says, "maybe I could take you to dinner sometime?"

"Sure. When?"

"How 'bout tonight?"

We both laugh.

"Or if tonight's not good—" he begins.

"No, tonight's fine. I mean, what are we waiting for?" I slip my arm through his. "We've done this opening. Let's go."

We make our way over to Church Street, chatting amiably. We end up at Bersani's, dining on designer pizza. You know the kind: sourdough crust topped with caviar, cilantro, and lemon rind.

"Are you originally from Toronto?" I ask, taking a sip of my beer.

"Ottawa," Jeff says. "My lover was transferred here in '87. We'd been together since university."

"When'd you split up?"

"Bryan died. Last October."

"Oh. I'm sorry to hear that. How long was he sick?"

"A few years. I kept him at home as long as I could, but in the end I just couldn't keep up with it all. Then"—he snaps his fingers—"he was gone. Just like that. It was all over. Everything was quiet. I thought I was prepared. You're never prepared. I really went off the deep end for a while." He laughs wearily.

"What'd you do?"

"Developed an unexplainable hatred for people in good health."

"I can relate."

"One day I really went berserk. Almost stabbed one of my co-workers with a letter opener just for making a bad joke. That's when I realized it was either time to cash it in or find some way to rejoin the living."

"I'm glad you chose the latter."

"Well, if you're a survivor, you ought to survive, right?"

"Right."

"I take it you've been tested?"

"Yeah, about a year ago. Along with everyone else I know. I'd always assumed I was positive, so it was no great surprise. Still,

11

having the news confirmed wasn't exactly easy. It gave me terrible dreams. I'd see myself all shriveled up like a little mummy, sick and broke. Stuck in some cheap hotel room with nothing but a soiled mattress."

"I won't let myself get to that point," says Jeff.

"That's what my friend Randy always said. Then when he was there he didn't even know it."

Jeff shivers. "I have to keep reminding myself that we're lucky."

"We all have to keep reminding ourselves."

"There's a lot more available now than there was even a year ago."

"I know. The good ol' early intervention medicine show."

"You got it, sister. Procure your bag of anti-virals, magic potions, and get on with it."

We toast. Another sip of beer.

A moment later, Jeff says, "Sorry, Zero. I didn't mean to get into all that."

"Don't worry. It's where every conversation ends these days."

"Well, not this one. Tell me about your column."

"What do you want to know?"

"How'd you ever get the idea?"

"Just stumbled on it, really. And I was fortunate enough the magazine was interested in publishing such a thing."

"And you support yourself from it?"

"More or less."

"You *are* lucky."

"Well, don't think I didn't put in my time in the steno pool."

"My first love is the piano," he says. "I gave it up some years ago when my teacher convinced me I'd never be a virtuoso. Stupid of me. But I've started back now."

"Classical?"

"Uh-huh."

"I'd love to hear you play sometime."

"Well, we can go over to my place after dinner if you want, and I'll give you a private concert."

"Sounds great."

We smile at each other, titillated by the thought of where this night may lead.

We finish our beers.

* * *

Jeff unlocks his apartment door, flicks on a lamp. In the middle of his funky living room is a shiny baby grand.

"Nice," I say. "I'm impressed."

"Something to drink?"

"Whatever."

"Glass of wine okay?"

"Fine."

He disappears into the kitchen, then returns with two wine-glasses, each filled halfway with white wine.

"A toast," he says. "To unexpected meetings."

"Unexpectedly."

"Sit down." He indicates a chair next to the piano and settles himself on the piano bench. Bends back his hands. Rubs them together to get them ready. "Any requests?" he asks.

"Oh, whatever you feel like."

"In that case," he says, "how 'bout the Andante to Mozart's Piano Sonata in D Major? Do you know it?"

"No."

"You will now. The Mozart sonatas are the most soothing music I play."

He takes a sip of wine, pauses for a moment to gather his concentration, then launches into it.

He plays beautifully, and his hands move over the keys with a wonderful grace. I imagine them moving over me in much the same way and wonder when the last time watching someone play the piano felt so much like sex.

Jeff sits with perfect posture, eyes closed. When he finishes, he looks as if he's just woken from a dream.

"That was exceptional!" I say.

He laughs. "You must not know much about classical music."

"No," I admit, "I don't. But more, please. Educate me."

"Okay." He grins. "You asked for it. This piece is by Ravel, another favorite of mine."

It's an equally beautiful piece, though completely different, and I tell him so.

TIME AND OTHER BOMBS

"You're sweet," he says, rising from the piano, carrying his wine over to the couch.

"What's wrong with the way you play?"

"My touch is too heavy. That's what I'm working to improve."

"Do you take lessons?"

"Yeah. Over at the Conservatory." He pats the spot next to him on the couch. "Don't be such a stranger, Zero."

I get up and join him. I feel shy, and laugh nervously.

He rests his hand on my shoulder. Sips his wine. I gulp mine. He grins. "Comfortable?"

"Sure I'm comfortable. I'm just . . . unsure as to what's about to happen. That's all."

He leans in toward me. "I could kiss you," he says, then does.

"Those are some lips," I murmur.

He kisses me again. The passion grows as the kiss continues, wetter and hungrier. We snuggle up against each other and start to hug. Pulling each other's shirttails out. Running our hands along the flesh of the back, the sides.

"It's been a long time since I've done this," I say.

"Me too. If you don't want to, if you think it's too soon—"

"Oh no. I want to. I want to very much."

"What do you mean when you say you haven't done this in so long?"

"I don't know, made love, I guess. Just after I moved out of David's, I moved in with this guy, Clay. We had a really good sex life, but weren't very compatible, if you know what I mean. It didn't last long. Just a few months. And over this past year . . . Well, I've gone to the sex clubs. I've had my fun. The hot, dark nooks and crannies. You know, nice and anonymous and quick and safe."

"Searching for the moment, not a lifetime?"

"You've been there, huh?"

"I certainly have."

"After all, a guy only has so many lifetimes to give."

"You've got that one right."

An hour later we find ourselves in the bedroom, laughing and still kissing. Playfully, I push him onto the bed. He lies there before

14

me, motionless except for the slight twitch of his erection pinned in his jeans. He thinks that's what I'm after. He's wrong.

I reach for his socks and pull them off.

" 'My,' said the wolf, 'what beautiful feet you have.' " Gently, I begin to suck his toes.

"Have you a fetish?" He giggles.

"Several," I tell him.

I reach up. Press my hand against his full crotch. He squirms. I undo his belt. Unbutton his jeans. The head of his cock protrudes from the waistband of his underwear oozing pre cum. I circle my finger over the tip, which makes him even harder.

He lifts his hips and I pull off his pants. Take him in my mouth, caressing his chest as he moves in and out of my throat. He goes with the rhythm, then arches his back. "You'd better stop that," he says, "or this is gonna be over much too quickly."

"Well, we don't want that, do we?"

I get up, discard my clothes. Then we slide beneath the covers. We come together in a tight embrace beneath the cool of the sheets. He feels so good that it makes me shiver.

"You're beautiful," he whispers.

Sweet words fall from the heat of his breath, sending more chills up and down my body.

"God," I pant.

Soon, I'm sitting on top of him, feeling his cock against my ass. Rubbing myself against it, enjoying the thrill. "Where do you keep your condoms?" I ask.

He reaches over to the bedside table, grabs a rubber and a tube of K-Y, and hands them to me.

I sit back on his thighs, squirt a little lube into the tip of the rubber, then sheathe him. Another squirt for me and I'm ready.

His flesh sinks into mine.

"Comfortable?" he asks.

"Yeah, it's heaven. What a fit!"

"Yeah, it is."

Several times, he almost comes. I feel it begin to happen, a sudden throb at the heart of me, then all his movement stops. Frozen and rigid. He doesn't dare to breathe.

TIME AND OTHER BOMBS

I bring him to this point again and again, then finally tell him, "Go for it."

His hands dig at the cheeks of my ass. His thrusts becoming wilder. And I ride him, laughing with pure pleasure.

He reaches his peak and gasps. I reach mine: pearl white tears spilling out onto his belly. I crumple on top of him and die.

When I open my eyes the next morning, Jeff is stretched out beside me, reading a book. Our legs are intertwined and my head is resting on his chest. "I would've made coffee," he says, "but I couldn't pull myself away."

I give him a squeeze, looking sleepily around the room. "I really should go."

"What's your hurry? You're not gonna get all weird on me, are you?"

"No. It's just that I didn't take my pills last night, and I don't have any for this morning, either."

"What do you need?"

"Couple of AZT, couple of acyclovir."

"I happen to have that very medication in my personal stock." He hops out of bed. Goes into the bathroom and returns with the capsules, the tablets, and a glass of water. "That'll cost exactly one kiss," he says.

"Forget it. My breath is terrible."

"I don't care."

"I do."

He kisses me anyway.

"Now, that wasn't so bad, was it?"

"No." I smile. "It wasn't."

He climbs back in bed. "Quite a night last night, huh?"

"Certainly was."

"Sleep well?"

"Like a little baby."

"Feel like breakfast?"

I roll on top of him, biting his lips. "Do I ever."

* * *

16

A few hours later, I walk home along Church Street, thinking about Randy. Randy sits in my mind. He's shrunk down to about five inches, and we talk.

"You've gotta deal with my apartment, Zero. You keep putting it off."

"I know. I just haven't been in the mood for it. I haven't even been over there but once since you died."

"Really? When was that?"

"Never mind. You'll just think it's silly."

"Tell me!"

"The night I got back from Vancouver. I wanted to sleep in your bed."

"I don't think that's silly. I think it's sweet. God, I hope the sheets were clean."

"They were. Clean enough. And don't worry. Clearing out your apartment is at the top of my list."

I look in the window of This Ain't the Rosedale Library. They've got a new display, featuring the novels of Eastern Europe and a cardboard rendition of the Berlin Wall broken in two.

"Monumental history," says Randy. "But just you wait. George Bush and Brian Mulroney will soon be crying, 'Hoo-ray, hoo-ray! Communism is dead. We won, we won!' That's what makes me glad to be out of here. It makes me sick."

"I've gotta go across the street for some juice and stuff."

"To the Superfresh?"

"I know, it's the rudest store on the block, but they have the best prices on beverages."

As I'm standing in the lineup waiting to pay, I glance at the tabloid headlines.

ACADEMY AWARD WINNER DIES IN GUACAMOLE ACCIDENT.

That makes us both laugh.

HUMAN SOUL WEIGHS ONE-THIRD OF A THOUSANDTH OF AN OUNCE.

"Is that true?" I ask Randy.

"What does it matter?" he says. "Weight doesn't have a damn thing to do with it."

* * *

TIME AND OTHER BOMBS

The light on my answering machine is blinking with half a dozen messages. Stay home and no one calls; go out and your entire cast of characters checks in.

I pour a glass of Perrier, grab a piece of paper and a pen, then sit down to play my own best secretary.

"Zero," says caller number one. "It's Trebreh. Guess what? I'm on the road promoting my new video. Going to bars across the country, doing my strip routine, signing autographs, you know the story. Anyway, I'm in Chicago tonight, and it seems to me that's somewhere near Toronto. Just thought I'd give a call on the off chance you might be free to come down and catch the act. Besides, there's somebody kind of special I'd like you to meet. I don't have a local number yet, but if you call my place in L.A., I check in there regularly. Hope to hear from you soon. Later, guy. Bye."

Caller number two: "Son?" says a voice in a thick Southern accent. " 'Tis your mother! Gimme a call when you get a chance. There's something I want to talk to you about. Hope everything's okay, but if it's not, let me know."

Caller number three: "Precious, it's Snookums here. I am just swamped this morning with deadlines and wondered if we could change our eleven o'clock meeting to twelve-thirty? I'll assume it's a go if I don't hear from you. Sorry to have missed you last night. David says you left with a suitor. Do tell! Can't wait to hear all about it."

Caller number four: a hang up.

Caller number five: the same.

Caller number six: "Is that Zero?" says a hesitant voice. "Zero, it's Dorothy Evans, Randy's mother. My husband and I are going to be in Scarborough visiting my sister later this week. I wondered if we could get together and talk. If you wouldn't mind calling me back on this, I'd certainly appreciate it."

Dorothy is followed by an extended beep, then a gurgle of the tape, which means that's it for communications at present.

For the moment, I ignore them all and call Alan in Vancouver. He answers, sounding sleepy.

"Alan, it's Zero. I hope I didn't wake you."

"It's all right," he says. "I need to get going."

"I keep forgetting about the time change."

"What's up? Did the ashes make it?"

"Yeah."

"In one piece?"

"Several pieces. Listen, it looks like I'll be meeting the Evanses later this week."

"What for?"

"Well, they *are* Randy's parents. They probably want to talk more about his headstone."

Alan sighs. "So let 'em get a headstone. There's a provision for it in his will."

"I've got it right here in front of me. It simply states that they have to use the epitaph Randy wrote for it."

"Do they know what the epitaph says?"

"Not yet."

Alan laughs. "You're gonna have fun breaking that to 'em, Zero."

"I know." I groan. "How would you like to become the executor of this estate?"

"No thanks, the duty's all yours. I was merely the lover; you're the best friend."

"Hey, you just used the past tense. Congratulations."

"I've been seeing a counselor."

"Have you been able to take some time off work?"

"No. I'm glad to be busy. The busier the better."

"Any word on Randy's movie?"

"They're still editing."

"God! Are we ever gonna get to see the thing?"

"That depends on our life span."

"Can't you get a rough cut?"

"Darling, I am only an art director. They don't even return my calls. There was talk about premiering it at the Festival of Festivals in Toronto next fall, but I don't know."

"Wouldn't that be something! We'd have to get a big gang of people together, rent a limo, and go."

"Well, don't hold your breath. Ninety-nine percent of these things never pan out."

"I know. But I can't help wanting to see him on the screen. It's so exciting. It's like there's a part of him that's still alive and it's in that movie. By the way, is there anything you want from Randy's apartment?"

"Not that I can think of. I'm not even sure what's there."

"We'll put together a little package for you then, okay?"

"Sure. I'll look forward to it. I miss him, you know?"

"Yeah, I know."

"Hang in there, Zero."

"You too, Alan."

"Bye, buddy."

"Bye."

David's kitchen table is from the Saskatchewan farmhouse he grew up in. Its surface has been worn smooth by anxious hands worrying about the weather, the price of wheat, and the ways of the world.

"Coffee?" he asks. He doesn't wait for an answer. He just pours a mugful and sets it, steaming, in front of me.

"I didn't hear you come in last night," he says.

"Were you listening?" I ask.

"I can always hear when someone goes up or down the staircase. Did you have a good time?"

"A very good time."

"He's cute, that Jeff Lake."

"I'm glad you approve."

"I do, Zero. I think it's good for you to start seeing people again."

"I see people all the time."

"You know what I mean. You've really been a hermit since you broke off with Clay."

"Don't mother me, David."

"I'm not mothering you. I just hope——" He stops himself.

"What?"

"Oh, never mind."

"What were you gonna say?"

"I just hope you don't plan on moving out."

"After one night?" I cackle. "I hardly think so."

"But you might want to someday, Zero. And I just hope you'll think about it before making the jump. We've got a pretty good thing going here."

"Yes, we do."

"Me with my apartment, you with yours."

"David, no matter how deeply I fall, I'm not moving out. Ever, ever again."

"Well, I'm happy to know you feel that way."

"I'm touched you were worried."

"Not worried, exactly. It's just that we're getting to be of an age. And there's our health to think about."

"Yes, our ever-present health."

"Friends are important."

"You're telling me?"

I glance at the kitchen clock: 11:35.

"Hey, hadn't you better go if you're gonna make that demo?"

"Aren't you coming?"

"I can't."

"Zero!"

"I've gotta be down at the magazine. Snookums changed our meeting on me."

"What if it was you who needed ddI?"

"I'd still have my meeting."

David gives me a stern look.

"All right. Point taken. It won't happen again."

"Afternoon, precious," chirps Snookums, breezing into the office half an hour late. In one hand he carries a cup of coffee, and in the other, a stack of copy.

"Been waiting long?" he asks, dropping the work on the desk, then prying the lid off the Styrofoam cup.

"It's all right. I brought a book."

He glances in the mirror affixed to the back of his office door and pokes at his turban. "Damn it," he says, "I still haven't mastered how to tie these things. I really ought to sue my mother."

"What does your mother have to do with it?"

"She's the one who insisted I make the purchase, the last time

TIME AND OTHER BOMBS

I was home in Trinidad, visiting her. To think of the crimes we have perpetrated against ourselves in the name of vanity."

"No one knows better than you."

"Correct me if I'm wrong, but that doesn't sound much like a compliment."

"Trust me, Snookums. The turban looks a lot better than that ill-fitting toupee you used to wear."

"But toupees are so much more comfortable."

"Though not nearly as colorful. Or dramatique."

I hand him a manila envelope containing my column.

He sits down at his desk, peeks into the envelope, and says, "Oh, goody! Something I actually look forward to reading."

"Let's hope," I say.

"What's the matter? You're not having a confidence crisis, are you?"

"I'm just finding it a little difficult to produce amusing copy."

"It doesn't have to be amusing, Zero."

"That's fortunate, because this episode certainly is not."

"Is it about Randy?"

"Sort of. But if you don't mind, let's talk about something else."

"All right," he says, setting the envelope aside. "Let's talk about me!"

"Fine."

"I am convinced this magazine is driving me crazy. When I agreed to take over as editor, I was assured it would get easier with each issue. Guess what? They lied!"

"What now?"

"Where shall I start? There's the new art director, for one."

"The board went and hired the ex-Jesuit?"

"Of course, they hired him! He'll work for half the wage, so why not?"

"Good god."

"He is the most neurotic creature I've ever worked with. He makes the rest of us seem as calm as the Dalai Lama."

"Surely you can find some way to get him under control."

"Nothing short of crucifixion, I'm sure."

"I'll make a note of that. Hammer and nails for Christmas."

We both laugh wickedly.

I pick up the current dummy of *City Magazine* and flip through it. "You know," I say, "his designs don't look half bad."

"Half bad? They're works of art! And after a million changes, tantrums, and personal confessions, they damn well should be."

"Sounds like he needs to get laid."

"Laid? Precious, he needs to be plowed by Godzilla."

"Don't we all?" I chuckle.

"Come now," says Snookums. "What about this fellow you met last night?"

"Jeff Lake? So far, he's perfect."

"Oh, what I wouldn't give for a decent lover."

"What about your thing with the Attorney General?"

"That? Ha! That's been going on for too many years to excite me. Every Tuesday, and we always do the same thing. Sit on a double-headed dildo from eight to nine P.M. while I listen to all his problems. No, precious, I envy you. And I envy your position, working for this outfit on a free-lance basis. Think of it. To be exempt from the day-to-day hassles of office politics. You do your work, you deliver it, you leave. That's why you have a life."

"That's right. No job to report to every morning at nine A.M."

"You were never here by nine."

"Okay, ten."

"And you can thank me for that!"

"I do, Snookums. Every morning I perform a little ritual in your honor."

"You do?"

"Um-hum. You know that picture I have on my fridge from Halloween? The one where you look like Gandhi?"

"I was supposed to be Daddy Warbucks. That's a terrible picture!"

"Well, every morning, as I'm waiting for my coffee to drip, I press my nipple right up against your cute little face."

"Precious, please! That's enough to make an old girl moist." He squirms in his seat.

"Meeting adjourned?" I ask.

"Well, it'd better be!" He fans himself with a file folder.

TIME AND OTHER BOMBS

"I'll see you later."

"I look forward to it."

Urn shopping proves to be a virtually impossible task. I go through a dozen stores before finally finding two raku pieces the right size, shape, and color.

I take them home, dump Randy onto my kitchen table, and separate him into two equal piles. I put one pile in each urn, then carry the urns over to the mantel and start arranging my favorite books between them.

The phone rings. I hate being interrupted midtask, so let the machine take it.

The volume is still turned up from when I listened to my previous messages, so I hear the caller, my cousin Trebreh, again say, "Hey, Zero! Guess what? Chicago was a bust. I'm on my way to Buffalo now. I've looked at a map and I'm thinking about coming up to Toronto over the weekend. Saturday, Sunday, maybe Monday, depending on how things go. See you then. Bye."

Mystified, I stare at that goddamn machine. I don't hear from my cousin for three and a half years and now I get two calls in two days.

Trebreh and I grew up together. We were raised in the same house. He was my first affair. That happened when he was fourteen and I was twelve. We'd just come back from visiting our Uncle Markus in New York. We were playing a game of *Gone With the Wind* up in the attic, using Great-Grandmother's hoopskirts. It was hot as hell. I was Melanie; he was Scarlett. And on this particular day, he kept insisting we do the part where Melanie has her baby. I protested at first, but Trebreh was always a charmer. He assured me, "It's all right, Melly. We're cousins." He lifted my legs, rested them on his shoulders, and began to assist with the birth. Though I couldn't see exactly what he was doing, I could feel it. And one thing led to another.

We kept at it from that moment on. We even had a special hideaway a couple of hours south of Little Rock at our granddaddy's fishing camp near Calion. We'd ride down there on Trebreh's motorcycle, go into the cabin, and spend the afternoon just seeing how many times we could do it. Then we'd lie around together and talk. That was the best part. Mainly we talked about the future. The future was where all the injustices of childhood balanced out. Or so we thought.

Though Trebreh was two years older than me, he'd been held back in school and was only one grade ahead. The day after he graduated, he climbed on his motorcycle and left for L.A. Trebreh didn't have time for college, and my grandmother didn't push it. He'd never been the academic type. No, Trebreh was gonna be a movie star. Live larger than life in the light of the silver screen. Then we could all say we knew him. Then.

His departure was a real heartbreak for me. Of course, I couldn't mention it to anybody. I just had to try and forget him.

On the rare occasions when we'd see each other, we invariably ended up together. Talking, carrying on, having sex. Then every time he'd leave, it'd be the same thing: this great emptiness.

The summer after I finished college, I was down in Florida, visiting Uncle Markus and his friend Jack. They had moved there some years before to start their dinner-theatre empire. One night, I found a bunch of skin magazines stashed in the back of the guest-room closet. I was horny and intrigued and started looking through them. Every last one featured Trebreh. I was shocked!

During our twenties, Trebreh and I hardly saw each other. But when Treb turned thirty, he instigated a reunion. He was in New York and flew me down from Toronto. Took me out to Fire Island, to some friends' place in the Pines. It was like the best of our old days. Crazy sex, laughing, eating, drinking, dancing in the discos, cruising boys, walking on the beach and talking. We had come full circle, I thought. I'd learned to enjoy Trebreh for what he was, just as I'd learned to accept love in its many variations.

After that visit, we talked regularly on the phone for a while. Then, the next time I was out seeing friends in San Francisco, he insisted I come down to L.A. When I got there, he was gone. Some business in Hawaii. He left a note on the door of his house, explaining how to get the keys and telling me to make myself at home.

Ever since then, it's been one missed connection after another. I know he won't show up this weekend. I know it.

With the urns perfectly arranged, I pick up the phone and call Jeff.

"Hi," he says.

"Hi. Nice to hear your voice. I was getting kind of lonesome for it."

"Me too. It's been about five hours."

"You busy?"

"Not terribly. Just got home from the doctor's. Why, what'd you have in mind?"

"Well, I've got a great big old-fashioned bathtub, and I was just thinking how nice it'd be to smoke a joint, get in it, and have a soak together."

"I'm on my way." He starts to hang up.

"Hey, Jeff?"

"Yeah?"

"Hadn't I'd better give you my address?"

"Oh. Right."

"So what were you doin' at the doctor's?" I ask, climbing into the tub.

"Getting my latest test results." He settles in behind me. "A little hotter?" he asks.

"Sure."

He reaches up with his foot to adjust the flow of water.

"And how were they, your test results?"

"Well, let's just say I hope you're not falling for the wrong guy." I stroke his legs. "Now, what do you mean by that?"

"My T cells have dropped to just below two hundred. And you know what they say, anything below two hundred's the danger zone."

"Good God, mine have never been above two hundred, and you know what they say then? They say the numbers don't really mean anything. Science is very flexible, Jeff." I pick up the shampoo. "Feel like washing my hair?"

"Sure."

"Anyway, it's too late. I've already fallen. With me, when it happens, it happens quickly." Oops. "Maybe I shouldn't've said that. I hope that doesn't scare you."

"No." He sculpts my hair into horns. "Should it?"

"I don't think it should. Not that I want to get married. I just want to enjoy . . . whatever."

"Me too."

We relax in the water awhile. Then I say, "You know what's funny?"

"What?"

"People who are really sick keep telling me: Put nothing off. They say if there's something you want to do, do it. You know what it is I want to do? Feel like I've done enough."

He laughs. "And do you?"

"Let me put it this way. I've never felt more alive than I've felt in this last year. I don't know if it's age or AIDS, but something in me is just burning."

"I have a friend who calls that the final burst of life."

We lie there until the water cools. Then we climb from the tub and dry.

The bath has made us groggy. We go to my bedroom and lie down.

Jeff dozes in the crook of my arm.

"I love you," I whisper to no one in particular, yet the sentiment is meant for everything my senses can register.

Randy's mom wants me and the gang to come for dinner Thursday night. She tells me over the phone that Thursday is her sister's night to curl, so we'll have the place to ourselves.

"Do we need the place to ourselves?" I ask jokingly. "Is it gonna be that bad?"

"I don't know, Zero," she says. "Forty-one years, and I still don't know what to expect from my husband."

"Well, I can't say I'll look forward to it, but it'll be nice to see you, Dorothy."

"You too, Zero."

Searcy can't make it on account of the Gong Show, but David and Snookums agree to go with me as reinforcements.

Dorothy has made tons of food, her homemade Chinese. Pity none of us has much of an appetite.

"Oh, it doesn't matter," says Dorothy. "My sister will eat it."

Snookums offers to help clear the table. I offer to help as well, but he motions me to sit back down and start dealing with Mr. Evans. David observes the scene silently, like a great sage enchanted by the mysteries of human behavior.

"Excellent dinner," I say.

"Dorothy sure can cook," replies Mr. Evans. "And now that we've got that established, let's cut the crap."

"Okay. Maybe you'd like to fill me in on what you wanted to talk about."

"I want you to let *us* handle things from here on out."

"But *I* happen to be Randy's executor."

"My lawyer says you can just sign that over to me."

"If Randy had wanted you to do it, don't you think he would've appointed you?"

"So you're gonna hold us to those documents he signed in the hospital?"

"He didn't sign them in the hospital. He signed them before he left Toronto. And they are his will and his last wishes. He knew exactly what he was doing."

Mr. Evans grunts and rises from the table. He walks to the picture window, cracking his knuckles. "My son and I may have had our differences, but he was still my son."

"I don't deny that."

"His mother and I intend to get him a headstone for our family plot. It's most important to both of us."

"Randy's instructions have a provision for that. You simply have to use the epitaph he wrote for it."

"What epitaph?" he asks suspiciously.

I hand him a piece of paper on which the two lines are written. Stoically, Mr. Evans takes it in.

"Well," he finally says, "my son was clearly out of his mind when he wrote this."

"I don't think so. He wanted something humorous and sexual to counter the usual impression people have of this disease. It's political, in a way."

"It's filth!"

November 1989

"What's filth?" asks Snookums, poking his head in from the kitchen.

"Yes," asks Dorothy. "What?"

"This," says Mr. Evans, handing his wife the paper.

She reads it, then gives it back. "Am I missing something?" she asks.

"For his goddamn headstone!" roars her husband.

"I'll explain it to you in the kitchen," says Snookums.

"Surely you don't expect us to have that engraved in granite?" Mr. Evans says.

"Yes," I say, "I most certainly do. I love Randy very much. I intend to see that his wishes are carried out. Of course, this only applies if you insist on getting a headstone. He's already been cremated. Why not just let it go?"

"All our dead for the last five generations are in that plot. Five generations! He knew what it meant to us. Damn it! He always has to have the last word, doesn't he?"

"If that's how you want to look at it."

"How else can I look at it? Every time I go to the cemetery, there it'll be, bigger than life. To think of the things I dreamt of for that boy."

"You had a wonderful son," I say through tight lips. "If you had taken the slightest interest in him, you'd've known that."

"I took interest, plenty of interest."

David gives me a look that says I've made my point and to let it drop.

But I will not let it drop. "Is that why you refused to visit him the first two times he was in the hospital?"

"I went eventually," Mr. Evans mutters. "I don't have to discuss this with you."

"Nor do I have to discuss Randy with you. I came here of my own free will to try to reach some kind of agreement."

"What if we choose to disregard those ridiculous instructions?"

"I'll drag you through every court in the land. This is not a pleasant position for me to be in, Mr. Evans, and it's not one I asked for. You and Randy parted ways long ago. All the ranting in the world is not gonna change that, nor is it gonna bring him back.

29

Personally, I hope you never get over it. I hope your pigheadedness gives you nightmares, ulcers at the very least. But that's just my personal view. As far as Randy's concerned, it's much simpler. You want the headstone, you get the epitaph. No epitaph, no stone."

"Oh, what does it matter?" asks Dorothy, drying her hands on a tea towel. "I'm sure we can work something out."

"I want a copy of that will," says Mr. Evans. "And those instructions. We'll see what my lawyers have to say about it."

"I've already made you copies." I hand them over. "You'll notice Randy left you the residuals from that deodorant commercial he did."

"Oh, gee."

"It brings in a lot of money."

"It does?"

"Also some personal effects from the apartment. There is one other thing."

"What?"

"I happened to see that obit that went into the St. Catharines paper. I also saw the death notices in the *Star* and the *Globe.* None of them mentioned a thing about how Randy died, and Randy made it very clear he wanted the fact he had AIDS mentioned. He felt it was degrading to leave it out. To him and everyone else with the disease."

"But he didn't die of that. He died of a brain infection."

"As a result of AIDS."

"That's right," says Dorothy. "We must say it as often as we can."

"Well, then," mocks her husband. "I guess that just about settles that."

"Enough," says Dorothy sharply. She goes back into the kitchen, returning with tea and a tray of her special Chinese buns.

We eat and drink in silence.

Afterward, Snookums says, "Guess I'd better call us a cab."

"So soon?" asks Dorothy.

"I'm afraid so," says Snookums. "It's been lovely, but we get a little strange if we're still in the suburbs past ten."

"Really?" Dorothy is puzzled, intrigued by this new aspect of gay life.

The cab comes quickly. I hug Dorothy and thank her for going to so much trouble.

"No trouble at all, Zero. And if you need help with anything, we'll be in town through the weekend."

"Okay. I'll call."

Once we're out on the sidewalk, the sage David finally speaks. "I'd always assumed you and Randy were exaggerating about that man."

"Isn't he a pig?"

"He's an absolute Neanderthal."

"Let's just hope there's nothing his lawyers can find in that will."

"There's not," says Snookums. "Randy had it checked again before he went out to Vancouver."

"Where to?" asks the driver.

"Church and Wellesley," we reply in unison.

Then Snookums adds, "As if you couldn't tell."

My phone is ringing. I rush in to answer it, hoping it's Jeff Lake. "Hello?"

"How *are* you?" asks my mother, her voice glossed with pleasantry.

"Fine," I answer curtly. "And you?"

"Still here. Did you get my message?"

"Yes, and I was gonna call you back tonight."

"Remember, you promised to keep me informed about things, Zero."

"I keep you informed, Mom."

She takes a deep breath. "Do you remember Campbell Rodgers? Used to live up the street from us on Main?"

"Yes."

"Well, he died last week. Of AIDS. And his family didn't even know he was sick. They'd seen him the week before and just thought he was skinny. Can you believe that?"

"Unfortunately, I can."

"Have you had any more tests lately?"

"Not in a couple of months."

"Are you still taking your medication?"

"Of course I'm taking my medicine. God!"

"Well, you don't have to get so defensive."

31

TIME AND OTHER BOMBS

"Then don't grill me like some kind of police interrogation."

"I'm just trying to figure out what you're hiding."

"I'm not hiding anything!"

"That's not what it sounds like to me."

"All right, Mom. My arm fell off today."

"That's not funny, Zero."

"Is this the only reason you called?"

"No. I had a couple. The main one being that February tenth is your sister Doll's thirtieth birthday and I want you here. We're throwing a gala!"

"A gala?"

"Yes! At the Capital Hotel. Sparky has rented the mezzanine for the Saturday-night dinner. We're gonna have Hart Border play piano. We're gonna dance. We're gonna eat. We're gonna drink. We're gonna have a grand old time even if it kills us.

"We'll do Friday night at my new condo, a catered something. Everybody'll be here. The Houston gang, the Yoakums, Sparky, even your old brother and his sad clan. I just wanted to let you know about it in plenty of time—"

"Like three months?"

"Well, so you can put it down in your date book. I don't want any excuses for you not being here."

"Don't worry. I wouldn't miss it for the world."

"It's not a circus, Zero."

"It's not?"

"No, it's not. Now you know poor Doll's really gotten the brunt of the family problems. She never got to make a debut. And it doesn't look like she'll be getting married anytime soon."

"So you're throwing the wedding without the groom."

"No. And don't say that again. She's sensitive enough as it is. We're just gonna gather for the weekend to celebrate our baby turning thirty. Everybody's so anxious to get a look at you, too. They've all been so worried."

"I'll bet."

"They're sincere."

"So are vultures. Are you certain you're having this for Doll and not because you think the relatives won't get a chance to see me again?"

"Just when did you become so cynical?"

"I don't know. Must be a by-product of the virus."

"We just want you here! To join in the celebration. Period. Now, do you want to bring somebody with you?"

"Like who?"

"How 'bout that nice boy David you used to go with? Doll's awfully fond of him. And he knows the whole family. It's not like our behavior's gonna put him in shock or anything."

"Well, I'll have to check it out with him and get back to you on that."

"All right. But be quick about it. You know me, I'm already making plans."

"I'm sure you are."

Her tone shifts. "Now tell me the truth, Zero. Are you really okay?"

"I'm fine!"

"And there's nothing you're not telling me?"

"I'm hanging up now. Good-bye."

"Honestly, you make it so hard for somebody to care!"

Snookums, Searcy, David, and I spend Saturday sorting through Randy's apartment—books, records, tapes, knickknacks, dishes, towels, linens, artwork, furniture, appliances—deciding who to give what. By the time we finish, the place is cluttered with little piles, each tagged with the lucky inheritor's name. My pile is mostly journals, snapshots, and his papers.

Late Sunday afternoon, the few people we invited stop by to pick up their loot. Searcy shows up with two cases of champagne, turning the quiet little gathering into quite a party.

"To hell with Randall's wishes," he proclaims. "We need a decent blowout. At least *I* do. I damn well deserve a good drunk on his behalf."

"You'll get no argument from me," I say.

"Nor me," says David, inspecting the champagne. "And I'm pleased to see you got the best."

"Well, hon, you can hardly send a homosexual to the greater

beyond on Freixenet. It must be Moët Chandon or Veuve Clicquot, or you might as well not bother."

"I'll just have a modest glass," says Snookums. "I'm an alcoholic, remember?"

"How could we forget?"

"So cheers, everybody! May the dead wing on!"

That gives me a great idea. I go back to the bedroom and haul out a bundle of Randy's clothes. "Let's all put on something that belonged to the dearly departed."

"Oh yes," says Searcy. "Let's do!"

I grab a red corduroy shirt. The one he wore to clean house in and rarely bothered to wash. It still has his smell. Searcy picks a pair of green bikini briefs and wears them on his head like a beret. David goes for a turquoise T-shirt. Snookums, a stylish belt.

We take a few Polaroids, laughing wildly. Then, as the laughter subsides, Searcy says solemnly, "You know, I'm gonna miss that little bastard."

"Does that come as a surprise?" I ask.

"Oh, you know how he was always picking at me."

"That was just the special affection you inspired in one another."

"Is that what that was?"

Dorothy is our first official guest.

"Come on in," I say.

She seems a bit taken aback to see such gaiety in progress. "Gosh, Zero, I didn't know you were planning anything so lavish."

"It's not lavish, Dorothy. It just sort of happened."

"I have to apologize for my husband," she says. "He isn't able to make it."

In Randy's honor, I abandon all tact. "I really think that's for the best, don't you?"

"Well, probably."

Searcy gives Dorothy a glass of bubbly and Snookums leads her to the clothes pile.

"Oh," she says reluctantly, "I . . . I don't know. I just couldn't. My son and I were nowhere near the same size."

But they keep insisting, and finally she chooses a *Flashdance* sweatshirt, which she pulls over her matronly dress. "Is that okay?" she asks.

"Smashing!" says Snookums.

The Celebrity AIDS Person arrives next, followed by Dr. Susan Fieldstone.

I present each of them with a glass of champagne.

Dr. Fieldstone says, "I can't stay long, Zero. But I did want to drop by."

"As long as you like. There's no time clock."

I take the Celebrity by the arm. "Listen, there's a pile of stuff over here for the hospice. Would you be in charge of delivering it for me?"

"Is cab fare included?"

"Absolutely."

"Then sure. What are you giving 'em?"

"A few dirty magazines, a Walkman, some tapes, novels—the usual hospital amenities. Feel free to keep anything you want."

"Well, I could use a Walkman."

I pat him on the back. "It's all yours. Happy inheritance."

Dorothy says to Dr. Fieldstone, "Quite a group, huh?"

"Randy had so many friends. It always amazed me. One day there were fourteen visitors in his room at once."

"He was a popular boy, all right," says Dorothy. She sips her champagne. "Do you work exclusively with AIDS?"

"Almost. Though AIDS didn't exist when I specialized in infectious diseases."

"Dr. Fieldstone," I interrupt. "The pile for Sunnybrook is on the dining-room table. Don't forget to take it when you go."

"I won't, but I hope it's not much, because people will just walk right off with it."

"It's not. Mostly magazines and books."

"Oh, good. We can always use those."

I spot David standing out on the balcony. I join him. He's looking at the city, thoughtfully sipping from his glass.

"What's up?" I ask.

He shrugs. "Just thinking."

"About Randy?"

"More than Randy." Then he looks right at me. "Do you ever wonder how many times you'll serve as an executor before someone's doing the job for you?"

"It's crossed my mind, yes."

He looks down at the street. "I just loathe how we've been robbed of our future. Every day another one of us disappears. Remember Rob Reynolds? I hadn't seen him for months. Then there he was, walking up Church Street this morning, completely emaciated and carrying a couple of empty boxes. Packing up his apartment, I suppose. Another one of us crawling off to die."

"David," I say softly, reaching over to touch his hand. "You know this isn't pretty, and you know it isn't easy."

"Don't," he says, pulling back. "Just give me a minute, okay?"

"All right."

I go back inside and freshen up my drink.

Searcy's talking about the first time he met Randy. "We were both working at Stratford. Playing bit parts in *Henry V*. Oh, I took it so seriously! It used to drive me crazy how during the curtain call half the audience would just walk out. Then Randy said, 'Shakespeare or musical comedy, our job is to entertain. If they're that bored with what we're doing, they oughta walk out.' " Searcy laughs. "I wonder if he had any idea that that simple bit of advice would become the cornerstone of my theatrical philosophy and, I might add, what I owe my durability as a performer to."

"You owe your durability," says the Celebrity AIDS Person, "to a very unsuspecting public."

"Hush, you! The point is, Randall possessed an inherent wisdom most mortals don't even dream of."

"Which he got from me," says Dorothy proudly.

David slips in from the balcony. Searcy catches his eye, clues into his mood, and tries to pull him out of it by asking, "When did you first meet Randall?"

"Summer of '78," says David. "I was organizing a demo against an Anita Bryant appearance in Moose Jaw."

"How brave," says Searcy.

"I didn't meet him until '85," says the Celebrity. "We used to dance at Cornelius on Sunday afternoons. I also used to see him at the Roman Sauna. In fact, my most vivid image of Randy is in a steam-soaked towel running after some—"

"Excuse me?" says Dr. Fieldstone, indicating Dorothy.

"Oh, don't stop on my account." Dorothy laughs. "I'm used to it."

"Well, I'm not!" says the doctor. "I'll never understand why gay men have to talk like they've all slept together."

"Because we have," says the Celebrity AIDS Person, laughing.

"Speak for yourself," says Searcy. "Some of us have not been so lucky. Now, back to the tribute."

"Yes," says Snookums. "Let's hear from Zero."

I look around the crowd uncomfortably.

"Go ahead, precious. Say something."

"Somehow," I confess, "Randy is more a mystery to me now than he ever was. He was simply"—I shrug—"my friend."

"Well," says Searcy, "if no one has anything to add to that, I think it's a good note to end on. I suggest we move on to the knee dancing."

"What's knee dancing?" asks Dorothy.

"Oh, just regular dancing," says Snookums. "Leave it to a queen to put a pet name on everything."

The first musical selection is Yma Sumac's "Gopher," a surefire way to get even the most sedentary souls onto their feet. However, this group doesn't need much encouragement. In no time, we're writhing as a mad unit, even Dr. Susan Fieldstone, whose step seems the wildest of all.

That's when Jeff arrives.

I make my way over to the door to greet him.

"Glad you could make it," I say, giving him a kiss.

"Me too. Though I thought I'd find things a little more subdued."

"They were." I lead him into the group choreography.

"What do you call this?" he asks, moving among us.

"Raising the dead."

The party breaks up about nine. Jeff and I stay to clean up, and once that's under control, we stretch out on Randy's bed.

"Come here," he says, pulling me into a snuggle, giving me a kiss. "Think Randy would mind?"

"Randy would love it."

"Then why don't we get out of these clothes and under these covers?"

"Why not? He won't be home tonight."

Just as we get settled, what else? The phone rings.

"Shit," I say.

I reach for the receiver. It's David. "Sorry to bother you," he says, "but you'd better get home. Pronto."

"Why? My cousin didn't show up, did he?"

"No. Just trust me on this."

I sigh heavily. "Are you sure it can't wait?"

"I don't think it can."

"I'll be there in half an hour."

"Okay."

I hang up.

"What is it?" asks Jeff.

"I don't know." I sit up on the edge of the bed and pull on my socks. "He just said to get home, fast."

"Want me to come with you?"

"And ruin your glorious nakedness? No. You stay here. I'll be back as soon as I can."

David's lights are ablaze. I see him through the window, handing a mug of hot chocolate to a little girl whom I'd judge to be about fourteen.

I knock on the door.

"Sorry to have spoiled your date," David says.

The little girl smiles confidently and reaches out to shake my hand. "I'm Mary Bull Jackeye," she says. "Trebreh sent me."

"Trebreh?" I ask.

"He had to fly back to L.A. for a few days. He said you'd put me up."

"You were traveling with him?"

"Yeah, he's my dad."

"Your what?"

"My dad."

I look at Mary Bull, then at David.

November 1989

I go up to my apartment alone and dial my cousin's number.

"Hello," says his answering machine. "Sorry to have missed you. Please leave a message at the sound of the tone and I'll get back to you as soon as I can."

"Treb? It's Zero. When you said there was someone you wanted me to meet, I assumed you meant a lover. Who *is* this child? Explanations! You've dumped a lot of things in my lap, but this takes the cake. Phone me, you bastard. Soon!"

"I phoned," says Trebreh, picking up.

"Oh, monitoring our calls, are we?"

"I always monitor my calls. There're a lot of people I don't want to talk to."

"So just when did you acquire a daughter? And how come I never knew about her?"

"I only found out recently myself."

"What'd she do, fly out of the woodwork?"

"Of course not." He laughs. "Isn't she cute? Don't you think she's the spittin' image of Grandmother Hortense, those short little legs and that chunky torso?"

"She's very attractive in her own way, but don't change the subject. How the hell did you get a daughter?"

"It's a long story, Zero."

"I've got plenty of time."

"A few years after I came out to L.A., my bike was in need of repair. I was broke, but I happened to know a dyke mechanic who was in the market for a sperm donor. She considered me an excellent specimen and we made a simple exchange. She fixed my bike. I jacked off in a jelly jar. Her lover impregnated her with a turkey baster. And that was that."

"Then how come you never knew about her?"

"I didn't think turkey basters worked. I *knew* Mary Bull. I just didn't know she was mine."

"What makes you so sure she is?"

"She told me. And the minute she said it, I knew it was true."

"How long has she been traveling with you?"

"About six weeks."

"On your bike?"

"Is there any other way?"

"Well, what about her mother?"

"Big Ellen? What about her?"

"This Big Ellen just let her daughter hop on the back of your motorcycle and travel around the country while you gyrated from one bar to the next?"

"It wasn't quite that cut and dried, Zero. Big Ellen and I are old friends."

"Does she even know where her daughter is?"

"Not exactly. She thinks she's with me. She doesn't know I'm back in L.A., so she doesn't know Mary Bull's in Toronto. Look, it's no big deal. Think of it as a blessing. The chance to get to know the cousin you never knew you had."

"What if I'd been out of town? David said she'd been sitting on our steps for three and a half hours."

"She has some money. She's a big girl. She would've called me and I would've told her to go to a hotel. I was actually all set to leave her with friends in Buffalo, but she insisted. She wanted to meet you."

"Oh, I'm sure."

"It's true. Ask her."

"Damn you, Trebreh."

"Relax, Zero. I'll be there in a few days."

"So," I say to Mary Bull, "make yourself at home. All I can offer you is the couch, but it's pretty comfortable. God knows, I've fallen asleep on it enough times."

Mary Bull sets her bag down and looks around the living room.

"Hungry?" I ask.

"No, I had a couple of pieces of pizza earlier."

"Would you like to clean up? Take a bath?"

"No. Actually, I'm pretty tired." She smiles. "I want to thank you for taking me in. I told Trebreh he should've called you. But he didn't, did he?"

"It doesn't matter. I'm very happy to have you, Mary Bull."

I haul some bedding out of the linen closet and make the couch up for her.

November 1989

She goes into the bathroom to brush her teeth. She comes out in her nightclothes, an oversize fluorescent T-shirt that says STAR in huge letters across her belly.

"One blanket or two?" I ask.

"Two," she says.

I tuck her in.

"Cozy?"

"Um-hum."

"You sleep tight and we'll have us a good visit tomorrow morning, okay?"

"Okay. 'Night."

" 'Night."

Mary Bull has already made up the couch, dressed, and is sitting by the door to the deck, drinking a Coke, when I crawl out of my bedroom.

"Hi," she says brightly.

"Been awake long?"

"Yep. I'm an early riser."

"You and your father."

I put on some coffee. "I thought I'd make us some pancakes. Do you like pancakes?"

"I love 'em."

"Good, then you'll really love these. It's an old family recipe. Great-Grandmother's specialty. Only she used to add blue food coloring."

"Blue food coloring?"

"It didn't change how they tasted, only how they looked."

"Well, I don't eat things that are blue."

"Don't worry." I get out a mixing bowl and start dumping in the ingredients. "These won't be blue."

She finishes her Coke, belches subtly, crushes the can, then tosses it into the wastebasket. "Two points," she says excitedly.

"You some kind of basketball player?"

"Sometimes."

"At school?"

41

"No. At my mom's garage. We have a team."

"You do go to school, don't you?"

"Of course I go to school."

I set the fry pan on the stove and turn the heat on high. "Well, how'd you manage to get the time off to take this trip?"

"A lot of kids take time off to travel with their parents. I do my work by correspondence. It's easy."

"Have you ever been cross-country before?"

"Not on a motorcycle."

"Fun, huh?"

"I love it!"

I drop a hunk of butter in the pan, wait for it to sizzle, then spoon in several dollops of batter.

"I used to love riding on Trebreh's bike, too, though he'd never let me drive it."

"He had one when you were kids?"

"He's had one since he was fourteen. Bought it with the money he got when his mom died."

"I didn't know she died."

"Hasn't Trebreh ever told you about her?"

"No, he never talks about his family. Except for you and his uncle."

"Well, maybe it's not my place to say, but then again, what's the big secret? His mom hanged herself. In our attic."

"How awful!"

"Yes, it was. Especially since it was five days before anyone found her. She wasn't a very happy woman."

"What was wrong with her?"

"A million things. Her fiancé came home crazy from Korea. They got married anyway. She got pregnant. Then she came down with the German measles, which everybody thought was gonna make the baby retarded. Her husband took that as his cue to run off."

"So Trebreh never knew his dad?"

"Oh, sure, he knew him. We used to spy on him all the time. He lived in a trailer just on the edge of town. We used to bomb him with water balloons every chance we got."

I set the first batch of pancakes in front of her.

I plop some more batter in the skillet and pour myself a mug of coffee.

"Tell me how you found out about Trebreh being your father and all."

"About a year ago, I just asked my mom who my dad was, and she told me. She gave me a scrapbook she'd been keeping on him. Full of his clippings, ads for his movies, even a few of his photo spreads."

"Nice, educational material for a growing child."

"I'm not a child. I have no problem with the naked body. Besides, he's pretty good-looking."

"He certainly is. Have you been going to his performances since you're been on the road?"

"Sometimes. But they're all the same. Usually I stay at the hotel."

"Doing your correspondence?"

"That. Watching TV. And practicing."

"Not basketball."

"Oh, no, singing. I've studied voice and acting since I was nine. That's the main reason I came on this trip. Trebreh's gonna help me once we get to New York. It's our next stop. I'm planning to make the rounds."

"The audition rounds?"

"That's right. I already have a pretty good contact. My mom's ex-lover is a casting director there."

"Does she know you're coming?"

"Well, no. But she'll be glad when she sees me. We have a lot in common, me and Lily. My mom keeps trying to frustrate my ambition. She tried to do that to Lily, too. My mom thinks having a lot of ambition isn't normal, like she's some expert on what's normal."

"Then why did she let you come on this trip?"

"She didn't. But she agreed to let me decide for myself and promised to respect my decision. Still, almost every time we talk she threatens, 'One of these days I'm just gonna come rescue you from the patriarchy and drag you back where you belong.' She's something else, my mom."

"She must love you very much."

"She does. She just doesn't want me to grow up. And she doesn't understand what a competitive world it is. She's been working in that garage of hers since she got out of high school. She doesn't realize that if you're gonna get somewhere in this life, you've gotta get going before it's too late."

"You've got plenty of time."

"I'm almost fourteen!" she exclaims. "Some kids start professional training at three. Look at ballet."

"Is that why you had on that STAR nightshirt?"

"Not really. It's just a shirt."

She gets up from the table, goes over to the coffeepot, and pours herself a cup. "Um," she says, smelling the steam.

"Careful," I tell her, "it's pretty strong."

"That's how I like it."

"Milk or sugar?"

"Nope."

"How 'bout some more pancakes?"

"Sure."

"Great-Grandmother would be pleased by your appetite."

"I'm a growing girl, what do you expect? I've gotta build up my strength for New York." She pauses. "New York," she says dreamily. "I'm in love with New York. I'm in love with it already and I haven't even seen it yet. I should've been born in such a place."

I give her a look. "I used to feel the same way."

"You don't take me very seriously, do you, Zero?"

"No. I mean, yes. I mean, Mary Bull, you're just a kid."

"A kid, huh?"

"And I hope the reality of it all doesn't disappoint you. I also hope Trebreh doesn't."

"He won't. And I'm not going completely green. I have experience, you know. I played one of the orphans in *Annie* at the L.A. Civic Light Opera. I've also been in two commercials."

"I'm impressed."

"The only thing that worries me is my looks."

"You look fine."

"You don't think I'm kind of ugly?"

"You have a very unique appearance."

"I wasn't supposed to be unique. I was supposed to look like Trebreh. That's why Big Ellen and Lily chose him."

"Really? I would've thought they chose him for his background."

"What background?"

"Being from the aristocratic South and all."

"No," she says flatly. "That wasn't it."

"You have the qualities of a great character actress, and their careers last a lot longer than those of beauty queens."

"You think so?"

"I know so."

I sit down next to her with my plate of pancakes.

"Are you a lesbian, as well?" I ask.

She just about chokes. "Why? Do I look it?"

"No. Not really. It's just that I knew I was gay when I was sixteen years old, so I thought I'd ask."

"I bet you didn't go around announcing it, though!"

"No, Mary Bull. But the world is a very different place now. I didn't grow up a child of Stonewall in a Southern California women's garage. I certainly don't mean you any offense."

"My mom taught me about Stonewall. That bar in Greenwich Village where the police tried to arrest the drag queens, but the drag queens fought back. My mom's really hot on that stuff."

"I'd like to meet your mom someday. She sounds like quite the gal."

"Woman," Mary Bull corrects me.

"Woman," I repeat. "After she and Lily split up, did she raise you single-handedly?"

"Her and the women at the garage. My mom has lots of friends. They're really great. If only they were a bit more . . . worldly."

"Mary Bull, you don't know how lucky you are."

"So? Who ever does?"

David drops by and offers to take Mary Bull to the Royal Ontario Museum. She seems keen on the idea, and I insist she go.

Then Jeff calls.

"Oh god," I say. "You're not still at Randy's, are you?"

"No, Zero, I'm home now. I can't believe you forgot about me. What the hell happened?"

"You wouldn't believe it."

"Try me."

"My cousin Trebreh's thirteen-year-old daughter showed up. I didn't even know he had a thirteen-year-old daughter."

"Back up a minute. What kind of name is Trebreh?"

"Herbert spelled backwards."

"Why would anyone want to spell it backwards?"

"I don't know. Everybody in the family thought Trebreh was semiretarded. They let him get away with anything. The name just sort of stuck."

"Jesus, that's weird."

"Look, why don't you come over? I'll fill you in on all the details, then we can pick up where we left off last night."

"What about the thirteen-year-old?"

"She's at the ROM. Look, I'm really sorry."

"I should play coy to punish you, Zero."

"Jeff, don't do that."

"No, I won't. But only because you do something to me, you bastard. I'll see you shortly."

The weather has taken a chilly turn. Jeff arrives wearing a black leather jacket, black jeans, black boots, and a SILENCE = DEATH T-shirt.

"My! Don't you look butch!"

"My winter wardrobe." He starts to take off his jacket.

"No, no," I say. "Leave it on."

I push him toward the bedroom.

"I didn't know you had a thing for leather."

"Neither did I."

"Tel-e-phone," says Mary Bull.

I wake with a start. "What time is it?"

"Four in the afternoon," she says, standing in the bedroom doorway, arms crossed, pouting.

"Four in the afternoon?! Shut the door. I'll be out in a minute."

She rolls her eyes.

I disengage myself from Jeff, trying not to wake him. He makes a slight noise and rolls over.

Mary Bull holds the receiver just out of my reach, tantalizing me. "I heard you guys."

"Heard us what?"

"Moaning and groaning and making the sounds of love."

"You didn't hear any such thing."

"Did too."

"You were at the museum!"

"The museum was closed!"

I snatch the receiver from her, clutch it to my chest, and take a deep breath.

I debate further argument with her, then decide just to answer the call. "Hello?"

"Zero, how's it goin'? Mary Bull giving you any trouble?"

"Too early to tell, Trebreh."

"Listen, guy, I'm afraid I'm not gonna be able to get away as quickly as I thought."

"Am I surprised?"

"It's not what you think. My ex-manager broke into my apartment. Says he's entitled to ten percent of everything I've made since I've been using the Billy Rockett stage name. He's out of his fucking mind. He stole my mailing list and my last two boxes of Billy Rockett dildos."

"So when will you be here?"

"A week Friday at the latest."

"A week Friday!"

"It's not my choice, Zero. I'd much rather be back on the road than dealing with all this. Just help me out this once. It's not like I make a habit of it. At least not lately."

"All right. But if you're not here a week from Friday, I'm calling Big Ellen and putting this child on a plane home. That's the deal, take it or leave it."

"Look, I'll be there. I've even got myself a gig."

"In Toronto? Where?"

"A place called Colby's. Do you know it?"

"Sure. It's quite popular. Famous for its strippers, drag shows, and table dancers."

"Well, why don't you get a bunch of your friends together and come? My treat."

"With free dildos for all?"

"Sure. If I can get some back."

"I might just take you up on that. We could use a night out."

"Then it's settled?"

"Why not?"

"Be sure and give my girl a hug."

"Yeah. And you keep in touch, you hear?"

When I hang up, Mary Bull says, "So what's keeping him?"

"Something to do with his ex-manager."

"Oh, that again," she says sarcastically.

"What do you mean, 'again?' "

"I don't even think he has an ex-manager. When'd he say he was coming?"

"A week Friday."

"And I'm supposed to stay here?"

"Got any better ideas?"

"No. But I'll tell you one thing. I don't appreciate being left alone for an entire afternoon. When my mom spends the day in bed, she at least rents me a couple of videos."

"Mary Bull, I didn't even know you were back. And if you want some attention, you shouldn't creep around the house like a ghost. Make some noise."

"I made tons of noise. Only you were making more!"

Jeff walks in in his underwear.

Mary Bull takes one look at him and says, "Not bad." Then she tells Jeff, "I heard you two."

Jeff yawns and scratches himself. "Huh?"

"I'm Mary Bull Jackeye. Zero and I are related."

"Yeah, I've heard."

"That was my cousin," I say to Jeff. "He's gonna be performing at Colby's next week. Wants us to invite all our friends."

"What's he do?"

"Dances and strips," says Mary Bull. "He's really good at it, too."

"Funny I've never heard of him," says Jeff. "I'm up on most of the stars."

"You probably know him as Billy Rockett."

48

"Not *the* Billy Rockett?"

"The one and only."

"You mean I've been going out with Billy Rockett's cousin for almost a week and didn't even know it?"

"That's about the size of it."

Jeff and I cohost our first dinner party, in honor of Mary Bull.

Searcy arrives early and entertains her while we get things ready in the kitchen.

"Zero tells me you're a singer."

"That's right," replies Mary Bull. "I sure am."

"What do you sing?"

"Mostly things from musicals. But it depends. I like all kinds of songs. My idols are Ethel Merman, Dinah Washington, and Maria Callas."

"Well, I can tell we're gonna get along just fine! You're gonna sing for us tonight, I hope?"

"If you want."

"Oh, we want, we want. Don't we, boys?"

"Absolutely," I say.

"Have you heard her yet, Zero?"

"Why do you think I invited you over?"

"This is too exciting!" Searcy gives Mary Bull a little pat. "I adore being in the presence of budding talent."

"More wine?" asks Jeff, noticing that Searcy's glass is empty.

"No thanks, hon. One's my limit. Have to protect my little ol' T cells."

"Yeah," I say ironically. "He only has five hundred."

"Five hundred?" says Jeff. "How luxurious! Here, have the whole bottle."

"Well," says Searcy, "I think it's my weight that helps."

I laugh at the absurd notion, then laugh again because it may very well be true.

"Are you on AZT or anything?" Jeff asks him.

"No, hon. I'm not joining the AZT Club until I dip below four hundred at least. Maybe even three-fifty. I take vitamins, hypericin, and a special extract derived from Chinese worms."

This health talk has made Mary Bull serious. Her brow is furrowed and her face is all scrunched up. I walk over and smooth back her hair. She looks at me intently.

"Are you all right?" I ask.

"Yeah," she says. "Want me to do anything?"

"Why don't you run downstairs and see if David's home. Tell him we're ready to eat anytime."

She dashes out the door, taking the stairs like a tap dancer: ba-bump, ba-bump, ba-bump.

"Did I hear you say the magic word?" asks Searcy. "Dinner?"

"Almost," says Jeff.

"Fabulous," says Searcy. "I am simply famished!"

"What'd you do? Starve yourself all day?"

"Of course! A lady must always have a proper appetite or she risks insulting her host."

"Well, how 'bout throwing some silverware on the table?"

"Love to," says Searcy. "Love to be of help." He chants to himself, "Forks on the left, knives on the right, spoons in the middle so the rest don't fight. Is it just the five of us?"

"Yeah, Snookums couldn't make it."

"How come?"

"Had to work late."

"That job is gonna kill him!"

"Oh, he loves it. Everyone should be so lucky as to have a new challenge at fifty-five."

"To *live* to fifty-five," says Jeff.

"Ain't that the bloody truth?" adds Searcy.

"My goal is forty," Jeff informs us.

"Just forty? Mine's forty-five," I say. "I'd like to see the year Two Thousand."

"Actually," says Jeff, "I don't care about age. I just want to live while I'm still healthy enough to enjoy it. And when I'm not, I'd just like to disappear."

"Pity it doesn't work that way."

"Yes, a great pity."

Jeff pulls the casserole out of the oven.

"Ou, it smells divinely Italian," says Searcy excitedly.

"Lasagna," I tell him. "Jeff's recipe. Mary Bull's request."

"How marvelous! Are you also serving your wonderful salad concoction and your famous garlic bread?"

"You bet."

"Oh, wonderful! Should I run out and get some anchovies? You know how I love those salty little morsels. They almost make lettuce worthwhile."

"I've got a tin ready for you, Searce."

"You are a true friend, Zero. You humble me." He plants a kiss on my cheek, then flounces back to the couch. He plops down, his blousy shirt settling around him like a parachute. "What a day!" he announces with a sigh. "Do you know, I spent the entire afternoon rehearsing a new company of drag queens. There is nothing more exhausting!"

"What are you putting together?" asks Jeff.

"I'm just trying out some things . . . interspersing some production numbers into a Gong Show featuring some of our past winners. I'm also working on a personal tribute to Divine."

"Are you gonna play him?"

"Don't you think it was a part I was born for? Of course, I'm not as vulgar as he was. But acting should have some degree of challenge."

Mary Bull bounds back in with David behind her.

" 'Evening," says David, "and how is every little body?"

"Dying to eat," says Searcy. "What's been keeping you?"

"A meeting."

"What else?"

David comes into the kitchen and hands me a bag containing two pints of Häagen-Dazs. "My contribution."

"How'd it go?" I ask.

"Not entirely disastrous."

"What are you agitating for now?" asks Searcy.

"These student conferences I do for the school board. We've proposed one on homophobia and we're getting a lot of flack. The teachers and the bureaucrats say the students aren't ready. Which is a perfect example of why we need to have one. It's so maddening. Everyone deserves rights except when it comes to sexuality."

David pours himself a glass of wine. "I heard a bit of the news in a taxi on my way home. Did any of you hear it?"

"No, what happened?"

"More massive demonstrations in Prague. It looks like the government's about to resign. It's just amazing."

"Really," says Searcy, "it's like every country in Eastern Europe has decided to take off their chastity belt at once."

"I'd love to go to Prague," says Jeff.

"So would I," I tell him. "Ever since I saw a photo spread in *National Geographic.*"

"I saw that too," says Jeff, smiling. "I was about twelve, I think. Maybe we could go sometime."

"Maybe." I kiss the back of his neck. "You just never know."

Jeff cuts the lasagna into hearty portions and dishes it out onto plates.

"By the way," says David, "AIDS Action Now is having a demo Monday. For anonymous testing. I hope you'll all be there. It's very important and we need as many people as we can get."

"I hate demos," I whisper to Jeff. "I know they're necessary, but I just hate 'em. Marching in a circle, carrying signs, yelling slogans. There's gotta be a better way."

"Of course we'll be there," says Searcy. "Have we ever failed the cause?"

"Well," says David, looking slyly around the group. "Not in the long run."

"The first song I'll do," announces Mary Bull, "is 'Over the Rainbow.' "

"One of the greatest tunes ever written!" declares Searcy.

"I'll start in the style of Billie Holiday. In the bridge I'll go into Ella Fitzgerald. And I'll wind up as Aretha Franklin."

"Now, *this* I've gotta hear!"

"It is a pretty effective progression of styles," she says. "Well, here goes."

We all know a perfect performance when we hear one, and this was definitely perfect.

"Good lord!" exclaims Searcy. "What a set of pipes! And what an uncanny rendition of those great ladies' voices."

"Thanks. I've been rehearsing."

"Unbelievable," says David.

"You really ought to be in a school for gifted children," says Jeff.

"I had a great teacher in L.A. But she retired."

"I could put you to work right now," says Searcy.

"You could?" asks Mary Bull, wide-eyed.

"We'd have to lie about your age and say you were a man in drag. It'd be very *Victor/Victoria*, but—"

"She's only here till next Saturday," I remind him.

"More's the pity," he says, shaking his head. "But don't you worry, Mary Bull. You have a great career ahead of you. What do you plan to conquer first?"

"Broadway," she says without a moment's hesitation. "My dad and I are going to New York next week, and I plan on making the rounds."

"Then I must give you some advice."

"Oh yes, Searcy, do."

"First of all, get the trade papers—*Variety, Backstage*—and see what kind of auditions are going on. Anything you're even remotely right for, go to! Let nothing stop you. And I mean NOTHING. Not the lack of a union card, not the fact that you haven't been submitted by an agent. Just get in there and show 'em what you've got. You were born to sing, child. Born for it."

Mary Bull squeals with delight. "Yes!"

"It won't be easy. There're more rats in New York City than in the whole rest of the country."

"Oh, I'm used to rats."

"Then how 'bout giving us an encore?"

"What do you want to hear?"

"Anything. But in your own voice this time."

"What about 'The Hard-knock Life' from *Annie?*"

"Another one of my favorites!"

*   *   *

TIME AND OTHER BOMBS

Jeff, inspired by the genius of Mary Bull, goes back to his place to practice.

I do the dishes, then call my mother.

"David and I accept," I tell her.

"Oh, good!" she says. "I'm so excited. And Doll is just gonna wet herself! Now Sparky wants to put y'all up at the Capital Hotel, his treat. 'Course, I'd like to have you stay with me, but the condo's so cramped. And the new psychiatrist Sparky has me seeing says it just isn't good for me to sleep under the same roof as my children. Says it encourages me to revert to my old self."

"Since when did you become somebody new?"

"Ever since Sparky and I worked out our arrangement! I've decided not to worry anymore. Not about you. Not about money. Not even about Sparky's wife."

"Congratulations."

"Do you need me to send you a check for your airline tickets?"

"No, I believe we can manage. But I would like you to send an invitation to Trebreh."

"You've heard from him?"

"Have I ever. His thirteen-year-old daughter's been staying with me."

"His what?"

"His turkey-baster baby."

"What in god's name is that?"

"It's a method lesbians sometimes use to impregnate themselves. Trebreh was the sperm donor."

"I've got the picture. You needn't go into any greater detail."

"She's a wonderful child."

"I'll trust your judgment on that. What's his address?"

I read it off.

"I'd be very surprised if he came," I add, "but it'd be nice to invite him. After all, there hasn't been a big family do since your last wedding."

"We'll have no mention of that, thank you very much."

"Have you heard from Uncle Markus?"

"Oh yes. He called yesterday. He's coming, and bringing his new friend."

"Who?"

"The companion he took with him to Greece while his hip mended."

"You mean Jesus Las Vegas?"

"Do you know him?"

"I introduced them."

"Then maybe you could clear something up for me. Are he and Markus, you know . . ."

"Good question. Jesus is definitely in there helping him run those dinner theatres."

"You mean he's a gold digger?"

"He's a nice kid. You'll see."

"Well, I've also heard from the Houston gang. Cousin Betty's coming with her new husband, Peppy. Her mother and father are coming as well, and none of them have spoken since she married the guy. Carol swore they wouldn't make a scene. But I told her to go ahead. We love scenes, don't we?"

"We sure do." I laugh.

Then my mother asks, "Are you still feeling okay?"

"Don't start on that."

"I'm not trying to rile you up, Zero. I'm just asking."

"I'm feeling fine."

The five-inch Randy and I are traveling down the California coast road. It's a beautiful drive. Lush green cliffs and the roaring sea far below. I'm behind the wheel and Randy is lounging on a ball of cotton in the ashtray. We're yakking away, when all of a sudden the car veers off the road and over the edge of the cliff.

I wake to the sound of screaming. But they are not my screams. They are Mary Bull's.

I flick on a lamp, get out of bed, and go into the living room to check on her.

"Mary Bull?" I say, giving her a good shake. "You're having a nightmare. Wake up."

She executes a self-defense move that sends me crashing into the bookcase on the opposite side of the room.

"Damn," I curse, holding my aching arm.

"I want my mom!" she cries.

"Hush!" I say, losing patience. "You'll wake the whole neighborhood."

"I don't care! I want my mom!"

"Your mom's in L.A. You know that."

I turn on the overhead light.

"Too bright!" she whines, hiding beneath the mound of covers and kicking her feet.

"You're too old for this, Mary Bull. I want you to stop it."

"No! No! No! No! No! No! No!"

Fine.

What else can I do but just leave her alone? That, of course, straightens her up faster than anything. She soon throws back the covers and sits up, face streaked with tears.

"Listen," I tell her, "I was having a bad dream, too. It must've been something we ate. Probably those damn anchovies."

"I wasn't dreaming," she says pitifully. "I was wide awake. I just want my mom."

"Then why don't you pick up the phone and call her?"

"At this hour?" She sniffles. "She'd kill me."

"Then call Trebreh."

"I don't want to talk to him. Don't you understand plain English? I want my mom!"

She flips facedown in the pillow and wails anew.

I move to the edge of the couch and stroke her gently. "Mary Bull, come on. You're just homesick, honey, that's all. You had a nightmare. But you'll be all right. You'll see. Everything'll be better in the morning."

She looks up at me, wanting to believe. "Promise?" she says.

"I promise."

"Then will you tell me a story? To make me forget about it and everything?"

"A story?"

"My mom tells me stories."

"What kind of a story?"

"Any kind."

I think about it a minute.

"All right. This story features me and your father, and it's called 'Why I Don't Like Mayonnaise.' "

"Mayonnaise?"

"Yes, mayonnaise. It's also about the first time we visited New York."

"New York?"

"My mother had to go into the hospital for a hysterectomy. The doctor said she needed some peace and quiet around the house when she came home to recover. My grandmother sent my brother off to camp, my sister to our cousins down in Houston, and Trebreh and me to see Uncle Markus in New York. You can't imagine how thrilled I was. Me, a little hick from Arkansas, about to gain some New York sophistication. I was twelve years old. Trebreh was fourteen.

"We left Little Rock the morning Robert Kennedy was shot. I was too excited to sleep, so I was watching the early-morning TV shows. It was the only story. And when we got to Manhattan, the body lay in state just a few blocks from Uncle Markus's town house. Mary Bull, I'm telling you, we had arrived!

"I tried to share my enthusiasm with Trebreh, but he was going through a disagreeable stage."

"You must mean puberty."

"Something like that. Anyway, Uncle Markus lived on East Forty-ninth Street. A hulking butler answered the door and carried our bags upstairs. Trebreh wanted to know if he could carry us as well, but the butler didn't seem to understand English.

"Uncle Markus and his friend Jack were in the living room waiting for us. You wouldn't believe how Uncle Markus's was decorated. The walls were covered with fabric. Huge, naked marble statues were posed in every corner. Through it all ran a brook, complete with a miniature barge that worked by remote control and carried cocktails from one end of the room to the other. Uncle Markus and Jack were drinking martinis. Trebreh and I had Cokes, but in martini glasses.

"I was thrilled to see my uncle, but I was ecstatic to see Jack. He was the most handsome man I'd ever laid eyes on. Secretly, I imagined sweeping him off his feet, being ordered to slowly remove his clothing and join him for a nap.

"We dined that night at the famous Rainbow Grill, a posh supper club high atop Rockefeller Center, with first-rate entertainment. That night it was Duke Ellington. I was simply beside myself.

It was all so elegant and perfect. That is, until Trebreh ordered turtle soup."

"What's wrong with turtle soup?"

"Nothing, ordinarily. But when the waiter brought it, Trebreh fished through the bowl with his spoon, then promptly sent it back. The waiter brought a second bowl. Trebreh sent that back as well. Finally, the waiter said, 'May I ask what the problem is?'

" 'The problem,' said Trebreh, 'is that there's no turtle. If you're gonna charge seven-fifty for a bowl of turtle soup, I ought to at least get a turtle.'

" 'But we don't put whole turtles in turtle soup,' the waiter explained. 'We cut them up. We cook them. Look,' he pointed, 'that's a piece of turtle right there.'

" 'It is not!' said Trebreh. 'I know a turtle when I see one.'

"Uncle Markus had a word with the waiter, who removed the soup and asked Trebreh, 'May I bring you something else?'

" 'A cheeseburger.'

" 'We don't serve cheeseburgers. Perhaps a steak sandwich?'

" 'That'll be fine,' said Uncle Markus.

" 'Rare,' said Trebreh.

"Crisis averted, Uncle Markus began to rattle off the agenda he had planned for the week. Broadway shows, a concert, a ballet. Then dinner came, and we ate.

"Trebreh and I finished quickly and got up to go look out the windows and take in the spectacular view. The city seemed to go on forever, shimmering with light like a million exotic jewels."

"Oh, I can't wait to see it!"

"Next thing I knew, Trebreh was over talking to the Duke."

"What'd he say?"

"He gave him a dollar and asked him to play 'Hello, Dolly!' "

"And did he?"

"A little bit of the chorus. It was a popular song of the day." I pause. "Are you getting sleepy yet?"

"Not on your life!"

Just my luck. "Well," I continue. "The next day, Uncle Markus arranged for Jack to take us on a bus tour of the city. It was a whirlwind. We saw Lincoln Center, Central Park, the United Nations, the Empire State Building, Chinatown, Wall Street, and were at Battery Park by noon, waiting for the ferry to go over to the Statue of Liberty. Trebreh was still fixated on eating a cheeseburger, so Jack went and got us all one from an old man with a concession cart. They were the weirdest-tasting cheeseburgers I'd ever had. Horsemeat, blue rare. But I ate every bite, not wanting to seem ungrateful.

"My nausea grew with each lurch of the boat. I finally went below deck to the men's room and made myself throw up, which helped. I suggested Jack do the same, noticing the greenish tint to his handsome face, but he dismissed the idea. Only Trebreh escaped unscathed. On Liberty Island, he ran up and down however many flights there are between ground and crown merrily singing, 'They're Coming to Take Me Away, Ha-ha, Hee-hee, Ho-ho.' It was maddening.

"Back on Manhattan, Jack, claiming a need for fresh air, suggested we take a horse-drawn carriage back up to my uncle's. Now I was fully recovered! And I sat right next to Jack, scooting as close as I dared, hoping he'd at least put his arm around me. He probably would've, too, had the nuisance Trebreh not been snapping pictures of us, insanely giggling all the while. Unfortunately, there was no film in his camera, so I don't have any photographic evidence of that romantic ride.

"The carriage pulled up to Uncle Markus's place. Jack asked if we could see ourselves inside. I assured him we could, then said in my best movie-star voice, 'My cousin and I would like to thank you for a most enchanting day.'

" 'Oh, you're welcome,' Jack said dismissively, nudging the driver to get going.

" 'Perhaps we could do it again tomorrow?' I asked.

"Jack gave me a stunned look. I guess he didn't want anyone, least of all the carriage driver, to suspect there was something between us. 'Oh, no!' he said. 'Not tomorrow.' And the carriage pulled away at a fierce speed. 'But I'll be in touch.'

"What a gentleman Jack was!

"As we walked up the steps to the town house, Trebreh began imitating me: 'My cousin and I would like to thank you for a most enchanting day. A most enchanting, chanting day.'

" 'At least I have manners,' I snapped.

" 'Oh yeah? Why didn't you just sit in his lap?'

59

TIME AND OTHER BOMBS

" 'You don't know the first thing about how society works, Trebreh.'

" 'I sure know a decent bowl of turtle soup when I see one.'

"The butler opened the door. 'Nice day?' he inquired in a heavy European accent.

" 'It was enchanting,' said Trebreh, then he went promptly upstairs, removed his shoes and socks, and began soaking his feet in the living-room brook.

"For the remainder of the week, our daytime chaperon was a stern German lady. The only place she took us was the Museum of Natural History, which was fine for a day, but Trebreh and I began to grow bored with dusty relics. Uncle Markus continued to take us out in the evenings. We saw *Mame, Fiddler on the Roof,* the New York City Ballet, the Philharmonic. But on our last night, Uncle Markus had a business dinner that he just couldn't get out of. It was also the butler's night off. So I suggested that Trebreh and I just stay in the town house, eat some frozen dinners, and watch TV, to which Uncle Markus readily agreed. Actually, we had another plan in mind.

"The second Uncle Markus was out the door, Trebreh and I dressed for a night on the town. 'Something mod!' I insisted. We wore all plaid. Even tied plaid neckties around our heads like headbands. Our intention was to see the scandalous hit musical, *Hair,* which we'd heard so much about.

"I hurried Trebreh out of Uncle Markus's building and across Forty-ninth to the theatre district. When the man in the box office told us the price of the tickets, I informed Trebreh he would have to pay, as I simply didn't have that much money. Luckily, Trebreh has always been generous where finances are concerned.

"We fell in love with the show. It was so energetic and full of good music. But best of all, the three main characters—two men and a woman—were all in love with each other, if you get my drift."

"I've got it."

"They took baths together, they were always hugging on each other. Then when Claude, the hero, got sent off to Vietnam . . . Mary Bull, it liked to kill me.

"When the performance was over, I had the saddest feeling. A feeling that life, no matter how hard I worked at it, would never be as good for me as it was for that tribe of characters onstage. I had to depend on Trebreh to pull me out of it, and he did.

"With my last five dollars, I took us to Sardi's. We could only afford a plate of plain pasta, which we had to share, but it was worth every penny.

"Walking back to Uncle Markus's, we were propositioned by a man in the back of a limo, who mistook us for boy prostitutes. Trebreh and I were delighted. We giggled wildly. A perfect end to a perfect day.

"The next afternoon, loaded down with our New York City souvenirs, we flew back to Little Rock. When we got home, I immediately ran upstairs to check on my mom. I was so excited to see her that I jumped right on her bed. She screamed in agony, 'Zero! For god's sake, be careful. I just had half my innards removed!' And she held herself, moaning.

" 'Sorry,' I said.

"I told her I intended to move to New York someday. I told her I was gonna do everything I could to lose my hick twang. Trebreh had suggested I start calling information in Brooklyn and studying the operators' diction. I thought that was a pretty good idea. But Mom just said she was tired and would I please carry her lunch tray back down to Stellrita in the kitchen?

" 'Sure,' I said, and I picked it up from the side of her bed and left the room.

"She had hardly touched her dessert. A big bowl of half-melted vanilla ice cream, one of my favorites.

"I took a seat at the top of the stairs, the tray in my lap, leaned over it like a hungry dog, and gobbled up a bite. I gagged as my taste buds registered what the flavor really was. Not ice cream at all. Mayonnaise."

"Gross!" says Mary Bull, holding her stomach, rolling around on the couch, laughing. "That is so gross!"

"And that is the end of the story. Now go to sleep."

The night of Trebreh's show, Snookums offers to baby-sit Mary Bull.

TIME AND OTHER BOMBS

"I'm too old for a sitter," she informs him the minute he walks in the door.

"Well then," he replies, "you must think of me as a confidante."

"I don't need one of those, either. Why are you wearing that turban?"

"Fashion, precious."

"Let me try it on."

"Now, precious, you don't want to look like an old man, do you?"

"I won't look like an old man. I'll look like me, but with an old man's turban."

"Well"—Snookums throws me a look—"maybe later."

"But I'm a lesbian!" announces Mary Bull, full-out.

"Really?" says Snookums. "And you've only been in this house a little over a week."

"I was *born* a lesbian. So it won't matter whether I look like an old man or not."

"I'm not sure I follow your logic."

"About wearing your turban. I want to try it on!"

"Mary Bull," says Jeff, "give it a rest."

"You guys don't want me to have any fun," she pouts. "You won't let me go to my dad's show; you won't let me wear a turban—"

Jeff pulls five dollars out of his wallet and gives it to her.

"And now you're trying to buy me off!"

"I'm not trying to buy you off. This is for you to take Snookums up Church Street for a frozen yogurt later on, okay?"

"Do I get to keep the change?"

"If there is any."

"There'll be two dollars and thirty cents if we both get smalls."

"Let him get whatever he wants," says Jeff.

"What a precious thing she is," says Snookums.

"Oh, don't gush," says Mary Bull. "I hate it when gay men gush."

"And I hate it when children turn ornery. If you're in that bad of a mood, you ought to retire to your room."

"That's telling her," I say.

"But this *is* my room!" says Mary Bull.

November 1989

I kiss Snookums on the cheek. "You're a dear for spelling us off like this. We'll try not to be too late."

"Whenever. I've got plenty of work to keep me busy after this one goes to bed."

"I'm not going to bed until my dad gets here!" Mary Bull marches in a circle.

"You boys enjoy yourselves."

"You too."

Colby's is packed, the audience high on anticipation. To think that the famous hunk they've masturbated to so often is gonna be here doing it for 'em live.

A special table has been set aside at the front for our group. Jeff and I make our way through the crowd. David is already there, along with a handful of Jeff's friends: several artist types, a couple of style puppies, and a lone disco bunny whose head never stops bobbing to the blaring music. David seems to know one of the artists and is busy working his charm. I'd say they had an affair that never quite began or never quite ended and just might find itself on the revival circuit tonight.

We order our first round of drinks.

Half an hour passes.

We order our second round.

An hour passes.

I get up and mosey over to have a word with the MC, local drag queen Misty Morning.

"Any news of the star?" I ask.

"We're expecting him any minute," she says automatically.

"Wasn't he supposed to start at eleven?"

"You know these things never begin on time."

A chant, from the back of the bar, is gaining momentum:

> Bill-lee, Bill-lee, we want Bill-lee.
> Bill-lee, Bill-lee, we want Bill-lee!

The stage manager looks at Misty. "Do something!" he pleads.

"What?"

63

TIME AND OTHER BOMBS

"How should I know? You're a performer. Perform!"

"I am not getting up on that stage until Billy Rockett is at least in this bar. You can't hold a crowd with lipstick and heels when what they've come for is dick. That's a suicide mission if ever I've heard one."

"Did someone go to meet his plane?" I ask.

"Who the hell are you anyway, his mother?"

"His cousin."

"Yes, someone went to meet his plane. Sam, our manager. Do you know Sam?"

"Only to see him. Did the plane arrive on time?"

"Yes. They're probably just stuck in traffic. Must be something on at the Skydome." Misty nervously nibbles her fake nails.

I head back to the table.

Searcy arrives, fashionably late, dressed as a jumbo Jeanette MacDonald: frills, bonnet, hoopskirt, the works.

"I see the family's grown," he observes, taking in all the new faces at the table.

Jeff introduces him to the three artists, the two style puppies, and the lone disco bunny.

"I'm charmed," says Searcy. "So pleased to meet you all." Then he grabs the waiter by the arm. "A grasshopper, please, to match the green in my frock."

"And another round for the rest of us, please," I add.

Jeff drains his glass, leans over, and whispers in my ear, "Did anyone ever tell you you're a helluva lot sexier than your cousin?"

"In a word, no."

"I can't wait to get you in bed tonight." He presses his leg against mine.

"It has been a few days."

Under the table, he takes my hand and places it on his crotch.

"Looks like a goddamn fire over there," says Searcy. "Am I gonna have to hose you boys down?"

"No," Jeff assures him, "we'll behave." He bites my earlobe, then growls.

"When, oh when," asks Searcy, "is it gonna be my turn?" He

drums his fingers on the table. The waiter brings the drinks. Searcy takes a sip of his, then bellows out a high C.

On hearing this piercing note, Misty Morning sashays over and plants herself in front of Searcy.

"Miss Goldberg," she says, "I'll thank you to remember there's only one diva here tonight."

"Don't you worry, hon"—Searcy gestures broadly—"it's all yours."

"Yeah? I've heard that one before."

"I mean it."

"Convince me."

Searcy throws himself at Misty's feet, no small task considering his size and the hoopskirt.

Misty giggles. "Now that's what I call devotion!"

"You mean I get a prize?"

"Yes. I appoint you honorary dowager duchess to the district court of Club Colby's."

"Don't make me cry," says Searcy, hoisting himself up.

Misty hollers to the cocktail waiter. "Another round for the VIPs. On the house!"

"We're gonna be obliterated by the time we leave here," I say to Jeff.

"That seems to be the idea."

The restless chant for Billy Rocket resumes:

> Bill-lee, Bill-lee, we want Bill-lee.
> Bill-lee, Bill-lee, we want Bill-lee!

The stage is suddenly illuminated with light, which catches Misty off guard. "Uh-oh," she says. "My cue." She looks back at the stage manager.

"Start the intro," he mouths, "but stall, stall, stall."

"Charles Pierce, give me strength," mutters Misty, crossing herself. She steps onstage, picks up the microphone, and breathes into it to make sure it's turned on.

The roar of the crowd subsides.

"That's right," says Misty. "A little heavy breathing and every fag in town perks up."

Big laugh.

"Ladies and gentleman, welcome. This is what's known as an introduction."

"Take it off!" cries a voice from the back.

"Puh-leaze," says Misty. "If you had any idea how long it took to create this illusion, you wouldn't be so anxious to have it destroyed."

"Yes I would! Take it off! We want some flesh!"

"Bouncer, take that man to my dressing room, tie him up, and gag him. I'll deal with him later."

Another big laugh.

"What a nice audience," says Misty sarcastically. "But now I want you all to shut the fuck up, because Misty has a story to tell. A story of when Misty Morning was just a little boy in Burlington, Ontario, as normal as anybody could be. But after her lights went out, after her mommy and daddy listened to her sweet little thankful prayers, she dreamt of a man. Yes, a man named Billy Rockett, who'd climb through her window, spread her little-boy legs, and fuck the frigging freckles off her back."

"Something we'd all like to see!" That same heckler.

"I had an older cousin," Misty continues. "I'd give him a blow-job, and he'd give me his old dirty magazines. Most of them featured Billy. That's how we got acquainted. In fact, I'm very sentimental about Billy to this day. I don't think many people realize the person behind the star. Or the person behind Misty Morning, for that matter."

"Take it off!"

"That's enough out of you!" Misty snaps. "Never interrupt a drag queen when she's thinking, she doesn't do it very often."

"That's telling him!" someone shouts.

"Performing is one hard job, ladies and gentlemen, no pun intended. By the way, do we have any ladies with us tonight?"

"Yes," cry a bunch of college boys accompanied by a female friend.

"Where?" asks Misty, shielding her eyes from the stage lights and peering into the crowd.

"Here!"

Misty spots them. "Oh, hi, honey! And what's your name?"

The girl giggles. "Phyllis."

"Phyllis. Isn't that pretty? Are you straight or gay, Phyllis?"

"Straight."

"Oh yeah? Come on up to the stage and let Misty Morning get a better look at you."

Phyllis, unfamiliar with the antics of drag queens, does as requested.

Misty takes Phyllis's chin in her hand and moves her head from side to side. "No, Phyllis, I don't think so."

"I am!" she insists, laughing heartily.

"No way does Misty Morning believe that, not for one misty minute."

"It's true! I even have a boyfriend."

"Pulling rank, are we? Is he out there tonight?"

"No, he couldn't make it. I'm with some friends."

"Uh-huh. And I suppose you're gonna try and tell me they're straight?"

"Oh no, they're gay."

"Well, thank god for small favors. But I'd be careful, Phyllis. They're probably trying to recruit you."

"Or turn me into a fag hag." She giggles again.

"My! You seem to know a lot about the subject."

"Oh, I do."

"Are you also familiar with Billy Rockett?"

"Why else do you think I'm here?"

"Well, life is full of surprises, isn't it? You're a good sport, Phyllis. Ladies and gentlemen, let's have a big hand for that old dyke Phyllis."

"Thanks," says Phyllis, remaining on the stage, grinning at the audience.

"You can sit down now, honey."

"What?"

"I said, go back to your friends, girl, go!" Misty gives her a friendly push. "God!" she says under her breath, "anyone else wanta try to steal my act?"

TIME AND OTHER BOMBS

"Billy Rockett!" yells another heckler.

Misty rolls her eyes. "Not that again."

> Bill-lee, Bill-lee, we want Bill-lee.
> Bill-lee, Bill-lee, we want Bill-lee!

"And you'll get him," snaps Misty. "Really, you are so impatient!"

"He was supposed to be on at eleven. It's almost one!"

Misty peruses the front row. She plants a high-heeled foot in the lap of one of Jeff's style puppies.

"What's your name, honey?"

"Rog."

"And are you straight or gay?"

"Gay."

"When'd you come out, Rog?"

"A few years ago."

"What'd you do before that?"

"A lot of parks."

"You had sex with men in parks?"

"I had a dog."

"Now that *is* kinky."

"I walked my dog in the park. If I happened to meet a man cruising there . . ."

"I think I've got the picture. But what finally brought you out?"

"Therapy."

"You mean therapy is actually responsible for something positive in this world?"

"Well, it made me bisexual."

"And two halves don't exactly fill a hole, do they, Rog?"

"No, I had to go the rest of the way myself."

"Good for you!"

"Quit stalling!" cries another heckler.

> Bill-lee, Bill-lee, we want Bill-lee.
> Bill-lee, Bill-lee, we want Bill-lee!

Misty shoots a desperate look at the stage manager, who shrugs helplessly.

November 1989

A clone type appears at the side of the stage puffing nervously on a cigarette. It's Sam. I go over and ask him what the hell's happened to Trebreh.

"He wasn't on the plane," he says. "He wasn't on the goddamn flight!"

The chant from the audience is gaining a nasty edge:

Bill-lee, Bill-lee, we want Bill-lee.
Bill-lee, Bill-lee, we want Bill-lee!

"Christ!" says Sam. "I'm gonna have a fucking riot on my hands."

I go back to the table and say to Jeff, "He's not showing up. Let's get out of here."

Bill-lee, Bill-lee, we want Bill-lee.
Bill-lee, Bill-lee, we want Bill-lee!

The audience bangs their beer bottles and cocktail glasses in rhythm to the chant; they stomp their feet.

Sam calls Misty Morning over to the side of the stage and has what looks like desperate words with her. Lord knows what he promises her, but it must be good. Because after some confusion, a jazz version of "Let Me Entertain You" comes over the sound system. Misty returns to center stage and begins a strip.

The wig is the first thing to go. Then the eyelashes. Then she takes a jar of cold cream and walks the perimeter of the stage, rubbing the cream into her makeup. She grabs a wad of cocktail napkins from one of the tables and wipes herself clean. She presents the back of her dress to Searcy, who unzips it. With a bump and a grind, she shimmies it down her body. She kicks off her heels. She props her left leg on a chair and slowly rolls down a stocking. She props her right leg up and does the same thing. She is quite a handsome man, and the chant for Billy Rockett subsides.

Misty dances in his underwear, letting various gentlemen tuck bills into his waistband. Searcy gives him a twenty and says, "You've sure got balls, honey."

"Yeah, and now I've got five minutes to get good and hard."

TIME AND OTHER BOMBS

Misty slips the underwear down a bit, exposing his tan line. He shows some butt. He pulls the shorts up again and dances some more. When he finally sheds the underwear, he is plenty erect and well enough endowed to shush even the most discontented. He wraps up the strip like the best of pros. Then . . . blackout.

"All right!" whoops Searcy, jumping to his feet, starting a standing ovation.

Misty appears in his robe to take his bows.

I toss twenty-five dollars on the table and mime to David that Jeff and I are leaving. "Want to come?" I ask.

"No," he says, smiling at his artist friend. "I think I'll make my own way."

Snookums is sitting in the living room with the lights out, drinking.

"Was she *that* bad?" I ask.

"She's gone," he whimpers.

"What?!"

"Your cousin called. The tour's been canceled. He had me put her in a car for the airport immediately. Said there was a ticket waiting for her at the Air Canada desk. He wanted her to take the midnight flight back to L.A. She was perfectly livid, the poor child. Missing her chance at New York. She cursed the whole time she was packing. Lord knows what all she forgot."

I take the drink from Snookums' hand. "You don't really need this, do you?"

"No," he answers meekly. "It's just that I was so upset. I wonder if I did the right thing, letting her go?"

"What else could you have done? Trebreh's her father. He calls the shots."

"If you had been here, precious, it wouldn't've seemed that simple. There's nothing worse than seeing a child's heart break."

"Snookums, I apologize for this turning into such an ordeal. But it's over now, and you'd better go home and get some rest. You've got a magazine to run tomorrow."

"I'm sorry, precious."

"There's nothing to be sorry about."

"Oh, I hope so. I sincerely hope so."

I help Snookums with his coat, then he totters out the door and down the staircase.

Jeff and I take a minute to catch our breath.

"You okay?" he finally asks.

"I feel like I've been slugged in the stomach. Other than that . . ." I shake my head. "I should've known. It's just like him." I sigh. "I'm trying my best to look on the bright side."

"What bright side?"

"Who would've thought we'd have the place to ourselves tonight, huh?"

"Yeah, who would've thought?"

A SHINDIG IN LITTLE ROCK

February 1990

"Should I take my red bow tie or my yellow? What do you think?"

"The yellow," Jeff says.

"It's not too much? Even with a yellow shirt?"

"I like you in lots of yellow. You'll be the cutest one at your sister's birthday party. Trust me." He lolls in my bed.

I put the yellow tie in my suitcase, along with my blazer, a dress shirt, and a pair of decent trousers.

"What time's the airporter car coming?" he asks.

"Ten-thirty."

"I'm already lonesome."

"It's only for the weekend, Jeff. We ought to be able to survive that."

He smiles invitingly. "Oh yeah?"

"Stop acting so irresistible. You'll make me forget something."

"The only thing you're forgetting is—"

"Socks." I look around. "Now I set a pair of navy blue socks out last night. What the hell happened to them?"

"I didn't even know you owned a pair of navy blue socks."

"Sure I do." I open my dresser drawer. "Damn. All that's in here is white. I can't wear white socks with a suit."

75

A SHINDIG IN LITTLE ROCK

"Then don't wear any. I love a man in semiformal dress without socks. It's very sexy. That vulnerable bit of flesh peeking out between cuff and shoe."

"Sexy is not what I'm shooting for at this particular event."

"No?"

"Sex is the last thing on my mind when I'm with my family. What could've happened to those socks?"

"If you're so worried about it, Zero, take those gray argyles I had on last night. They'll do."

They're lying with the rest of Jeff's clothes on the bedroom chair. I pick them up.

"That way you'll have a little scent of me to take with you."

I clench them in my teeth. "And you know how I love your appendages."

He pulls back the covers, teasing me with his cock. He moves it from side to side as it begins to grow. "Happy three-month anniversary," he says.

"Three months? Has it already been three months?"

"To the day."

"Then I *must* be in love."

"Of course you're in love." He reaches for me, pulls me on top of him. "What else did you think this was?"

"I don't know. A mirage."

His erection springs between my legs. "This is no mirage."

"No"—I grip it tightly—"it's certainly not."

We kiss.

"I love your fat, soft lips," I say.

We kiss again.

A few minutes later, we're interrupted by a furious knocking at my apartment door.

"Zero?" calls David from the hallway. "I need a word with you."

"We're still in bed," I call back.

"It's important!"

"So is this!"

I hear him jiggling the doorknob. "Come on," he says. "Open up!"

I pad my way into the living room and let David in. "This better be good," I tell him.

"Have you seen the morning paper?"

"Of course not. Like I said, we're still in bed."

"Ontario's chief medical officer has recommended that the Minister of Health reclassify AIDS as a virulent disease."

"What's that supposed to mean?"

"That the government could forcibly detain people with AIDS up to four months without a trial."

"That's insane."

I go back to the bedroom and join Jeff under the covers.

David follows me, but has the good sense to stop in the doorway.

"And it's too early for politics, David."

"Dr. Schabas also said any seropositive who continued to have sex, safe or otherwise, should be quarantined. Which would include all of us."

"That'd be some camp," says Jeff.

"David, really, there's no way a recommendation like that will go through. These maniacs are always coming up with outrageous proposals. It makes the paper and that's the end of it."

"Don't be so sure. British Columbia and Alberta already have quarantine laws on their books."

"So what happens now?" Jeff asks.

"The minister either passes it on to Cabinet, or she kills it."

"Has the minister made any sort of comment?"

"No. She's in India for the month on holiday."

"That's convenient."

"That's government. Four community groups, and the Canadian AIDS Society, which is not known for its radical stance, have already demanded Schabas's resignation. There's a big demo in the works for tonight and I've gotta call everyone on my phone tree before we leave."

"But the car'll be here in half an hour."

"There's nothing I can do about it, Zero."

"Yes, there is," says Jeff. "I'll call them for you. Just leave me the information."

"You sure?"

"Sure I'm sure. It's the least I can do."

"Satisfied, David? Will you leave us alone now?"

A SHINDIG IN LITTLE ROCK

"Yeah. Sorry."

"I'll be downstairs with my suitcase as soon as I've had a chance to clean up. You can give Jeff his instructions then."

David's bag is by the front door, but he's sitting at his kitchen table doing voodoo. He's torn Schabas's picture from the newspaper and is piercing it relentlessly with pins.

"Does that really work?" asks Jeff.

"Believe it," I say. "He really knows how to put 'em through it. Just hope he never gets a bug up his ass about you."

"Well," says David, "anything I can do to help conquer ignorance. That's the list of people to be phoned. If you get an answering machine, go ahead and leave a message. But be sure to explain the situation as thoroughly as possible. Remember, most people don't read."

"Okay."

"There're a couple of press releases that need to be photocopied and dropped off at the CBC."

"No problem."

The car honks from the street.

"There's our ride."

"You guys enjoy yourselves," says Jeff.

"We'll do our best." I give him a hug. "I'll miss you."

"I'll miss you, too."

The flight is blessedly smooth and uneventful. An hour later, we land in Nashville, where we change planes for the short hop to Little Rock.

The second plane is much smaller, and it's packed. David and I don't get to sit together. I do, however, get a window seat, and after takeoff, I lean my chair back and watch for the mud-laden Arkansas River to come into view.

It slithers through the landscape of bluffs and pine trees like some kind of prehistoric serpent. I love to stare at it. It hypnotizes me. It gives me a sense of my whole life being one blazing moment. As we begin our descent, you can actually see the swiftly moving currents. Everything you could want, I think to myself, right there in front of you.

The flight attendant taps me on the shoulder. "Hello?" she says in a heavy twang. "Anyone home?"

I look at her with a blank expression.

"Yes, you, honey pie. I'm talking to you. We'll be landing momentarily. I need your chair in the upright position. Didn't you hear the announcement?"

"No," I mutter. "Sorry."

"That's all right." She smiles. "It's just that airline safety depends on each and every passenger observing the rules."

Inside the terminal, my mother's voice calls out to us, "Zero! David! Welcome to Little Rock!"

I wave to her. We make our way through the throng, then I give her a hug, careful not to muss her shellacked, helmetlike hairdo.

Her hands run over my back. "You feel mighty skinny, Zero. I can feel your ribs. You haven't lost more weight, have you?"

"Maybe a pound or two. But I'm sure I'll gain it back in the next few days."

"I certainly hope so."

"You're looking good," I tell her.

"Thank you."

She hugs David. "Good to see you, David. I'm so glad you could make it."

"Thanks for inviting me."

"You all just can't imagine how touched Doll is that you'd take the time off and spend the money to come all this way for her birthday. She couldn't be more thrilled."

"Where is Doll?" I ask.

"Oh, she had some meeting or other, some new crisis at the store. But she'll be joining us at my place for dinner later on."

We walk toward the baggage-claim area, Mom chatting excitedly about the weekend's festivities, who's getting in when, and what's on each menu.

When we get to the baggage carousel, she says, "I'll go out to the parking lot and bring the car up to the emergency lane just outside the door. That way, y'all won't have to carry your luggage all over kingdom come, okay?"

"Fine. But we don't have much luggage."

"Still, I don't want you to exhaust yourself!" She smiles, ever the gracious hostess, and traipses out the automatic double doors.

David and I exchange a conspiratorial look.

"Sure am glad we're staying at a hotel," I say.

"Me too."

We go out to the car.

Mom has her window rolled down and is chatting with an elderly black man who, it looks like, was just walking by. She sees us in the rearview mirror and releases the trunk. We throw in our bags.

"Boys," she says, introducing the man, "this is Leroy Jones. Leroy, you remember my son, don't you?"

He looks at David. "Why, yes, ma'am. I surely do. Fine lookin' young man."

"No, that's not him. That's his friend. Zero's the one who looks kind of like me."

" 'Course," says Leroy.

"Leroy used to deliver our dry cleaning when we lived on Main," Mom informs us. "He's here to pick up his daughter. She's flying in from New Orleans, where she works as a criminal lawyer. Isn't that something?"

"Not a job I'd want," I say, "but somebody's gotta do it."

"That's because you don't want any job. Not where you have to get up in the morning or make a decent living! Zero's in the arts," she explains to Leroy. "He and David have just come all the way from Canada."

Leroy smiles and nods, then glances at his watch. "Goodness me," he says. "I'd better get on down to the gate 'fore my girl thinks I've deserted her."

"Well, it sure is good to see you."

"You too, Miz MacNoo."

"Call me Edie."

"Yes, ma'am, Miz Edie."

Leroy saunters into the terminal as David and I climb in the car. I take the front seat; he takes the back. He immediately starts digging for his seat belt, which is deeply buried under the seat because my mother doesn't believe in them.

"I tell you," says Mom, pulling out of the emergency lane with a dangerous lurch, "dry-cleaning delivery just hasn't been the same since that man retired."

"I wonder if I should've rented a car?" I ask her.

"No, darling, I want you to use *my* car while you're here."

"Well, what'll *you* do?"

"Use Doll's. Until Sparky comes, then he always rents one."

She pulls onto the freeway, nearly getting sideswiped by a pickup truck. The driver swerves to avoid her, honking and cursing. Mom remains oblivious. "The traffic in this town just gets worse and worse," she says.

David continues his elusive search with a growing air of desperation.

"How do you think Doll likes being back in Little Rock?" I ask.

"I think she likes it fine," says Mom. "She loves her job, though she's buying for six departments and it's just about to kill her. But she's so conscientious. I just hope she didn't move back on account of me."

"She loves being close to you. You're her primary relationship, like it or not."

"I love it! It just worries me that she doesn't have any friends of her own, 'cept for the people she works with. Nor does she have any male companionship. Says every decent man she meets is either gay or married."

"But I thought she was seeing somebody."

"You must mean that redneck she met at her singles' club. That's purely biological. He's no match for Doll. Lives in a trailer, has a daughter named Taffy, and doesn't even know how to use a salad fork."

Downtown looms before us.

"I thought I'd swing by the hotel so y'all could check in and drop off your stuff."

Mom cuts across two lanes of traffic and exits onto Main Street. A couple of stoplights later, we're there. David still has not found his seat belt.

A SHINDIG IN LITTLE ROCK

"I've already put your room on my American Express," Mom says, "so don't let 'em charge you twice."

"Aren't you comin' in?"

"No. I'll just circle the block. No need parking the car when you're only gonna be five minutes."

We retrieve our bags, then walk into the hotel's magnificent lobby.

I ask the clerk at the front desk if we may have a room on the river side. He does some shuffling, adds ten dollars to the nightly rate, and says, "One key or two?"

"Two."

"That's Room 307. Need a bellhop?"

"I believe we can manage."

"The elevator's just around the corner."

"Thank you."

"You're gonna love this elevator," I say to David. "It's a vintage 1920 brass cage."

We step into it, then clunk our way up to the third floor.

Our room is beautiful. River view. High ceilings. Two very comfortable queen-size beds. And an old-fashioned tiled bathroom.

"Nice," says David.

"Isn't it? I think they did just a wonderful job renovating this place. You should have seen it when I was a kid. Barely hanging on. Nothing in it but a pool hall."

We hang up our semiformal duds, then head back downstairs.

We find my mother idling across the street in the taxi stand. Several irate cabdrivers are honking and making faces at her. She waves back at them, mouthing, "Sorry. I'll be gone in just a minute."

We get in the car.

"Your room all right?" Mom asks.

"Excellent."

"The whole family's gonna be staying down here."

"I'm sure they'll all be very comfortable. When's Sparky getting in?"

"I don't know."

"But I thought this whole weekend was his idea."

"It was."

"Then don't you think he should be here?"

"He'll be here. I just don't know when."

"That's strange."

"No, it's not. I never know when he's coming or going. And if I have to spell it out for you, it's his wife. Hilda's been keeping a pretty tight rein on him lately."

"What happened? Did she catch y'all again?"

"No. She didn't catch us. I just made a little boo-boo on Sparky's sixtieth birthday last month."

"What'd you do?"

"I'd really rather not discuss it."

"Aw, come on, Mom. I love to hear about your capers."

"It was not a 'caper.' It was an unfortunate accident and it's best forgotten."

"How can I forget something I don't even know?"

She shakes her head. "You are still a brat. Some things never change, do they?"

"I'm naturally curious," I correct her. "It comes with being a writer."

"That's exactly what I'm afraid of. But this is not for publication. You got it?"

"Got it."

She drums her fingers on the steering wheel. "Where to begin? A man only has one sixtieth birthday, and I just wanted to do something special. Sparky's been so good to me, he really has. Ever since my brief marriage to J.B., he's been a changed man. And I don't mean about the condo and the bills and things. I mean by figuring out what kind of relationship we can have and have now. No more waiting around for Hilda to either divorce him or die. He's made a point of being in Little Rock at least two days a week. And I wanted to show him how much I appreciated it. Problem is, he's got one of everything and two of most. Then I stumbled on the balloon idea."

"The balloon idea?"

"Yes. You know all these cute little balloon places that have cropped up in the last few years? Well, I decided to send him a balloon-o-gram. Sixty heart-shaped balloons accompanied by a gypsy violinist to serenade him with 'Laura.' That's our song," she explains to David.

"I had the balloons sent to his office, of course. His secretary warned me that he usually left early on his birthday, so I made sure they could make the delivery before three. But lo and behold, some mix-up occurred and the delivery didn't get there till three-thirty. Sparky had indeed left, and the secretary, trying to be helpful, sent the balloons and the violinist on to his house.

"Hilda answered the door, of course. She had a surprise party in progress. Seventy-five of their closest friends milling around, drinking champagne.

"The delivery girl asked for Sparky. Hilda called him. He came to the door, the girl handed him the balloons, and the gypsy violinist launched into 'Laura.' Hilda knew the minute she heard that who it was from. By the end of the song, she was fit to be tied. And Sparky was pretty cross with me for stepping over the home line.

"Hilda had all the wives come outside and hold the balloons down in the driveway while she got in Sparky's little red sports car and drove over every last one of them. Later that night, she called me. Luckily, I was out with J.B., having dinner at Graffiti's. But she left an incomprehensible message on my machine. Drunk, probably. Her usual state."

"You mean you still see J.B.?"

"Only when Sparky's not in town," says Mom perkily. "We're friends." Then she sighs. "It's difficult. All in all, you have to feel kind of sorry for Hilda. She knows her husband's been in love with me ever since we were children, and there isn't a damn thing she can do about it."

"I wonder if she knows about this weekend?"

Mom swerves into the condo's parking lot. "I wouldn't be surprised if she bribed Sparky's travel agent to furnish her with his complete itinerary."

"Well, what if she shows up?"

"Show up? She isn't gonna show up." Mom laughs at the very idea. "All the way from Denver? Are you crazy? I'm not even worried about that. And I'm certainly not gonna let it ruin our fun."

Mom leads us into the condo. "We call it 'Colonial Modern,' " she says, giving us the tour, "with an oriental accent. That's Sparky's touch. Doesn't it remind you of Williamsburg? Remember that summer we went there, Zero?"

"How could I forget? You crawled on hands and knees from one end of the historic section to the other."

"I did not! Though it *is* the prettiest place I believe I've ever seen."

"A Southerner's dream," I muse. "An entire town preserved in slave-day glory."

"Are you accusing me of being prejudiced just because I happen to like Colonial decor?"

"Heavens no. And I think your condo is very nice."

"Lovely," says David.

"Well, I'm so glad you both approve."

She waltzes into the living room and opens a louvered door, behind which is a luxurious, mirrored built-in bar.

"I believe we need a drink," she announces. "Now what can I get y'all?"

"Well, seeing as how we're in the South, how 'bout a bourbon and soda?"

"Two," says David.

"Okie-doke." Mom plops some ice cubes into crystal tumblers and starts pouring.

I look around the room, taking in the sight of the new turntable, receiver, speakers, cassette player, and five-disc CD carousel.

"Where'd you get all this fancy stereo equipment?"

"Oh, you know, every time Sparky's here he feels he has to buy something new. What a man!"

She hands us our drinks. Then, clutching a scotch, she plants herself on the couch. She kicks off her shoes and pulls her legs underneath her, carefully covering them with the skirt of her dress.

"Cheers!" she says, raising her glass.

"Cheers," we reply, and all take a sip.

"Tell me about your T cells," Mom says exuberantly, as though she were asking about my badminton game.

"Well," I gulp, "I still have some."

"Have you had 'em tested again lately?"

"I have 'em tested every few months."

"So what's the current count?"

" 'Bout the same as it was. A hundred and sixty."

She looks at me with great pity, like she isn't sure I'll make it through the weekend. "God, Zero," she says. "I'm about ready for 'em to go up, aren't you?"

"No kidding. But there's not much I can do about it that I'm not already doing. Anyway, the ratio's still the same, and they say that's more important than the actual count."

"What ratio?"

"T4s to T8s," explains David.

"Oh," says my mother. She swills her drink and rattles her ice cubes. She sighs heavily, then says, "I just can't help but feel there's gotta be a cure in sight."

"Really? What makes you say that?"

"Well, even the Little Rock Country Club had an AIDS benefit this year. For AMFAR. Elizabeth Taylor's group. Sparky and I sent 'em a huge check. It just seems like so much is being done. And by so many people."

"That doesn't mean there's a cure in sight."

"The whole thing," says David, "is management. Manage the infection and try to keep yourself on an even keel."

"Are your T cells as low as Zero's?"

"My T cells are all over the place. But"—he laughs—"I've still got my teeth."

"Lord!" says my mother. "To think you can even joke about it." She gets up and pours herself another drink.

"I still get that newsletter from that place you gave my name to in California. Which I read faithfully."

"You mean Project Inform?"

"Yes. And I always send them a check as well."

"Good."

"Did y'all see that article in the paper a few weeks ago about people who've tested negative after moving to the country and putting themselves through an exercise routine?"

"Don't believe everything you read," I say cynically.

"Well, it might help, Zero."

"Everybody's got their theories. But I have several competent doctors all doing their best to keep me in as good shape as possible. Like I said, I've been stable. What more do you want?"

"I want you to get well!"

"Unfortunately, Mom, that isn't the way it works."

"It's a pretty lethal virus," says David. "No amount of New Age hocus-pocus is gonna make it disappear. Not to say those things don't help some—"

"But not you?"

"It's good for people who've never given the choices they've made a second look," he says diplomatically. "For us, though, the best we can do is just get on with it."

"Well," says my mother, "that's a pretty depressing set of options. Y'all are a lot braver than I'd be."

"You never know," says David. "You might surprise yourself."

The front door opens. In barrels Doll. "Hey y'all! I'm here!"

I get up to give her a hug. "Hi."

"Hi!" she says. "I'm so glad y'all could make it. You sure are looking good!"

"Thanks. So are you."

"Must be all the excitement. Gives me an extra glow."

"Something to drink?" asks Mom.

"Yes," says Doll desperately. "Whatever you're having. But a double."

"Coming right up!"

"How's the new job?" I ask.

"Perfect!" Doll exclaims. "I just *love* it! Cohn's is the place for me. Though I have to admit, it's been a little hectic lately."

"How come?"

"Oh, the usual retail frenzy. They fired half the staff the day after Christmas and have me doing everybody's job."

"She's buying handbags, hats, socks, panty hose, costume jewelry, and hair ornaments," says Mom proudly, handing Doll her late-afternoon liquor.

Doll takes a sip. "Hair ornaments is my pride and joy," she beams. She turns sideways to show off a papier-mâché bouquet affixed to the back of her frosted 'do.

"Isn't that the cutest thing?" says Mom. "You see, hair ornaments is the new catchall phrase for anything that goes in the hair."

"I'm sure they figured that out," says Doll.

A SHINDIG IN LITTLE ROCK

"Well, excuse me," says Mom. "I'm just trying to help tell the story. Don't be too quick to get on your high horse, missy."

"Sorry," Doll apologizes. "Like I said, I've been under a lot of pressure lately. God, what I wouldn't give for a cigarette!"

"Don't let us stop you," I say. "Smoke away."

"Oh no," says Mom. "She quit."

"I was forced into it," mutters Doll.

"Sparky gave her a scholarship to Smokenders as one of her birthday presents."

"And how could I refuse, what with him putting on this weekend and everything?"

"You couldn't," says Mom triumphantly. "Anyhow, it's high time you stopped. It's a filthy habit and you know it."

"So is everything else that's any fun."

"Nice men don't like girls who smoke."

"Men," says Doll. "As if that's anything I need to be concerned about."

"How long's it been since you've had one?" I ask.

"A man or a cigarette?"

"A cigarette."

"Two days. And let me tell you, they're much harder to quit than men." Doll looks around the living room. "What happened to all the ashtrays?" she asks in a mild panic.

"I washed them."

"Mom," Doll whines, "you're not supposed to do that. You're supposed to keep them around so I can sniff 'em."

"Doll, I am not gonna have you goin' around here sniffing ashtrays all weekend."

"Meanie."

"You got it. Now drink your drink and entertain the boys while I go in the kitchen and get dinner on."

"Need any help?" I ask.

"No, no. Lutherette was here this afternoon to fry you a chicken and cook up some rice and greens. All I've got to do is make some gravy. It'll only be a minute."

I ask Doll if she's heard any news of our crazy father.

"Yes!" she says. "He's running for mayor. He thinks the aliens have taken over politics—that's why nobody votes anymore—and it's high time someone with some sense got involved. You'll be pleased to know I've started visiting him occasionally. When my guilt gets the better of me. Christmas, Father's Day——"

"Does he recognize you?"

"Are you kidding? That'd be way too normal for him. He thinks I'm from Welcome Wagon because I usually take him a present."

"What do you talk about?"

"He talks. Space travel, flying dogs, the theory of relativity. I never stay too long."

"Zero?" Mom calls from the kitchen. "Did you ever hear whether Trebreh got his invitation or not?"

"I'm sure he did if you sent him one, though I haven't actually talked to him lately."

"Well, I sent him one, and he's the only guest that didn't RSVP, not to mention send Doll a little remembrance."

"He doesn't have to send me anything," says Doll. "I don't care a damn about presents."

"Oh? I'll remember that."

"I was so tickled to hear about Trebreh having a daughter," says Doll. "What a relief someone in the family besides Norm is fathering kids. Did you hear the latest about Norm's kids? He's let 'em change their names."

"That is just another ridiculous attempt to try and win their affection," says Mom dismissively.

"They go by Rotten Dog and Little Cookie now. R.D. and L.C. for short."

"I don't call 'em that," says my mother. "I don't call 'em anything."

"But this Mary Bull," says Doll excitedly, "sounds like a much more successful experiment."

"Oh, she is," I tell her. "In fact, she's working in a Broadway show. She's the new Red Ridinghood for the *Into the Woods* tour."

"Sparky and I saw that the last time we were in New York," says my mother.

"Wasn't it good?"

"We didn't like it very much."

"Well, I loved it! And Mary Bull is perfect for that part."

"But you said it's the tour, not the one actually on Broadway?"

"That's right. They're in L.A. at the moment, doing an open-ended run. Ironic, because Mary Bull is from Los Angeles and she was trying to get out of there. Hence why she was traveling with Trebreh last fall and why she ran off to New York."

"Ran off to New York?" asks my mother, alarmed.

"Uh-huh. Trebreh had to go back to L.A. and left Mary Bull at my place. He promised to come back for her within a week, and their next stop was to have been New York. Well, he didn't come for her, but he called and said there was a ticket at the airport, and for her to take the midnight flight back to L.A. Apparently, what she did was cash in the ticket, buy one for New York, and keep the change. Treb called me at the crack of dawn the next morning wanting to know where the hell she was."

"That's scary," says Mom. "A little girl all by herself in that big city. Lord knows what might happen."

"You don't know Mary Bull. She's a tough customer. Plus her mother's ex-lover lives in New York. So it's not like she didn't have a place to go."

"Well, how do you reckon she ever got a job in a Broadway show?"

"Auditioned."

"Is she that talented?"

"No, Mom, she slept with the producer. Of course she's talented! She wrote me the cutest card. She said her mom, who runs a garage, had bought a whole block of tickets for her opening night. Said she was bringing all the women she knew and that most of them had never even seen a play."

"She has a six-month contract and an Equity card," says David. "She's really one hell of a singer."

"Well," says my mother, "I guess all those music lessons we wasted on Trebreh are paying off in the next generation."

"I guess so."

"Still, that's no reason for Trebreh not to observe the simple social manners."

"Trebreh just does things differently from the rest of us."

"Oh, it's no big deal," says Doll. "I'm just sorry we're not gonna see him."

"Me too," says Mom. "Who knows when the chance will come again?"

"My fortieth birthday?" asks Doll expectantly.

"Over my dead body!" says Mom. "Now come on, y'all. Dinner's on the table."

"Finally!" moans Doll. "If I can't smoke, I might as well satisfy my oral cravings with food."

"You be careful," warns Mom. "You want to still be able to fit in your dress come Saturday."

"Fit in my dress? Are you calling me fat?"

"No, but your time of the month's due any day and you know how you have a tendency to swell."

"God! My life with the Menstrual Police."

"Somebody's got to keep you in line."

Mom sits at the head of the table. She hands Doll the plate of chicken. "Don't take the pulley bone," she says. "That's for Zero."

David and I excuse ourselves after dinner and head back to the hotel. David flops down on one of the beds, flicks on the news, and immediately falls asleep. I'm not so lucky. Call it nerves or just plain agitation. Finally, I put on my jacket and go out for a walk.

Main Street is pretty deserted at this time of night. I pass the stores of downtown and wander over the freeway toward the house I grew up in.

I see the big porch that rings the place and Stellrita sitting out there in her rocker, just like I knew she'd be. Stellrita used to work for us until my granddaddy died and willed her the house.

"Feel like a little company?" I call from the gate.

"Who's that?" She squints at the street.

"Zero, Zero MacNoo."

"Why, sure. Thought for a minute my memories were playing tricks on me. Come on, sit down."

"What kind of tricks are your memories up to?"

"The usual. Everything just crazy and mixed up. My mind's like a tunnel, child. I remember things from a hundred years ago better than I remember yesterday. The longer I live, the more confusin' it gets. Time done snapped somewhere. 'Course, I try to mind my own b'iness, but the public won't let me."

"What do you mean by that?"

"When I had my birthday last, the governor come round with a bunch of reporters to present me with a certificate that says I'm the oldest living human being in the state of Arkansas."

"Congratulations."

"Ain't nothin' to be congratulated about. Publicity has a bad way of turning on you. Ruins your peace. Everybody comes back to haunt you. Like my daughter, Helen. Showed up here wantin' to take care of me. Said she had no idea I's still in this world and come runnin' as soon as she read about it."

Stellrita fires up a cigarette, a Salem Extra Long, takes a deep drag, then coughs terribly.

"It's probably good to have somebody with you."

"Yeah? What do you know? You some expert on people who live too long?"

"No. My expertise seems to be people who don't live long enough."

"Lot to be said for that."

"You'd have a hard time convincing them."

"Wouldn't even try. People gotta see it for themselves."

She takes another drag off her cigarette.

"Truth is, I was too old when I had Helen. I'd had my share of children and sure didn't need no more."

"How many did you have, Stellrita?" I've been trying to get this information out of her for years.

"Must've been fifteen, maybe twenty. I forget. I remember the first one 'cause it hurt like hell. I remember the second and the third, too. But once you get to the fourth and the fifth, you hardly notice. Just grows in your belly, then one day, out it falls. Helpless and crying and needy. Just one more thing for you to take care of. That's what all my birthing's taught me. Done never should've bothered."

"How old is Helen?"

"Forty, fifty. What does it matter?"

"Well, if you're a hundred and twenty—"

"A hundred and twenty-two," she corrects me.

"Well, if you're a hundred and twenty-two, that means you

would've been at least seventy or eighty when you had her. Surely you weren't still having children at that age."

"If I say birthed her, I birthed her. Don't bug me about it! I hope you didn't stop by here to hassle me. 'Cause if you did, I'll get out my shotgun. I'll fix you up good."

"No, no. Forget it."

"That's better." She reaches up under her skirt for her bottle, takes a generous swig. "Ah," she says. "Helen thinks I oughta put her up just 'cause I got me this big house. But when Helen was making money hand over fist in her high-and-mighty De-troit, do you think she sent me a cotton-picking nickel? 'Course not. And that's wrong, dead wrong. The way I see it, when a child succeeds, they owe a little bit of it to everyone who ever taught 'em. Everyone who contributed oughta share in the prize. I told Helen that and she said I was starting to sound like a communist. But I just want what's mine. I got my empire to think about."

She takes another pull off the bottle.

"Then again, maybe Helen's motivated beyond her knowledge. She got your granddaddy's blood coursin' through her. Maybe that's what it is."

"She's Granddaddy's child?"

"Who else, you idiot?"

"Did Granddaddy know that?"

" 'Course he did, fool man. Though he never admitted it. White man only admits to white babies. The mixed-up ones just have to belong to themselves. That's what I tried to teach Helen, and she just said I didn't appreciate her. But who appreciates something they got no choice about?"

"Well, is she livin' with you or not?"

Stellrita makes a vague gesture toward the house. "She's in there somewhere. I don't know. I just stay out here on the porch and don't bother with it none." She shifts in her rocker. I notice she's got her feet soaking in an old bucket.

"What's that?" I ask.

"My mud," she says. "If I don't die soon, I'm gonna bury myself in it entirely."

"Isn't it chilly, having your feet in a bucket of mud at this time of year?"

A SHINDIG IN LITTLE ROCK

"Do you think I care about temperature?"

"Well, it'd be a shame to catch your death of cold after all the living you've done."

"You *would* take that attitude. Here, have a sip of my drink. Might change your outlook." She hands me the bottle.

I take a swig. The minute I taste the foul substance, I spit it out. "What the hell is that?"

Stellrita cackles. "My miracle drink. Whiskey, pine needles, and camphor. Medical people keep comin' round wantin' to know what my secret is. I don't tell 'em, but that's it."

I hand it back to her. She helps herself to a little more, then lights another cigarette. After her coughing routine, she sighs and nods, then says, "On the other hand, maybe Helen came back on account of her boy. She had one when she was too young to know better and left him here with his daddy's side of the family. Maybe Helen's finally gotten curious about him. Maybe it done dawned on her the only real enemy we got's time."

"Time isn't our enemy, Stellrita. Either you've got it or you don't."

"You're getting to be a real thinker, ain't you?" She laughs.

She reaches into the bucket, grabs a handful of mud, and starts rubbing it up and down her arms. "But me, I'm just waiting to die. Just waiting to leave all this behind. I am so tired of it, I don't think I'll miss a moment. 'Cept maybe my cigarettes. Cigarettes are the one thing that hasn't disappointed me. Yet."

"Mama?" queries a kind-sounding voice from inside the screen door. "Who you talkin' to?"

"See?" says Stellrita. "Don't give me a moment's peace. It's Zero, Helen. Zero MacNoo."

"Oh." Helen steps out onto the porch. "Hi. You must be in town for your sister's birthday party. Doll sure has been excited about it. Hardly talks of anything else."

"How do you know?" snaps Stellrita.

"I work for Doll down at Cohn's, Mother. Remember, she was kind enough to give me a job when I came back to town."

"But not kind enough to pay you decent."

"I can't complain," says Helen sweetly. "Except about how much you keep me hoppin'."

February 1990

"I don't need nobody lookin' over my shoulder, damn it!"

"Nobody's lookin' over your shoulder."

Helen takes a cigarette from Stellrita's pack, then sits on the porch steps to smoke it. "Awfully warm for February," she says. "Must mean we're in for a scorcher of a summer."

"Who cares?" Stellrita caps her miracle drink and puts it away.

"I was just in there watching the news," says Helen. "They're supposed to release Nelson Mandela this weekend."

"Who's that? Another one of your jailbird boyfriends?"

"I wish." Helen laughs. "He's only the head of the African National Congress. Been in a South African jail for the last twenty-seven years. You are familiar with apartheid, aren't you, Mother?"

"I got no concerns past this porch."

"That's right. You just stay in your little haze and let the whole world pass you by."

"Don't you be tellin' me, child. And don't you be addin' things to my head. I got all the facts in here I need. Just when'd you get so high-minded on news and stuff anyway?"

"I've always been high-minded on news. That's why I left this place, why I went to Detroit, remember?"

"I don't remember nothin'."

"I envy you that talent." Helen smiles slightly, then grinds out her cigarette beneath the toe of her sandal. "What am I gonna do with you, Mother?"

"Leave me be, I hope and pray."

"Well," says Helen, "at least for tonight." She gets up to go back into the house.

"Bring me another bucket of my mud first."

"You've had enough mud for one day."

"Devil!"

"Good night, Mother. 'Night, Zero. Have a pleasant visit."

"Thanks, Helen."

"Damn," spits Stellrita.

"I'll get you some mud."

"No," she says emphatically. "I want Helen to do it or I don't want it at all."

"Okay. Have it your way."

We both look out at the street, trying to disperse the sour mood.

A SHINDIG IN LITTLE ROCK

I pull a Baggie out of my jacket pocket and set it in her lap. "I brought you something."

"Did? What is it?"

"A scoop of my best friend's ashes."

"Now, that *is* interesting." She examines the bag, holding it up to the dim porch light. "Was a handsome fellow, wasn't he?"

"Sure was."

"Can I put him in my mud bucket?"

"I wish you would."

She dumps in the contents and stirs it with her feet.

"Ou, that feels good," she says. "That's fixin' me up real good."

"Morning!" chirps David.

He sits on the edge of his bed, waiting for me to open my eyes.

"Morning," I croak, then bury my head beneath my pillow.

"It's almost ten," he says.

"So go for a walk," I mutter.

"I've been for a walk. I've also read the paper. From cover to cover. It's time for you to get up, Zero, and entertain me."

"Since when did you need entertaining?"

"Since I agreed to accompany you on this trip."

I sigh. "All right. Call room service for a pot of coffee, and when it comes, I'll get up."

David picks up the phone and dials. "We need a pot of coffee and two continental breakfasts. Room 307. . . . Thanks." He hangs up. "Ten minutes."

"Great. Ten more minutes of precious sleep."

"Do you think it's too early to call Jeff?"

"David, please."

"I just asked a simple question."

"What do you want to call Jeff for?"

"To hear how the demo went. Don't you want to talk to him? Don't you miss your lover boy?"

"Fuck off."

"Don't you even want to say hello?"

"Not until I've had a cup of coffee!" I climb out of bed. "Congratulations, you've successfully woken me up."

February 1990

I go into the bathroom and splash some cold water on my face. Pull on my bathrobe.

David has thrown open the curtains. It's a blinding bright day.

"Jesus!" I say, shielding my eyes. "You are such a pain in the ass."

"I'm calling Jeff now," he says. "What's the number?"

I rattle it off; he dials.

He waits for Jeff to answer, twisting the cord around his fingers.

"Jeff? Hi, it's David. . . . Oh, we're fine, got here without a hitch. Listen, how was the demo? . . . You're kidding, six hundred people? Was the media there? . . . Front-page coverage, a picture, and an editorial denouncing the recommendation? Why, that's fantastic! Be sure and save the articles for me. . . . Okay, thanks, Jeff, thanks a lot. Want to say hello to Zero? He woke up a real grump, but—"

"Give me the goddamn phone."

I snatch it out of his hand.

"Room service," announces a voice from the hall, followed by a crisp rap at the door.

David lets in the waiter, who carries the tray to the table and sets it down. As he turns to leave, he faces me and exclaims, "Zero!"

I look up. "Lance?"

"I don't believe this," Lance says. "What a coincidence."

"Yeah," I fumble, making a vain attempt to pat down my morning hair. Then I say to Jeff, "Listen, let me call you back. Things are a bit hectic at the moment. . . . Okay. I'll talk to you tonight. . . . Love you, too. Bye."

Lance plants his hands on his hips. "Thought you were gonna let me know the next time you were coming to town."

"Actually, I was gonna call you today."

"A likely story," he says cynically. Then he grins. "You're looking good."

"So are you."

"You gonna introduce me to your friend?"

"Sure. David, this is Lance. Lance, David."

They shake hands.

"Lance and I met when I was down for my mother's wedding a couple of summers ago."

"More than met," Lance says.

A SHINDIG IN LITTLE ROCK

"How long have you been working at the hotel?"

"Since last May. I've been trying to get it together to do grad school, but in the meantime I gotta make a living."

The beeper on Lance's belt sounds.

"Shit," he says. "Gotta run. But listen, you guys, I get off around three. If y'all are gonna be here, why don't I stop by for a visit?"

"Sure," says David.

"Great," says Lance. "I'll see you this afternoon."

"Lance," I add. "I really was gonna call you."

He laughs. "Yeah, I'll bet. Anyway, it's good to see you. Both." He catches David's eye.

David grins for all he's worth. The minute Lance is out of the room, he sighs, "What a dreamboat!"

After breakfast, David and I go out for a walk. A deranged-looking man wearing a sandwich board that says I HAVEN'T ACCOMPLISHED A LOT LATELY, BUT IT'S TAKEN EVERY MINUTE OF THE DAY TO DO SO is standing in front of the hotel, panhandling. David and I move to avoid him. Then, on second glance, I realize it's my father.

We look at each other suspiciously. Then, for lack of anything better to say, I ask if he thinks he's gonna win the election.

"What election?"

"You're a candidate for mayor, aren't you?"

"I am the mayor! Always ready to serve my fellow creatures. What may I do for you, sir?"

"Nothing. My companion and I were just going for a walk."

"A walk?" he says incredulously. "Today is no day for a walk. Today is a day for a spaceship ride!"

"Oh? David, how would you like to ride a spaceship?"

"He'd love it!" snaps my father. "Come on."

Dad discards the sandwich board. "Stay right here," he tells it, then he scampers across the street toward the river.

The spaceship turns out to be a barge, the same one that takes tourists for rides.

"Our connection," Dad says.

"Clever of the aliens to disguise it as a riverboat," I venture.

"Yes, sir. They're pretty clever critters."

He leads us down the plank.

"Hey!" yells the captain. "Gotta have a ticket to ride this boat."

Dad stops in his tracks. "Don't you know who I am?"

A woman working the concession stand says, "It's okay, Captain Andy. It's just 'the mayor' brung us a few more customers."

"See," confides my father. "The aliens recognize me."

"Five bucks each for the two young 'uns," says the woman.

"Well, don't just stand there," Dad orders. "Pay up!"

David reaches into his pocket for a ten and gives it to her.

"So what are we waiting for?" Dad barks. "Blast off!"

The barge lurches out over the muddy water. It's decorated with Confederate flags and an assortment of rickety folding chairs advertising Budweiser beer.

"This is what they come for," my father says with a sweeping gesture.

"Boat rides?" I ask.

"No. Mud. They like their water to have lots of mud. Helps weigh 'em down. They're light, the aliens. And there's not much liquid in outer space. That's how I got to be mayor. I'm the one negotiated the deal."

"What deal?"

"To dam up the Arkansas River and send the water to the sky."

"I see."

"No, you don't. Nobody sees but the all-seeing goddess. The aliens left her here years ago. She lives among us like a lot of 'em live among us." He pauses. "You're not aliens, are you?"

"Not that I know of."

"That's a relief." He laughs uproariously. "In that case, I proclaim it refreshment time. Since you gentlemen seem civilized enough, I'm gonna let you buy me a beer."

"Gee, what an honor."

"Not everyone's allowed to buy for the mayor."

"One for you, David?"

"I think I'd better."

By the time we get off that boat, we've listened to two solid hours of Dad's ravings: evolution, politics, economics—you name it. And his theories grow wilder with each beer consumed.

He walks us back to the hotel to retrieve his sandwich board.

A SHINDIG IN LITTLE ROCK

I'm totally exhausted and go up to the room to rest. The message light on the phone is blinking. The message is for me to call my mother.

"Where have you been?" she asks.

"Riding up and down the river," I tell her.

"The river? Well, I've been callin' and callin'. I was beginning to think y'all'd already had enough of us."

"Did the Houston gang get in?"

"Yes. Doll and I met 'em at the airport, took 'em to lunch at the Little Rock Club. Carol, Will, Eunice, and Doc, that is. Betty and Peppy decided not to fly, but to drive. Apparently, Peppy has some business in Fayetteville."

"Fayetteville? But that's two hundred miles out of the way. What is it Peppy does, exactly?"

"Carol says he's in real estate. But you'll meet him tonight. We're having cocktails and dinner at the condo. I want y'all here about six, and wear something nice, okay?"

"Don't worry."

I hang up.

"I have a headache and I'm taking a nap," I say to David.

"What about Lance? He should be here any minute."

"You entertain him."

"Edie!" squeals Aunt Eunice. "I just *love* your new condo. Especially the Jacuzzi! Why, I'm of half a mind to take off my clothes and just jump right in!"

"Go ahead."

"Oh no, you don't," counters Aunt Carol with the authority of a four-star general. "You keep your clothes on tonight. This isn't one of your nudist camps."

"Are you still going to those things, Eunice?" Mom asks.

"Not as much as I used to. Doc's a little shy." Doc is her new husband.

"I'm not shy," says Doc. "Take off your clothes wherever you want."

"We're just like two peas in pod." Eunice beams.

She catches sight of me and David coming in the door. "Zero!" she exclaims. "You're here!"

"Hello, Aunt Eunice. Good to see you."

"You too!" She pecks at the air on both sides of my head, saying, "Kiss-kiss. And aren't you looking so *healthy?*"

"Thanks. You remember my friend David, don't you?"

" 'Course I do. Hello there, David. You were at my place in Houston for dinner once."

"That's right. The first time Zero brought me down here."

"Didn't we have fun?" she coos.

"Fun?" says my mother. "That was a visit from hell if ever there was one."

"Oh, nonsense, Edie. Everybody had a marvelous time except you."

"Mom just thought," says Doll, "that if she was hateful enough to David that Zero would decide not to be gay."

"I am not proud of the way I acted," my mother admits. "And I've been trying to make up for it ever since." She looks sheepishly at David.

"No problem," he tells her.

"Doc?" says Aunt Eunice. "Come on over here and say hello to my darling nephew and his darling friend."

"Hi 'do," says Doc, extending his hand and smiling amiably. Doc has several chins and a substantial set of jowls, which jiggle as he speaks. Eunice grabs a pinchful.

"Isn't he the cutest thing?" she says. "I just love all his extra skin."

"Eunice, you're embarrassing me."

" 'Course I had a little facelift to get rid of mine," she confides. "But on Doc, well, I think it suits him."

"*A* facelift?" roars Aunt Carol. "You and you alone are responsible for keeping the plastic surgeons of Greater Houston up to their scalpels in mink."

"Surgeons don't wear mink, Carol. Unless they're women. And I've only had male surgeons."

"I don't know why you just won't let your age show. Who cares if we look like a couple of old turkey buzzards at this point?"

"You said it, Carol, not me. And don't give away any more of my secrets!" Aunt Eunice laughs gaily. "Ain't life grand?" She clasps her hands together. "Isn't it *wonderful* to be together again?"

"Yes!" cries Doll. "I don't know why we don't do it more often."

"Because it's too damned exhausting!" says Carol.

One of the waiters walks through with a platter of boiled shrimp. Carol takes one, then carries it over to her husband, my deaf uncle Will. She's stationed him in a corner, out of the line of traffic.

Carol yells at him, "How you doin', honey?"

Will looks like he's just been reeled in from another world. "Want a drink," he mutters.

"Why do you always ask for things you know you can't have?"

" 'Cause I still want 'em."

"Even after the open-heart surgery you've been through?"

"Even then."

"You know the rules, Will. No alcohol and no butter."

"I'd be happier dead."

"Will! Put that thought right out of your head! Attitude's half the battle."

"I just want a drink."

"You're too deaf to drink! Here, have a shrimp."

"Shellfish gives me a rash."

"Better a rash than a heart attack. A rash I can cope with." She pops it in his mouth.

I sneak into the guest room, where the bar is set up, and order three martinis. One for me, one for David, and one for Uncle Will.

When I hand it to him, he says, "Bless you, Zero. You always were a good boy."

"Anytime."

"Tell me, Edie," says Aunt Carol. "Who did this marvelous catering?"

" 'Member Mary Mack from Pine Bluff?"

"You don't mean she's still alive?"

"Alive and cookin'!"

"Well, it's just delicious."

"I'll tell her you said so."

"I want to know where the Yoakums are," says Aunt Eunice.

"They couldn't make it tonight," says my mother.

"Why not?"

"If you want to know the truth, I think Lorna's punishing me."

"Punishing you? For what?"

"My . . . circumstance with Sparky. She's convinced I'm crazy. And she's probably right."

"Lorna always was so moralistic," says Eunice. "Why, the first time I went to a nudist camp, she wrote me a ten-page letter condemning my judgment. I answered it by sending her a copy of our group photo."

"It's strange," says Doll. "She used to be so much fun."

"She's still fun," says my mother. "She just spends too much time nursing Aunt Tula, not to mention taking care of four grandkids. That'd be enough to dull anyone."

"She needs to get a life," proclaims Eunice.

"Well, you'll have to be the one to tell her that," says Mom. "She stopped listening to my advice after my first divorce."

"But you're so close."

"As close as any two sisters can be."

"Hey!" sounds a voice from the front door, followed by a wild laugh. "We're here!"

"Betty!" says Doll, jumping up to give her cousin a hug. "I'm so glad you could come."

"Thanks, Doll. You know I wouldn't've missed it."

Betty introduces the squat, swollen-faced man accompanying her. "Hey, everybody," she says, "this is my new husband, Peppy."

Peppy looks at the assembled crowd, grunts a few hellos, then asks if he may use the telephone.

"Certainly," says my mother. "Right this way. There's a private extension in my bedroom."

Aunt Carol rushes over to her daughter. "Betty, honey, what have you done to your hair?"

Betty laughs. "Peppy cut it."

"Cut it? Why, it looks like he just yanked it out."

"Oh no, Mother. He used scissors."

"What a relief!"

"Betty," says Mom merrily. "May I get you something to drink?"

"She doesn't drink anymore," says Aunt Carol.

"Yes, I do," says Betty. "Vodka, Edie. No ice."

"Right away."

"How was your trip to Fayetteville?" asks Aunt Carol.

Betty looks at her, confused. "Fayetteville?"

"Isn't that where you were all day? Isn't that why you drove instead of coming with the rest of us on the plane?"

"Oh yeah," says Betty. "It was fine. Just fine."

"What'd you do up there?"

"Went to see some friends of Peppy's."

"What for?"

"He had some business with 'em, Mother."

"Real estate business?"

"What is this, the third degree?"

"I just want to know."

"Yes, real estate business. He's sellin' some land."

"In Fayetteville?"

"Wherever. They have land all over."

Mom hands Betty her drink. Betty swills it and immediately asks for another. Aunt Carol shakes her head and walks away. Betty lights up a cigarette, then goes over to say hello to Uncle Will.

"Hey, Daddy."

Uncle Will doesn't seen to notice her chopped-off hair, her heavy makeup, or the quiver in her long, thin hands. "You look beautiful," he murmurs.

"You're looking pretty good yourself."

"Much better now that you're here."

"I'm much better now, too."

"A cigarette!" Doll exclaims, noticing Betty's. "I'm so glad someone still smokes. Let me have a whiff off that."

"You can have one of your own, if you want."

"No, she can't," says Mom.

"What'd you do? Quit?"

"Three days ago," says Doll glumly. "I was forced into it. But god, doesn't that smell good! When you butt it out, leave the ashtray by me, okay?"

Betty looks at her like she's really missed something. "Sure, Doll. Whatever. It's your birthday." Betty laughs nervously, then swills the second vodka.

"Aren't you drinking a little quickly?" asks Aunt Carol.

Betty looks at her empty glass. "Not at all, Mother. Actually, I'm a little behind myself tonight."

"Have you forgotten that your father and I have paid good money on several occasions for you to dry out?"

"How could I? It seems to be your favorite subject. 'Scuse me while I get another cocktail."

"Doll," coaches my mother. "Tell about the store. Tell about how you're buying for six departments!"

"Oh, it's nothing," Doll says. "But it keeps me busy."

"I'm just so proud of you!" says Aunt Eunice. "I want to know when you're gonna take us down there shopping."

"How 'bout tomorrow?" asks Doll. "I can probably even get you a ten-percent discount."

"Really?" asks Aunt Carol.

Peppy pokes his head in from the bedroom. "Betty? Where's Betty?"

"Betty?" calls Aunt Carol. "Your husband wants you."

"Comin'," says Betty, traipsing back through the living room, sloshing her fresh drink. "What is it, Pep?"

"I need you in here a minute."

Betty makes a mysterious face, then disappears into the bedroom, shutting the door behind her.

"How very cryptic," observes Aunt Eunice. "Maybe they want to try out your bed, Edie. Being newlyweds and all."

"Who is that man?" asks Uncle Will.

"Your new son-in-law," yells Carol, moving toward the bedroom door in an attempt to eavesdrop.

The caterer whispers a few words to my mother, who then announces that it's time to eat.

Laid out on the dining room table is a glorious spread of rare tenderloin of beef, homemade rolls, horseradish sauce, potatoes au gratin, marinated artichokes, and numerous salads.

David and I load up our plates, then sit with Doc and Eunice in the living room.

"I understand Zero's in the arts," says Doc, "but what is it you do, David?"

"Human rights," he says.

"Human what?" barks Carol, leaning in from the armchair.

A SHINDIG IN LITTLE ROCK

"Human rights," Eunice tells her.

"Oh," says Carol. "That's something to do with the blacks, isn't it?"

"Can be," says David.

"Well, I'm a Republican," Carol announces.

"Everybody we know in Texas is a Republican," says my mother.

"You mean you're not?" asks Aunt Carol.

"No, ma'am," my mother states. "I'm a Democrat, through and through."

"Then let's not talk about politics."

"No," says Eunice. "Politics and religion are two subjects families should avoid."

Aunt Carol pats David gingerly on the knee. "Barbara Bush and I belong to the same garden club. She sent Betty the nicest present the first time Betty married. 'Course, that was before George became President. We're still in touch, though. And the next time I get up to Washington, I'm gonna have dinner at the White House."

Betty emerges from the bedroom, looking flustered. "Peppy had to slip out," she says. "Had to get back to the hotel. To meet some people."

"What'd he do?" asks Mom. "Climb over the terrace wall?"

"Yes." Betty laughs. "That's exactly what he did."

"Honey," says Aunt Carol with strained patience. "Don't you think Peppy is just a little socially inept?"

"No!" says Aunt Eunice. "I think he's just *darling*. I think all you young people are as darling as can be."

"I need another drink," says Betty.

"Anything you want," enthuses my mother.

"I am really sad to see you drinking like this," says Aunt Carol. Betty ignores her.

I get up for some more horseradish sauce. Betty latches onto me. "Hey, Zero. How you doin'?"

"Pretty good."

"You know, one of these days I'm gonna come up to Canada and visit you. I'm just gonna show up at the airport and there I'll be."

"Well, you might want to call first. You know, in case I'm out of town or something."

106

"Call?" She grinds her teeth, looking at me as if I couldn't have insulted her more. "Why would I want to call?" Then she bursts into that wild laugh again and staggers up to the bar.

After we've done our best to clean our plates, Mom presents Doll with her birthday present: a chest full of my grandmother's silver.

"Lord!" says Doll. "Why, thanks! 'Course I seldom cook and I never entertain, but I sure will enjoy having this in my apartment."

"So will your insurance company," Aunt Carol informs her. "Your premium just went up fifty dollars a month."

"What?"

"Yes, ma'am. Burglars just love silver. They melt it down and sell it by the weight."

"But fifty dollars a month?" says Doll. "I can hardly pay my bills as it is."

"Don't you worry, princess," says a deep, drawling voice from the entrance hall. "You know where to look for help when you need it."

"Sparky!" exclaims my mother, rushing to greet him. "You made it!"

They embrace madly, then my mother whispers, "Is everything all right on the home front?"

Sparky chuckles. "Don't worry about it, Edie."

Mom winces. "What's that supposed to mean?"

"I'm here, aren't I?"

"Yes, thank goodness, you are!"

"I *love* the silver chest," Doll tells him.

"I'm glad," says Sparky. "And don't worry about the insurance."

"Oh, I'm not."

"Come on," says Mom, pulling Sparky toward the living room. "Come on in here and let me show you off."

En route to the hotel, David asks to be dropped off at Discovery, the big gay disco. "I told Lance I'd meet him."

"You didn't get enough of Lance this afternoon?"

He says nothing.

A SHINDIG IN LITTLE ROCK

"Good god. All you need is to fall in love with another guy from Little Rock, Arkansas."

"I am not about to fall in love, Zero."

"No? Looks to me like you already have."

"Just drop me off, okay?"

"No problem."

I pull off Cantrell and go down the little access road that leads to the Discovery parking lot.

"Don't do anything I wouldn't do," I tease as he hops out.

"That leaves me a pretty wide berth."

I drive over to Stellrita's.

"Where you been?" she asks.

"Oh, big family dinner."

"Hell, ain't it?"

"It's exhausting."

"Did I ever tell you about the time they put them streetlights in?"

"No, I don't believe I've heard that one."

"It was the summer Hortense found herself pregnant with your daddy. She went down to El Dorado to spend a month with her peoples. Took your Uncle Markus with her. He was about ten. So I was here more 'n usual looking after your granddaddy. Never had been streetlights on this part of Main. Know why? 'Cause Walter Jackson MacNoo didn't want any. And since he had the biggest house and the most money, the city let him have his way. Plus, it saved on the municipal funds.

"Then Pinchback Dupewley got himself 'lected mayor. That was exactly one year before he got kicked in the head by a parade horse and died in the middle of the street. And Pinchback didn't give a damn whether Walter wanted streetlights or not. It was Pinchback's intention to light Main Street, and by god, he was gonna do it.

"Your granddaddy and me was sitting at the dining room table, eating some pork chops I'd fried. See, when Hortense wasn't around, I ate at the table, not in the kitchen like I usually had to do. We was sittin' there like any two civilized people, when on comes this light. Walter cursed, set his silver down, and went over to the window. His face was red with fury. You know how it could be. Said he was gonna get his shotgun and shoot the sons of bitches right out of their sockets.

" 'Sit back down and eat your dinner,' I said. 'Ain't no reason you can't live with streetlights just like everybody else. Ain't nothin' but a little extra light, and it's free, too.'

"He sat there sulkin' and eatin' with no manners to speak of, looking at me like I personally put them lights in. Finally, I thought to hell with it and went into the kitchen to get a head start on the fry pan. A good pork chop always sticks to a fry pan. A good pork chop wants to ruin a fry pan if you let it. Well, I wasn't gonna let it. So there I was at the sink scrubbing away, when he comes in. And do you know what that man did? He hit me. Right across my face. Don't nobody go hittin' on Stellrita.

"Walter looked scared, real scared, like he knew he'd gone too far. I dropped that fry pan lickety-split, dried my hands, fetched my pocketbook, and came out on this here porch to wait for my ride.

"Walter started beggin' me through the screen door, tellin' me he was sorry, and to come on back in and make it up. But there wasn't no way in the world I's gonna do that. Then he said, 'Too many 'squitoes for you to be waitin' out there.' I said, ' 'Squitoes don't bother me none.' Then he said very quietly and very sincere, 'I'm sorry.'

"Child, that got to me more than anything. I'd known that man the better part of forty years, and I'd never heard him apologize to anyone, and there he was apologizin' to me. Not that it was enough. Not with the sting of his hand still on my face. 'You may be sorry,' I said, 'but you'd do it again. No matter how long we live you'll always have that power over me. First, 'cause I works for you. Second, 'cause I'm colored. Third, 'cause you the man. I quit your service, Walter Jackson MacNoo. I quit this job, here and now.'

"Wasn't an easy thing for me to do. I'd worked for your family since I was a girl of twelve, and I'd been tied up with your granddaddy almost as long.

"Walter moved like he was gonna open the screen door, but I said, 'You better not. You come out here, I might do something crazy.'

"He disappeared in the house somewhere. Came back a few

minutes later with a little box from the jewelry store. 'If you ain't comin' back,' he said, 'might as well take your birthday present.'

" 'Keep it,' I told him. 'Ain't no present I want from you.'

"But he gave it to me anyway. Was a watch inside. A really nice one. When my ride came, my younger brother Carl, I gave it to him. 'Take this down to the pawnshop and buy you something good.'

"I didn't come back to work for Walter until the first time he almost died. Had the fever and it served him right. But I figured a grudge didn't matter much at that point. Besides, I needed the money. So I come back to take care of him. Hortense wasn't much good at that.

"The fever played some mean tricks on Walter. Things didn't flow right through his brain. He was about as intelligent as a bowl of grapes by the time it was over. He'd shrunk a mighty lot, too. Didn't weigh over sixty pounds, and we had to keep him in a crib. The only thing that'd get him to respond was a candy bar. He loved his chocolate, and I loved to tease him with it. I'd hold a piece just outside his reach and really make him snap for it.

"Then one morning I found him a-whimpering. I had the feeling real strong that death was in the room. And I was sorry, so sorry I started to cry. Not so much for Walter as for the way things are. Don't seem right somehow. Seem like you oughta get a little more from livin' than that.

"Then"—she cackles—"Walter started to pee himself. Had his gown hiked up and peed all over him and me both. Had more water in him during the end of that fever than anything I ever saw. I had to take to visitin' him in a slicker. And that's how I knew my magic was beginnin' to work. That's how I knew I'd saved him.

"Sure enough, few days later he was back to his old self. Crotchety as ever, and never once thanked me. Never once believed it was me who made the difference."

"You must've been furious with the old goat."

"No, child. A woman can't regret what she do with her magic."

Stellrita sets her chair to rocking. "Don't make much sense, lookin' at them streetlights now, do it?"

"No," I say. "It doesn't."

She takes a scoop of mud and rubs it on her face. "Help yourself," she says. "You don't have to listen to your ol' Stellrita, not with a perfectly good bucket of mud sittin' here."

I take a little of it. Mold it in my hands. It feels good and warm.

"I saw Dad today," I tell her. "Do you ever see him?"

"See him? I got him livin' in my attic."

"What?"

"Sure. After Helen moved in, I figured I might as well open up the place and make me some rent money. I charge him his monthly welfare check. And he gives it to me, no questions asked."

She slaps her thighs, laughing. "Yes sir. Stellrita's got all you MacNoos headin' right where she wants you."

I get back to the hotel about two A.M.

David is standing on his head in the middle of the floor, stark naked, and Lance, also naked, is reading him Auden.

"What the hell is this?" I ask.

"Oh, hi, Zero. I hope you don't mind. I invited Lance to stay over."

"Mind? Why should I mind? I just hope you'll keep it to a minimum."

"Don't worry, we've already done that."

"Twice," says Lance.

"So what are you doing on your head?"

"It's an experiment," says Lance. "Poetry and the flow of blood."

"How silly of me not to have recognized it."

I'm the first one up in the morning. David and Lance are sleeping in a tight, tangled togetherness. They look so cute, I get out my Polaroid and snap a few pictures.

I call room service for our breakfast necessities, then go into the bathroom for my shower.

When I come out, Lance is gone.

"Where'd he go?"

"Had to work." David yawns pleasantly. He flops his arm toward me, holding out his hand. Wants a squeeze. I give him one.

"Enjoy yourself?" I ask.

A SHINDIG IN LITTLE ROCK

"Um," he says. "And you were right. I've been shot in the ass with Cupid's arrow for sure. I don't think I've been in this much danger since I met you."

"Rest assured you'll make a lovely bride."

Languorously, he hugs his pillow. "Lance, Lance, Lance."

There's a forceful knock at the door.

I open it, assuming it's room service. But it's my brother, Norm, and his two unruly kids.

"Hidy, Zero," he says. "Y'all awake?"

"Zero!" yell the kids, dashing past their father and jumping on my bed as if it were an Olympic-size trampoline.

"Rotten Dog, Little Cookie," warns my brother. "Y'all be careful. Y'all don't want to break anything."

"Yes we do!" says Rotten Dog. "Our mission is to destroy this whole hotel!"

"Yeah!" agrees Little Cookie.

They jump higher, singing, "There's a man in here, there's a man in here. Zero's gay, Zero's gay."

"They're a little energetic this morning," explains my brother.

"I could give 'em a Valium," I suggest.

Norm laughs. "Always the joker, aren't you?"

"Rotten Dog," I snap, "Little Cookie, I want you off that bed this minute."

"No way, egg face, we're glued." Rotten Dog lands with bent knees. He does a little jiggle to add force to Little Cookie's next jump. It practically sends her through the ceiling.

"Wow!" she squeals. "Great springs, man!"

"Aren't they cute?" Norm beams.

"I don't believe I'll answer that."

A rap at the door. "Knock-knock. Miss Scarlett? Miss Melanie? Y'all's breakfast is ready." Lance sashays in with the tray. "Oops," he says, "didn't know y'all was entertaining."

"Just set it on the table, Prissy."

Little Cookie emits a bloodcurdling scream, stunning us all except for Rotten Dog, who's busy inspecting the orange-juice glasses.

"No way, L.C." Rotten Dog gloats. "Not even a crack."

Little Cookie screams again.

"That is enough!" I say, grabbing her by the wrist.

She bites me.

"Ouch! Do something," I say to Norm.

"She just wanted to show you how she could break a glass."

"I don't want her to break a glass!"

"These are much too thick for L.C., Dad."

"Uh, later," says Lance, slipping out to safety.

As calmly as possible, I pour myself a cup of coffee. "Listen, R.D. and L.C., did you know that if you run down to the lobby as fast as you can, the man at the desk will give you a dollar?"

"Really?"

"Wow!"

"Let's go!" And they're off.

"God, Zero, you didn't have to lie to 'em."

"Cup of coffee, Norm?"

"No thanks. We had breakfast hours ago. I just stopped by to see if we could get a little time together. You know, for a brotherly talk."

"Sure, Norm. Why not?"

"When's good?"

"How 'bout I stop by your room in an hour or so?"

"Great. Well"—he shrugs, heading out the door—"see you then."

I hand David a cup of coffee.

"Amazing," he says.

"What? That after all these years my brother still doesn't speak to you?"

"No. How you have to get a license to do everything in this world except have children."

Norm drives me to River Dam Park, on the outskirts of town. We get out of the car and sit on the bank, side by side. He folds his hands, and with a serious expression asks, "Zero, are you happy?"

"I'm happy enough. And you?"

"Oh, I'm happy. Real happy. Finally."

"Good, Norm. I'm pleased to hear that."

He's silent for a moment. He seems to be studying the currents in the water. Then he says, "I want you to know I didn't come here on account of Doll's birthday."

"You didn't?"

"No. I came on account of you. Your health," he says ominously. "Barbie convinced me not to miss this opportunity to say good-bye."

"Good-bye?"

"Well, this may be the last time we see each other. Not that I think you're gonna die tomorrow. Hell, I could be killed in a car wreck on the way back to Denton. But I just wanted to let you know I loved you."

"Great. I'll file that away for a rainy day."

"Zero, I'm trying to open up to you. You don't have to be so sarcastic."

"Then let's talk about something else."

"Why? Don't you want to be close?"

"Norm, it's been sixteen months since I got my wonderful news, and this is the first time you've even mentioned it. You haven't called, you haven't written—"

"Communication isn't my strong suit."

"No kidding."

"I'm much better in person."

"Bullshit! And when I drop off the face of this earth, it isn't gonna affect your life two bits. This is no time to come running in with a bunch of sappy sentiment. This is the time to cut the crap."

"That's what I'm tryin' to do. I've got a few HIV patients myself. Not homosexuals, mind you, hemophiliacs."

"Of course. No one in your practice could possibly be gay, could they?"

He shrugs. "Well, they could be. But none I know of."

He looks out at the river and takes a deep, put-upon breath. "It's just that I spent my whole childhood being a big brother to you and Doll, and I've got a family of my own now."

"You've got several."

"I wanted to say all this now, Zero, instead of waiting till you're on your deathbed."

"If and when I'm on my deathbed, don't feel like you have to say a thing. You're off the hook, Norm. I absolve you. Completely."

"Still, that doesn't mean I don't love you."

"If you say that one more time I'm gonna push you in the river."

"You'd really do it, wouldn't you?"

"Try me."

"God! I wish someone would tell me why homosexuals feel they have to be so belligerent about everything."

"Because we all come from families full of assholes like you!"

"I am a liberated man."

"That's right. I forgot. You took that seminar when you were married to Tettie and earned a certificate."

I stand up in disgust. "I'm ready to go back to the hotel now, Norm. Are you gonna drive me, or shall I hitchhike?"

"Zero, please. I wanted to talk."

"We have nothing to talk about."

"Nothing?" His facial expression becomes so wounded and juvenile that I actually relent.

"Oh, all right. Look, I know you mean well. At least I think you do. You just try too hard, Norm. It's embarrassing. If you want to talk, talk. But let's keep it simple, and let's leave matters of life and death out of it."

"Whatever you want."

Silence.

Now we're both studying the currents in the river.

"Barbie and I sure have a good sex life," he says out of the blue.

I look at him, warily. "So do Jeff and I."

"I don't think I want to hear about that." He laughs.

"That's because you're homophobic."

"Huh?"

"You expect me to listen to you go on about Barbie, but I can't mention Jeff."

"Oh."

Back to the currents in the river.

"I hear you've been in touch with Trebreh," he says.

"Trebreh's been in touch with me," I correct.

"Did you two have a falling out or something?"

"I just have a new policy about people I can't depend on."

"Trebreh really burned me good when I was divorcing Tettie."

"What'd Trebreh have to do with it?"

"He was in Dallas with some promotional thing, and we met for

115

a drink. I told him about hiding out in Tettie's flower bed with my video camera, trying to get some footage of her staggering around the house drunk. But every time I was there all she was drinking was a Coke. So I had to jiggle the lens to make it look like she was unsteady. Then I had to have the video doctored to change the Coke can to a beer."

"God, Norm, Tettie hardly ever drank."

"It's not how much you drink, Zero, it's what it does to you. My lawyer thought if we could prove Tettie was an alcoholic, it'd be easier for me to get the kids. But Trebreh called her up and told her the whole plan. Thanks to him, it took me over two years and almost a hundred thousand dollars to get those kids back. Barbie got so impatient with the whole process, I had to buy her two diamond rings and a fur coat."

"You need your head examined."

"Why? It's only money. Besides, they're great kids. They'd be really hurt if they thought you didn't like 'em. They look up to you, Zero."

"They don't even know me."

"Sure they do. We talk about you all the time, mention you in our prayers every night."

"I am really ready to get back to the hotel now, Norm."

"Okay." He throws his arm around my shoulder and gives me a stiff squeeze. "But I'm glad we had this time together. You can't say I didn't try."

David and Lance are back in bed.

"Resting between shifts," says Lance.

"I'll bet."

"He's working again tonight," clarifies David.

"Bartending your sister's birthday party," says Lance.

"Aren't you the lucky one?"

"Yeah." He yawns. "And I've gotta be down on the mezzanine by four-thirty to set up. What time is it?"

"Just after three."

"Have a good visit with your brother?" asks David.

"It was wonderful. He took me down to the river to tell me he loved me, in case I died before he saw me next."

"Nice guy. You been with him all this time?"

"No. I stopped downstairs for some lunch, then went for a long walk. This place depresses me."

"Guess who we saw?" asks Lance.

"I can't imagine."

"Jesus Las Vegas."

"And your Uncle Markus," adds David. "They want us to drop by their suite about five."

"Fine. But in the meantime, I've gotta lie down and leave this life behind."

"Uncle Markus, you look wonderful! What happened?"

"Thank you, Zero. I owe it all to Jesus Las Vegas. He's brought youth back into my life. A remarkable young man."

"You don't have to tell *me*."

"Well, come in, come in."

"You remember my friend David, don't you?"

"Of course. Hello, David."

"Hey, guys," says Jesus, coming out of the bedroom. "Good to see you."

"You've put on a little weight," I observe. Jesus pats his slight paunch and grins. "And so many gold chains!"

"One for every month we've known each other," says my uncle. "Sit down, boys. Take a load off your feet. Can I get you something to drink?"

"No thanks," I say. "I believe I'll hold off until this evening."

"Have it your way," says Uncle Markus, pouring himself a martini.

"How was Greece?"

"Heaven on earth," says Jesus dreamily. "Over the course of the year, the cruise took us to twenty-two islands. Your uncle's hip mended as good as new."

"Though recovery was a little longer coming than I'd planned," says Uncle Markus.

"We read," says Jesus. "I lounged by the pool, tanning my

beautiful body"—he giggles—"and meeting so many interesting people."

"The Cruise Set," says Uncle Markus. "You wouldn't believe how strangers flock to this boy."

"Oh yes I would. I've seen him in action."

"Greece is one of my favorite places," says David. "Zero and I had a wonderful time there in 1980."

"When did y'all get back?" I ask.

"We flew into New York late October," says Uncle Markus. "Stayed a couple of weeks to do some business."

"Took in some shows," says Jesus. "It was so much fun."

"Always anxious to find fresh properties for my dinner theatres," says Uncle Markus. "I secured the rights to a wonderful new musical."

"With a country-and-western score," adds Jesus.

"Which Jesus is slated to star in." Uncle Markus is beaming.

Jesus crows, "Isn't that something, Zero? After eight years on the drag circuit, I'm finally going legit!"

"What's it called?" I ask.

"*Gimme Back My Pork Chop*," announces Jesus.

"Doesn't sound so legit to me."

"It's about family greed in the Deep South," explains my uncle.

"How appropriate."

"I play the matron of a rooming house," says Jesus excitedly.

"The matron?"

"Well, yeah. Just 'cause I'm goin' legit, don't think I'm gonna start playin' men."

"He'll be splendid," says Uncle Markus. "It's all the rage now, cross-dressing in the theatre."

"You bet," says Jesus, patting my uncle's knee.

Uncle Markus asks about Mary Bull.

I fill him in on the details.

"I simply can't wait to meet her," he exclaims.

"She's eager to meet you, too. Especially after she heard you'd won the Tony Award."

"Eons ago," he says dismissively. "I just hope she doesn't get too famous before I can persuade her to come work for me."

"Guess who's touring in *Into the Woods* with her?" I say.

"Who?"

"Julie Mercer."

"No!"

"They've got her playing the witch."

"What an ingenious bit of casting."

"Isn't it? I'll never forget meeting her when you two toured together in *Company* and it came to the Robinson Auditorium. What a lady."

"A lady and a pro. I'm so pleased to hear she's come out of retirement."

"She's done four recordings in the last few years."

"I have every one of them. The greatest song stylist working today. Mary Bull's lucky to be exposed to her." Pause. "But what about Trebreh?"

"He's the same as ever, as far as I can tell. He was supposed to be in Toronto last fall, but never showed up. He has a new video out."

"Yes, I've ordered it."

The phone rings.

"Excuse me a minute," says Uncle Markus, picking up. "Hello? . . . Well, hello, Lorna Yoakum, greetings to you too. . . . I think that's a splendid idea. We'll be down in two shakes."

He hangs up.

"The Yoakums are already here," he informs us. "Lorna wants us to come down to the mezzanine, have a drink, and pay our respects to Aunt Tula. Apparently, Tula's so deaf she can't hear thunder. So it's best we attempt a little chat before the party's in full force."

"Now which one is Tula?" asks Jesus.

"Tula is the last living member of her generation," I tell him. "The grande dame and the family's undisputed matriarch."

"Undisputed?" asks my uncle with a raised brow.

"Undisputed on my mother's side of the family," I clarify.

"On my side," says Uncle Markus, "we have all kinds of matriarchs. Including me!" He laughs gaily.

"In that case," says Jesus, "I'd better change for the evening."

"What are you wearing?" asks Uncle Markus.

"I was thinking of my sailor suit," says Jesus.

"Splendid! You look wonderful in that. And I'll wear blue to set you off."

"Why don't we just meet y'all down there?" I suggest.

"Good idea," says Uncle Markus.

He sees us to the door. "We'll only be a minute."

Aunt Lorna clearly wasn't expecting to see me or David. Not yet, at least.

"Oh!" she says, spilling some of her drink. "You!"

"Hello." I give her an awkward hug. "Aunt Lorna, you remember my friend David, don't you?"

"Why, yes. And don't you both look so . . . healthy!"

"Thanks. So do you."

"Some would call it fat," she says, turning to her husband. "Ron, go over to the bar and get that nice colored boy to make Zero and David a drink."

"What'll y'all have?" asks Uncle Ron in a pinched voice.

"Two martinis, straight up."

Uncle Ron walks over to the bar like he's been frozen from the neck down.

"Is he all right?" I ask.

"Oh, he's just recovering from a little hernia operation," Aunt Lorna explains. "He's in a lot of pain. Don't pay any attention to him."

She leads us over to Tula, who's planted in a simple armchair not far from the bar. Her white hair is charmingly curled, her dress is immaculate, and her gnarled hands rest patiently on top of her cane.

Aunt Lorna braces herself. "Mother!" she shouts. "It's Zero and David!"

"Who?" Tula shouts back.

"Zero!" I holler. "What's the matter? Don't you recognize me?"

"Oh," she says, looking me over. "You married yet?"

"Not yet."

"Got a girl at least?"

"No, but I got me a new guy."

"You're always getting yourself a new guy. What you need is to get yourself a girl!" She bangs her cane for emphasis. She looks at David. "Who's that?"

"My friend."

"He looks familiar."

"That's because you've met him before, several years ago."

"I'm too old to be meeting people."

"I said, you've met him before."

"You say, who's at the door?"

I try a different approach. "You sure are looking good."

"Don't make fun of me."

"I mean it."

"I've had cancer. Lost both my breasts. My gas is about to kill me. And I've got giant brown things growing all over me."

"They're moles, Mother," says Lorna. "And they're not that big."

"Some of 'em are the size of golf balls."

"Why don't you have 'em removed?" I ask.

"I've been tryin', but no one'll operate."

"The doctor says it just isn't worth it," says Aunt Lorna. "Not at her age. They're not hurtin' anything. Just old-lady moles."

"They hurt my pride," says Tula.

Uncle Ron doles out the drinks, handing Tula a screwdriver.

"I hope it's not too strong," she says. "You know I don't like it strong."

"Tula, I've been fetching you screwdrivers for thirty-eight years. I believe I know how you like 'em by now." Uncle Ron heads out to the terrace for a smoke.

"I'll never get used to that man," mutters Tula.

Aunt Lorna just shakes her head.

I ask Tula what she's been doing with herself.

"Not much. Dominoes keeps me busy. Most of my friends have died though, so I have to play with my enemies. I don't enjoy that very much. Still, I have my car. That's my one consolation."

"You're still driving?"

"Sure. They can take away your license, but they can't take away your car!"

"Isn't that kind of dangerous?"

"She doesn't go far," says Aunt Lorna. "Mainly to Baskin-Robbins and back."

"Gotta have my ice cream," says Tula.

"Oh, look!" says Lorna. "Here comes Markus!"

"Who?" says Tula.

A SHINDIG IN LITTLE ROCK

"Markus MacNoo," Lorna shouts. "Edie's brother-in-law from when she was married to Charles."

"See," says Tula. "I told you somebody was at the door."

"Mother, there is no door. We're on a mezzanine. It's a big wide-open space that looks down onto the lobby. See?"

"I see doors," says Tula. "Lots of doors."

"Those doors don't go anywhere except out onto the terrace."

"Paris?"

"Terrace!"

Lorna sighs with great exasperation, then greets Uncle Markus. "It's wonderful to see you again, Markus. You look marvelous."

"You too, dear. As ravishing as ever."

"Flatterer!"

Lorna takes in the nautical sight of Jesus Las Vegas. "And who have we here?" she asks.

"This is my traveling companion, Jesus Las Vegas."

"What a cute name! Ron?" She looks around. "Where did he go?"

"Right here," Ron calls from the terrace.

"Get that nice colored boy to pour Markus and Jesus Las Vegas a drink."

"What'll they have?"

"Martini," says Uncle Markus.

"Mint julep," says Jesus.

"You'll have to excuse Ron," says Aunt Lorna. "He just had a little hernia operation, and he isn't too thrilled to be here."

Lorna leans against the back of Tula's chair, gearing up for another shout. "Mother! Here's Markus come to see you!"

"Humph!" says Tula. "Who's the girl?"

"That's not a girl! That's his friend, Jesus Las Vegas!"

"Jesus?" Tula flinches. "Lord have mercy. I know I haven't been too nice in this life, but I'm not ready to go on to the next one. Not yet. Let me make it up to my family first. Then I'll go. Without a struggle."

Jesus giggles. "Sure, honey, whatever."

Lorna scowls. "Oh, Mother, for heaven's sake, it's Jesus Las Vegas, *not* Jesus Christ. Markus's friend."

Tula looks confused. "Where am I?"

"Just drink your drink," says Lorna. "What does it matter where you are?"

"How can I drink my drink in front of all these biblical characters? Something's happening to me, something I don't like. I don't know where I am!"

"You're at the Capital Hotel," Lorna snaps. "In Little Rock, Arkansas." She turns to the rest of us and says, "This is what I have to put up with, day in and day out."

"You could do something about it if you wanted," says Ron, handing Markus and Jesus their drinks.

"I heard that!" cries Tula. "He's bound and determined to put me in a home. I'm your mother, Lorna. Don't let him do it."

David and I look over at the bar and roll our eyes.

That nice "colored boy," Lance—busy making setups, plopping ice cubes into glasses—winks.

In the center of the lobby is an enormous butter sculpture, which Sparky has commissioned, featuring a gigantic lobster, Doll's favorite food, with the words HAPPY BIRTHDAY etched on its tail.

The entire family (excluding Tula, who has remained in her armchair, and Betty and Peppy, who are simply "absent") lines a path leading from the lobby up the grand staircase to the mezzanine.

Sparky pulls up in front of the hotel in his rented Cadillac. My father, masquerading as a doorman, opens the front passenger door. My mother steps out. Dad salutes. "Hail, great sanctimonious one!"

"What are you doin' here?" she asks, horrified.

"Workin', ever heard of it?" He grins maniacally.

"Oh!" she growls. "You just have to ruin everything we try to do right, don't you?"

"I'm on a mission," he informs her.

Sparky hops out of the car, thrusts a two-dollar tip into Dad's hand, and rushes around to open the door for my sister. But Dad beats him to it, pulling a magician's flower bouquet from his coat sleeve and presenting it to his daughter.

Doll is so moved by the gesture that she bursts into tears. "Why, thank you, Daddy. Thank you!"

Dad helps her from the car.

A SHINDIG IN LITTLE ROCK

Doll has on a red-and-black patterned dress accessorized with a string of pearls, a jade necklace, and a large opal brooch pinned to her bosom. Her hair has been blow-dried into a monstrous haystack held in place by several clusters of hair ornaments. On her fingers are at least a dozen rings. On her wrists, infinite bracelets. And to top it all, thrown over her shoulders is a floor-length emerald green cape.

"Doesn't she look gorgeous?" says Mom, squeezing Sparky's arm as they join the family lineup.

"Yeah," David whispers, "like she just stepped off the trading floor of 'Let's Make a Deal.'"

With tears of joy cascading down her cheeks, and the sweetest, most sincere smile upon her face, Doll makes her entrance.

Sparky glances up at the mezzanine to cue Hart Border to start playing "Thank Heaven for Little Girls."

My father, still outside, has his nose pressed to the window and is watching the procession with great interest.

Doll glides across the lobby to the staircase. Rotten Dog and Little Cookie try to trip her, but Doll deftly stays afoot, ascending to the mezzanine in perfect time to the music.

Mom follows on Sparky's arm. Then David and I. Then Norm and Barbie. Then R.D. and L.C. Then Aunt Lorna and Uncle Ron. Then Aunt Eunice and Doc. Then Aunt Carol and Uncle Will. And finally, Uncle Markus and Jesus Las Vegas.

Doll reaches the top of the staircase, approaches Tula's armchair, and bows. Tula, who seems completely confused by the whole thing, quotes a short passage from *Li'l Abner*, then waves her away.

Sparky takes Doll by the hand and leads her onto the dance floor for the opening waltz. The rest of us stand around the perimeter, and after the final note has been played, applaud politely.

"Oh, thank you, Sparky," says Doll, still in tears. "That was just beautiful!"

"Doll," says my mother. "Why don't you come on over to the table and take a look at your stack of presents?"

"Oh, no!" squeals Doll. "Nobody was supposed to bring me anything."

"Nonsense," says Aunt Eunice. "Doc and I have a little charm for you that we got in Mexico. It's been blessed by a fortune-teller."

"Oh, how sweet!"

"Your Uncle Will and I got you a life insurance policy," says Aunt Carol. "That's one thing everybody needs. Eventually."

"I'll treasure it forever," cries Doll.

"We bought you some earrings," says Norm dully. "You can exchange them if they're not to your taste."

"And a little bottle of perfume," adds Barbie, referring to the free sample the store gave with the earring purchase.

"L.C. and me got you two cans of Play-Doh," says Rotten Dog.

"And I picked the color," adds Little Cookie.

"Here's an envelope from me and your Uncle Ron," says Aunt Lorna. "A practical gift."

"This is from Jesus and me," says Uncle Markus. "Something we picked up on our travels. One of those Greek vases depicting various gentlemen enjoying the ancient athletic pastimes."

"Why, thank you, Uncle Markus. I'll think of you every time I look at it."

"This is from Zero and me," says David.

"It's so heavy!" exclaims Doll. "What is it? A crystal ball?"

"Why, that's exactly what it is," I say. "How did you know?"

Another gush of tears. "Oh, gosh! Y'all are just too good to me. I can't stand it! This is the happiest day of my life. I don't know what to say except . . . God, *I need a cigarette!*" She buries her face in the closest ashtray, sniffing mightily.

My mother forces a cheerful laugh. "Doll's just quit smoking," she says. "Doll, honey. Try to restrain yourself. It's just not ladylike."

"But I'm so overwhelmed!" Doll cries.

"Do you think maybe we ought to go to the powder room and freshen up our lipstick?"

"Yes," Doll says. "Let's."

"We'll be right back," says my mother. "Y'all belly up to the bar and get yourself a drink!"

That sets off a stampede. Poor Lance is so swamped with orders that David has to help him pour.

"Bloody Mary!"

"White Russian!"

"Whiskey sour!"

"White wine!"

"Vodka tonic!"

A SHINDIG IN LITTLE ROCK

"Double bourbon!"

"Piña colada!"

Doll returns, somewhat subdued, and orders a double Dewar's. Lance pours it and sweetly says, "Happy birthday."

"Thank you."

Hart Border strikes up a jitterbug, which packs the dance floor with the older couples spinning and twirling. But it's Mom and Sparky who specialize in the step and show everybody else what they're made of.

Aunt Carol sits Uncle Will next to Tula. "There you go, honey. You two can have a nice chat. Say anything you want because neither one of you can hear a word."

"Where's Betty?" Uncle Will asks pitifully.

"I don't know," Aunt Carol snaps. "And we're not gonna worry about Betty. This is Doll's night. We're here to celebrate. And I've decided to allow you one drink. What's it gonna be?"

"Martini," he says.

"And for you, Tula?"

"I'll have another one of these screwdrivers," she says, somewhat cross-eyed, handing Carol her empty glass.

"You guys need any help?" I ask David and Lance.

"No," says Lance. "I believe I've about got it under control. Go on back and join the party, David."

"I prefer this party," he says.

"You are bad."

"Excuse me," says Aunt Carol. "I need a martini, a screwdriver, and a glass of white wine."

"Comin' right up."

Rotten Dog and Little Cookie are over at the dining table, rearranging the place cards.

Norm says to Barbie, "Aren't they creative?"

"Yeah," she says. "Two regular geniuses." She tugs at Norm. "Come on, let's dance."

"I don't feel like it just now."

"Well, I do! I want to be seen. Do you realize not one person in this family has even spoken to me yet?"

"They're just distracted," says Norm.

"Distracted my ass. They're out of their minds. To put on this

126

lavish spread for a thirtieth-birthday party when they couldn't even be bothered to send us a wedding present. Now come on!" She drags him to the dance floor.

Aunt Lorna leans lazily against the bar. She seems to be quite tipsy, and has been listening to Norm and Barbie's conversation. She says to Aunt Carol, "I can sure see why Norm divorced Tettie. That new wife of his is some looker."

"Isn't she?" says Aunt Carol. "And a real take-charge kind of gal."

Rotten Dog and Little Cookie are now blowing their noses in the dinner napkins and cleverly refolding them.

I go over and threaten them. "If you two don't straighten up—"

"What?" they say in a smart-aleck tone. "What'll you do?"

"I'll bang your heads together until your brains squirt out!"

"Will not! Will not!"

"What's goin' on?" asks Doll.

"R.D. and L.C. are doing everything they can to sabotage your party."

Doll glances at the place cards. "No problem," she says. "A lady always memorizes her seating plan." She rectifies the situation.

"Is a lady the same thing as a woman?" asks Little Cookie.

"Depends," says Doll. "Every girl becomes a woman, but a lady takes cul-ti-vation."

"Barbie says you're not a real woman," challenges L.C.

"What does Barbie mean by that?" asks Doll.

"Barbie says you're not a real woman until you have a baby of your own."

Doll flinches.

Little Cookie continues, "And you aren't even married yet. You don't even have a date for your own party."

"I don't need a date," says Doll bluntly. "I don't need to be married either. Men have never given me anything but grief."

"Come on, L.C." says Rotten Dog. "Let's go torture somebody who appreciates it."

"Let's get the old lady."

"Yeah, let's get her!"

"Feel like dancing?" I ask Doll.

"Love to."

A SHINDIG IN LITTLE ROCK

Aunt Eunice introduces Doc to Uncle Markus.

"Markus, darling. I hear you've been to Greece."

"Yes," says Uncle Markus. "Broke my hip and went for a cruise while I was on the mend."

"Well, I can't think of a better reason to break a hip than that. Can you, Doc?"

"No, Eunice. I sure can't."

"I just love the idea of Greece. Did you, by any chance, hear of any nudist colonies over there?"

"No, though there's a nude beach on Mykonos."

"Child's play," says Eunice dismissively.

"Charge!" commands Rotten Dog. He and Little Cookie attack Tula, poking her chair from behind with cocktail stir sticks. Tula is not so much aware of the invasion as of a vague discomfort. She moves to get up, and rocks forward a couple of times. But in trying to find her feet, she misses and tumbles onto the floor.

"Good lord!" she exclaims. "I'm drunk!"

"Hello there, Mother," says Lorna, stepping over her. "Having fun?"

"Somebody spiked my orange juice!"

"Well, you just lie right there. You'll be fine." Lorna wanders over to the dining table to locate her seat.

"Let's tie her up!" says Rotten Dog.

"Yeah," says Little Cookie. "Gimme your belt."

I go to Aunt Tula's rescue.

"Uh-oh," says Rotten Dog. "The terminator."

"Retreat!" yells Little Cookie. "To the maid's closet."

"Yeah!"

My mother, on her way to the bar, says, "Zero, I wonder who they remind you of?"

"Who?"

"Rotten Dog and Little Cookie. It's you and Trebreh all over again."

"Thanks a lot."

"You're welcome," she says brightly.

"Can I help you up?" I ask Aunt Tula.

"No, Zero. I'm very comfortable, thank you. Quite a hotel they've got here. Look at that ceiling."

February 1990

Jesus takes me aside. "David just told me about Randy. I'm sorry."

"Thanks. He was quite fond of you."

"It was a mutual admiration," he says. "I don't know if I ever told you this, but that was one of the best times of my life, that summer I worked in Toronto and met you guys."

We look at each other a moment. I shake my head and sigh. I miss Randy. I miss so many people.

"What's Searcy up to?" asks Jesus.

"More of the same."

"Be sure and tell him I said hello."

"I will."

"It's really nice to see you again, Zero."

"You too. And I think you've worked wonders with my uncle."

"It was the time away more than me. The man hadn't had a day off in fifty years."

"I just hope you're finding . . ." I pause, searching for the right words.

"What?" he asks.

"Well, life with a seventy-three-year-old must not be too terribly fulfilling."

"We're not lovers, if that's what you mean."

"Oh? I didn't know that."

"He thinks of me as a son."

"Many do."

"I even have my own apartment. We're friends. I hadn't intended to go home with him to Florida. Once my job as traveling companion was done, I assumed we'd go our separate ways. Then *Pork Chop* came along and he made me an offer I couldn't refuse." Jesus grins. "A starring role. Your uncle's a smart man. But then again, so am I."

"Jesus?" calls Uncle Markus.

Jesus pats me briskly. "If you'll excuse me, I'd better get back to my duties."

Hart Border plays several more numbers. The guests order several more drinks. Then Sparky announces it's time to sit down for the first course, oyster soup.

"What's this gross stuff?" asks Rotten Dog, tossing an oyster at Little Cookie.

A SHINDIG IN LITTLE ROCK

"Stop!" she screams.

Lance comes around with the wine.

Ding-ding-ding. My mother taps her spoon against her glass. She stands at the head of the table. "May I have your attention, please? I just want to welcome each and every one of you to Doll's thirtieth birthday. I can't begin to tell you how honored we are that you'd take time out from your busy lives to be with us this weekend: my wonderful children, my dearest relatives, my friends, and of course, the man who's made it all possible: Sparky." She raises her glass in a toast.

Sparky, seated to her immediate right, rises. "Why, thank you, Edie." He dabs his napkin to his mouth, then looks at it strangely. "I want to welcome everybody as well. As most of you know"—he looks at Mom—"I've loved this remarkable lady since I was a little boy. Life has taken us in very different directions, and now we're together again. I know many of you don't understand our relationship, or approve, and I'm not asking you to. But rest assured there has never been greater love between man and woman. Someday I'm gonna marry you, Edie. Someday I'll make you my wife."

Mom smiles, tears in her eyes, then gulps down a little wine.

"As for Doll," Sparky continues. "I like to think of Doll as my 'chosen' daughter. And Doll, I wish for you the happiest of birthdays and the brightest of futures."

Another toast, followed by a round of applause.

Cousin Betty staggers in. She weaves over to the table, then sits in one of the two empty seats.

Aunt Carol whispers, "Where's Peppy?"

"Who?" Betty asks.

"Your husband!"

"Down at the bar. I think."

"You think? Either he is or he isn't."

Betty pulls her napkin apart with some difficulty and sets it in her lap.

"What's the matter?" asks Aunt Carol. "Isn't he gonna join us? Or don't we merit his lovely company?"

"He has some business to do."

"I don't like this, Betty. I don't like it at all."

Lance removes the soup bowls and starts bringing the salads.

Sparky looks at him arrogantly and calls him over. He says in a quiet hiss, "We could use a little more time between courses, boy."

"I know, sir," Lance whispers back, "but the chef says the lobster thermidor's about ready, and you wouldn't want it to get cold, now would you?"

"No, I certainly wouldn't."

Mom rests her hand on Sparky's and suggests, "Why not just bring it all at once? I think we're more than ready to eat."

Lance looks at Sparky for his approval.

Sparky waves his hand. "Sure, boy, go ahead."

Lance dashes back down to the kitchen.

Sparky goes over to have a word with Hart Border, requesting an upbeat version of "Laura."

"Our song!" squeals my mother, hearing the opening notes. She gulps the rest of her wine, then glides onto the dance floor into the arms of her man. They hop around like two jumping beans, swinging this way and that.

"Doll?" asks Norm. "Care to dance with your eldest brother?"

"Sure."

"I wonder," says Aunt Eunice, "if I ought to go down to the bar and give that Peppy a piece of my mind. I can't stand to see the women in this family mistreated. I mean, if you're gonna bother to marry a man, the least you ought to get out of it is a decent escort and a pleasant dinner companion."

"Best to let the young people sort these things out for themselves," says Doc wisely.

A cool wind blows against the back of my neck. I turn around and see one of the terrace doors has come open. Uncle Ron must have left it ajar when he went out to have his last smoke. I get up to shut it. Then I notice a lady's shoe wedged in the bottom. I follow the shoe up the leg, up the torso, and finally, to the face. It's Sparky's wife, Hilda! She offers me a friendly, drunken smile. Then she pats me on the shoulder, slurring, "Excuse me," and staggers into the room. In one hand she carries a flask. In the other, a small handgun.

She looks around the mezzanine to get her bearings. She sees Sparky and my mother out on the dance floor. She hears the sound of "Laura," raises her gun, and takes aim.

I force my voice out of my throat. "Watch out!"

A SHINDIG IN LITTLE ROCK

Barbie is the only one that seems to hear me and cries, "Norm!" But what with the music, the dancing, and all the table conversation, Norm doesn't hear her.

Little Cookie does, though, and she screams her high-pitched battle cry, shattering half a dozen wineglasses, which gets the attention of everyone still seated at the table.

"Wow!" says Rotten Dog. "Radical!"

Aunt Carol sees Hilda and says, "Uh-oh. Looks like Edie's 'bout to get her due. Take cover!"

Carol, followed by Uncle Will, Doc, Uncle Markus, Uncle Ron, and Aunt Tula, ducks under the table for protection. David and Jesus get up to stalk Hilda. Aunt Eunice and Betty are the only ones who remain seated. Slowly, Aunt Eunice begins to undress.

Hilda pulls the trigger. *Bang!*

We look around in a panic, trying to follow the trajectory of the bullet. Blessedly, Hilda seems to have missed.

Sparky and my mother, so caught up in their dance, remain completely oblivious to the intrusion until Sparky swings my mother out on a count of three and comes face to face with his wife. Stunned and shocked, he freezes, letting go of my mother's hand. And Mom keeps right on with her enthusiastic dance, flying over the mezzanine rail in midstep.

There's an awesome moment of silence.

Hart Border, who used to teach with Mom in the school district, keeps playing, but stands up and has a look over the rail.

"Oh my god!" screams Aunt Lorna. "She's fallen!"

Doll lets out an anguished cry of "Mommy!" and races down the staircase, followed by Sparky.

Norm dashes after them. "Stand back!" he yells. "I'm a doctor!"

Hilda disappears back onto the terrace.

"Get her!" says Aunt Lorna.

David and Jesus go after her.

Betty refills her wineglass and says, "Was this all planned?"

Heads begin to poke out from under the table.

I'm squeamish about blood at the best of times, and the idea of seeing my mother's cracked-open head or broken neck is more than I can bear. Still, I force myself to look down into the lobby.

February 1990

I can't believe it. Mom has landed smack-dab in the butter sculpture. It seems to have melted somewhat and broken her fall.

"I think she's all right," says Norm, checking Mom's pulse, lifting her eyelids.

"It's a miracle!" cries Doll. "A birthday miracle!"

Sparky covers my mother's face with kisses. "Edie, oh Edie, you're okay."

I run downstairs.

Several of the relatives crawl out from under the table and go over to the rail to see for themselves.

Hilda comes weaving into the lobby.

Mom opens her eyes, murmurs, "What's goin' on?" sees Hilda, and faints.

Norm busies himself reviving her.

Lance emerges from the kitchen with plates lined up and down his arm. "What the hell?" he says, absorbing the scene in front of him.

"Call the manager," says David. "The woman's got a gun."

Hilda advances toward Sparky and my mother, a vengeful smirk on her face.

"Easy now," says Sparky. "This is no way to solve our problems. You've already earned yourself a few years' time, but if you hand over the gun now, I can probably get you off on mental anguish."

"Mental anguish?" she says. "I am way beyond mental anguish. This is what's called mental revenge."

"Give me that gun," demands Sparky.

"You and your philandering."

"I said, give me that gun!"

Again, Hilda fires. *Bang!*

We all look around, holding our breath.

Another miss.

Peppy appears from the bar, waving a pistol of his own. "Where are they?" he raves. "You ain't gettin' any of my goods without the money first, damn it. Where are they?!"

Hilda points her pistol at him haphazardly and fires.

Peppy goes down, clutching his shoulder. "She got me! The stupid bitch got me!"

Betty races down the staircase to his side. "Peppy, for god's sake, I told you this would happen! You can't just sell a friendly little gram, can you? You've got to step on everyone's territory. Get us on every death list from here to L.A.! God, help me! He's bleeding to death!"

"No, he's not," says Norm, pressing a napkin to the wound. "He's just been grazed. He'll be fine. We need some ambulances here," he calls out. "We need some ambulances!"

"Ambulances!" Betty calls, rushing to the front desk. "Help! Help! Ambulances!"

Patrons of the fancy restaurant downstairs come out to see what all the commotion is.

Sparky takes advantage of the momentary confusion and tries to jump Hilda. A noble idea, but he slips on a stray piece of butter and lands splayed at her feet.

Hilda points her gun at that most tender spot between his legs. "No!" he says.

"Time to put out the fire, Spark."

Bang!

Sparky lets out an anguished cry, grabbing himself. Blood pours between his fingers. He passes out.

"Oh my god!" screams my mother, scrambling out of the butter sculpture, chunks of it stuck to her dress and hair. "You've shot the best part of him, you insane woman!" She rushes to his side. "Sparky! Sparky, speak to me!"

"Freeze!" rasps a voice from the doorway.

It's Stellrita, followed by my dad. She's got her shotgun propped against her shoulder, her eye squinting as she aims. She orders, "Put down your weapons. I've got mine and I'm coverin' you all."

"Gladly," says Hilda, taking a seat. "I've done what I came to do." She sips from her flask, then offers it to me.

"Uh, no thanks," I say.

"Peppy's got a gun, too!" yells Aunt Carol.

"Gather 'em up, Charles," Stellrita tells my father.

"Yes, Goddess." Dad does as he's told.

Then he and Stellrita take the weapons and duck out.

Aunt Eunice, stark naked save for her high heels and jewelry, meanders down the staircase singing "St. Louis Blues" in a sweet, faint voice. The restaurant crowd listens politely, then offers a warm round of applause, to which Eunice bows.

Three ambulances arrive: one for Sparky, one for Peppy, and one for my mother, who protests, "But I'm fine! I didn't hurt a thing. Honest! I don't need to go to any hospital except to be with Spark."

"They've got to check you out," Norm tells her. "You fell twenty-five feet. You may be in shock."

"I am not in shock! I'm fine!"

Forcibly, the paramedic straps her onto the stretcher.

"Oh, for heaven's sake," Mom says as they start to carry her out. "Well, y'all go on back up and enjoy your dinner. Doll, you're the hostess now!"

Doll looks at her, stunned. "But Mom, don't you want me to come with you?"

"No, I don't want you to come with me! We didn't go to all this trouble to have the whole party ruined at this point."

Doll looks lost for a moment. Then she takes a deep breath, steadies herself, and troops back up the staircase, saying, "The excitement's over, everybody. Come on. Let's eat."

"Great party," says Rotten Dog.

"Yeah," says Little Cookie. "On my next birthday, I want one just like it!"

After spending a good hour in the Capital Hotel bar recounting the evening's events to the police and various members of the press, I go over to Stellrita's.

"How'd you know there was gonna be trouble?" I ask her.

"Your daddy came and got me. He was watchin' the whole thing."

"Well, the police don't think too highly of people taking the law into their own hands."

"I was trying to get the law *back* in my hands."

"They're gonna want to talk to you, Stellrita."

"They ain't gettin' nothin' from me."

A car pulls up and Helen steps out.

"Where you been?" asks Stellrita.

"To a meeting, Mother. Like I told you earlier."

"What kind of meetin'?"

"Nothing you'd be interested in. About Mr. Mandela."

A SHINDIG IN LITTLE ROCK

"Bring me another bucket of my mud."

Helen walks to the side of the house to fetch some, then pours it over Stellrita's feet.

"Oh, that feels good. If that ain't heaven, I don't know what is."

"Pretty night," says Helen, looking out at the yard.

"Ain't over yet," says Stellrita.

Two figures approach from the street.

"If that's the police, tell 'em I just left this life." Stellrita lets her head fall forward, playing dead.

"It's not the police," says Helen, "it's Lance."

"Lance? What's he doin' here?" I ask.

"He's my son," says Helen.

"Your son?"

"I may not have raised him, but we're trying to make up for that now."

"I've known Lance for a couple of years, but I sure didn't know we were cousins."

"Half cousins."

"I hope he doesn't want to move in with us, too," says Stellrita. "Who's that with him? Don't he know it's bad luck to bring strangers round at night?"

"That's not a stranger," I tell her. "That's David."

" 'Evenin'," says Lance, handing Stellrita a doggie bag.

"What's this?" she asks.

"Lobster thermidor."

"Ain't that sweet of you? And I'm as hungry as I can be. Gettin' off this porch really revs up my appetite."

"How was the rest of the party?" I ask.

"Wound down pretty quickly," says David. "Though we had a hell of a time getting your Aunt Eunice back in her clothes."

"Yeah," says Lance. "I've worked a lot of these things, but I ain't never seen so many people have to be carried out."

An explosion sounds from the roof. The yard is suddenly illuminated with a burst of fireworks. A few minutes later, my father runs out on the porch, Roman candles strapped around his waist. "Goddamn it!" he raves. "The aliens have tricked me again!"

He becomes aware of the assembled group, turns from one face to the other, then says directly to me, "No holes, I hope?"

"No. And thanks for helping us out."

"Always ready to serve my fellow creatures. It's those aliens that are driving me crazy." He runs down Main Street. "Come back, you little critters. Come back, and fight like a man!"

Lance hands Helen an envelope.

"What's this?" she asks.

"My tips for the night. I told you I was gonna donate 'em to your Free South Africa Fund."

Helen looks in the envelope. "Honey, there must be two hundred dollars in here. You don't have to give all this."

"I want to."

"You're some prize kid," says Helen. "I don't know through whose fault, but I sure am glad of it. If Mandela gets out tomorrow, we're gonna march down Main Street."

"I'll be there," says Lance.

Helen goes into the house, carrying the envelope.

"You should've give that to me," says Stellrita.

"Sorry, Grandma. Some other time."

"That's what you always say. If it's money, it's some other time."

"Zero," says David, "would you mind if Lance stayed at the hotel again tonight?"

"Not at all. In fact, I was thinking of stayin' here."

"That's right," says Stellrita. "We always did keep the best company, didn't we, Zero?"

"Pretty good," I say. Then, to David: "We ought to be at the airport around ten. I'll be back about nine to pack."

"Okay."

" 'Night all," says Lance.

" 'Night."

They walk down the sidewalk, hand in hand.

"Ain't that cute?" says Stellrita. "Life is full of sorrow and love is the spark of life."

"Listen, Stellrita, I wonder if you'd let me spend the night in my old room."

She looks at me suspiciously. "What for?"

"I just want to, that's all."

"It'll cost you. Can't do nothin' for free."

"How much?"

"Oh, ten dollars oughta be a fair price."

I reach in my pocket and hand her a bill.

She takes it from me, grinning. "Nothin' I like more than receiving compensation for a job already done. Go on in, child. You know the way. You just go right on in whenever you're ready."

She laughs to herself. "Ten dollars. Got myself a ten-dollar bill!"

THE PRESSURE OF DREAMS

May 1990

F*lip.*

That is the word that keeps going through my mind as I listen to my doctor tell me about my latest test results.

He drew eighteen vials of blood and none of them have revealed very much. Except that my hemoglobin's down. "Not dangerously so," he says. "But we want to keep an eye on it."

Flip.

"What about my T cells?" I ask.

"Well," he says, "that's why I called you." My file is open in front of him. He picks up the lab-results sheet and pushes it my way. With his gold monogrammed pen, he circles the number: ninety.

"Ninety?" I ask. "That's quite a drop."

"I know," he says. "You've been stable around one-sixty since you started treatment. I'd like you to go back to the lab for another count. Make sure it's not a fluke. But I think it's very possible you've grown resistant to AZT. I see a lot of that after a year and a half on the drug."

"What then?"

"We'll put you on ddI. We can get it through the study, no problem."

"But doesn't ddI cause seizures, and make your feet and hands go numb?"

"Not seizures, neuropathy." He smiles, amused at my ignorance of medical jargon. "But that's just in extreme cases. You did well on AZT; I don't see why you shouldn't do well on ddI. Besides, it's not nearly as toxic to the bone marrow."

"Gee, I can hardly wait."

"I wouldn't be too worried about this, Zero. Not yet."

"Do I look worried?"

"I fully expect you to be here in a year's time. I would be surprised, though, if you didn't come down with some kind of an opportunistic infection." He puts the lab report sheet back in my file.

"Then weight loss, the odd fever, knee problems, thrush, and rashes don't count, huh?"

"It's all part of the syndrome. Which reminds me. I want to send you to a specialist for that facial rash."

"Not another specialist, please. You've already sent me to three. And each one gave me a different prescription. None of it's helped. The last dermatologist recommended something with the consistency of Vaseline. How many people do you see running around with Vaseline all over their face?"

My doctor laughs.

"And my knee," I continue. "You said it was a torn ligament. The sports doctor you sent me to said it was a swollen lymph node. And Dr. Fieldstone just shrugged and said, 'You're lucky it's not anything worse.' "

"You are lucky, Zero. You're quite lucky."

"Yeah, I'm lucky. Take a picture, quick, and remind me to buy a lottery ticket. You know as well as I do it's just a matter of time. That's what this is all about: time and management. So when something specific is wrong, just give me something to take care of it. I don't need to see a zillion specialists. I'm sick of spending the better part of every week at a doctor's office."

"You don't spend that much time at doctors' offices, believe me."

"So I'm being a prima donna again?"

"I'll give you some Dermovate," he says. "That'll take care of the rash, but use it sparingly. And you need to be careful about letting your attitude get too negative."

"Negative? I'm trying to be practical."

"Just remember, we're all doing the best we can. And nobody, not even the most informed scientist, knows very much."

"It's all so comforting, isn't it?"

My doctor takes a deep breath. He folds his hands in front of him and calmly looks at me. "Have you considered meditation or visualization?"

"Are we to that point?" I have to laugh. "Sure, doc. Don't forget I used to live in California. We did all that stuff."

"And?"

"I have a hard time sitting still. I find it virtually impossible to 'empty my mind.' I mean, if we were meant to have empty minds, don't you think we would've been born vegetables?"

"If we were meant to fly, don't you think we would have been born with wings?"

"Look, I know what you're trying to say. But I'm at ease with myself; I know myself. What you're talking about is something that gives you a break, something that makes you see things in a new way."

"And what does that for *you?*"

"A good book. A play. Music."

He makes a note in my file. Probably that I'm hostile. He fills out the various blood-work forms, then hands them over. "I'd like you to have this done as soon as possible."

"I'll do it tomorrow morning."

"We'll call you when the results come in."

I walk out of his office, full of jitters and nerves. They say a cat has nine lives. How many does a gay man have? One for every address he's lived at? One for every career he's tried? One for every illness he's endured? One for every death?

I get in the elevator, thinking about those long-term survivors who've never taken AZT, never taken any kind of antiviral. Most of them don't even believe AIDS is caused by a virus. What if they're right? And if they are, what is it that's happening to me?

The doctors say those of us on the medications *seem* to do better than those of us who aren't, but what the hell does anyone know?

Fuck it. I'll just forget about it until my next set of results.

THE PRESSURE OF DREAMS

Now, would you call that denial, or would you call that practical? Write me. I'd really like to know.

I walk out of the doctors' building onto University Avenue. The air is full of spring, and the planters along the median are full of tulips.

A man passes me in the crowd. He catches my eye. We both try a flirtatious smile, but it doesn't quite come off.

We are losing.

I walk over to Yonge Street, up to Dundonald, then head over to Jeff's, cutting through Cawthra Park. It's full of the usual assortment of seminaked neighborhood boys getting a head start on their tans. Bare feet, baskets, and ghetto blasters. Tiny Speedos and shiny, shiny skin.

The front door to Jeff's building is unlocked. I walk up the two flights of stairs to his apartment. From the hall, I can hear him practicing. He's been working on Ravel's "Pavane for a Dead Princess," a lovely piece of music.

I stand outside the door and listen to him play. He's got the first part down much better than the last. Why are we so much more adept at beginnings than endings? It's the same with my column. I can always get started, but it's where the piece goes and how it finishes that's the trick. True, you have to start things before you can finish them. So you work more on the beginning than the end. I don't know, maybe we're all just suffering from terribly short attention spans.

Jeff hits the last note. I knock.

"Who is it?" he calls.

"Me."

"Hey, me," he says, opening the door. "What a nice surprise."

It's hot in his apartment. Direct sunlight and no air-conditioning. Jeff has on an old pair of gym shorts.

I give him a hug, then walk over to the baby grand, sit on the bench, and depress one key. "You're really coming along on that piece," I say.

"What, the 'Pavane'? It's tricky, but I'll get it. Eventually. What have you been up to?"

"Oh, the doctor's."

"What'd he have to say?"

"That my T cells have dropped. To ninety. He wants me to have 'em retested to make sure it's not a fluke. Funny how they think it's a fluke when they go down but not when they go up, isn't it? I'll probably have to start on ddI."

Jeff sits beside me. "Well, that's not the greatest news, but it's not the worst either."

"Except that this wasn't supposed to happen."

"What wasn't supposed to happen?"

"All that crap about early intervention was supposed to maintain me."

"You've been on a pretty even keel, Zero."

"Been, Jeff. Past tense. Been."

"Look, there're declines and reprieves. You know that."

"Yes, I know that. And you're stable at two hundred. But I feel like I'm falling, Jeff. Falling over a big cliff with nothing at the bottom."

He feels my shoulders. "You're tight."

"Of course I'm tight."

"Want me to give you a massage?"

"What I want is for all this to be over with! What I want is to do something with the rest of my life besides wait to get sick."

"Come on." He unbuttons my shirt, slips it off my shoulders. "Lie down on the couch."

He starts along my spine.

"Ouch. Not so hard!"

"Breathe into it, Zero. Go with it."

"But you're killing me."

"I'm not killing you, you big sissy."

"Massage is supposed to be a pleasure, not a torture."

"They don't call it massage therapy for nothing." He goes after my shoulders. "It has to hurt a little, especially if you want it to do any good."

He does a sweeping motion from my shoulders to the top of my butt.

"Now, *that* feels good."

"That's because you're starting to loosen up."

"Or you've put the magic back in your hands."

"Be quiet. Just enjoy it."

"Okay. I won't say another word."

And I don't. But I start thinking again about my doctor and where this is all heading, and finally I can't stay quiet. "Jeff?"

"Yeah?"

"You know the thing that really drives me crazy?"

"What?"

"When the moment is gone, it's gone. Snap. No souvenirs, no postcards home. That's it. Finito."

"That's the way life is, Zero. Has that just dawned on you?"

"No. But it's just that time, or the shortness of time, makes it all the more maddening. And don't feel like you have to Pollyanna me. Just let me bitch a little bit, okay?"

He grins. "Sure." Then he goes after my neck.

"Ow!"

"Relax."

"I am relaxed!"

"No you're not. Not very."

We make love.

Then we split a sandwich he's got tucked away in his fridge. We sit in the middle of the living room floor, eating, laughing.

"Don't forget we have to make dinner for David and Lance," I say lazily.

"I haven't."

"We oughta get a move on."

"I'm ready when you are."

We dress and leave the apartment.

We pick up groceries along Church Street and head over to my place.

"Doesn't look like they're back from the airport," Jeff says, noticing that David's apartment is dark. "I thought Lance was getting in this afternoon."

"He was, but his connection was through Chicago, which guarantees a late arrival."

"After three months of love letters and long distance calls, I bet David's getting pretty anxious."

"You don't know the half of it. He's been flying around the house all week like a nun in heat."

"I just hope the visit isn't a letdown."

"It won't be. David is very mature. He's hardly expecting a mail-order bride. Besides, Lance is just coming for a two-week visit."

"And how'd you end up living here, Zero?"

"I came for a—"

"Two-week visit!" Jeff laughs. "I'm on to you."

"Well, what difference does it make? What happens between them is their affair, not ours."

I start unloading the groceries.

Jeff opens the door to the deck. "What do you say we eat out here? It's plenty warm enough."

"Sure, but you'll have to wipe off the table. I haven't gotten around to it this spring."

Jeff gives it the index-finger-across-the-surface test. The pad of his finger comes up the color of tar. "It's gonna need more than a wipe," he says.

He fetches the scrub brush and fills a bucket with hot, soapy water. He carries it out to the deck. "To work miracles," he says. "How 'bout putting on some music?"

"That Chet Baker CD?"

"Sounds good."

I put it on. It's a reissue from Chet's youth, when he had such a sweet voice, and phrased lyrics the same way he played the trumpet. I hum along, dicing garlic and onion to mix in with the hamburger.

Jeff pokes his head from the deck. "You know, you could put a very nice garden in up here."

"You're not supposed to eat things you grow in the city," I tell him. "Something about lead in the rain."

"Not a vegetable garden, silly, a flower garden. It'd be absolutely beautiful."

"Well, I'm not the gardening type."

"I am. And I don't have a deck at my place."

"Then be my guest. Feel free to do whatever you want."

"You're on." He smiles. "Victoria Day weekend. That's the time to plant. I'll make you a wonderland, Zero. Window boxes full of petunias, pots of begonias, all kinds of geraniums, nasturtiums, portulaca, lupine, lilies, sunflowers, ferns, nicotiana, lobelia—there's nothing more beautiful than lobelia: five colors of little flowers streaming down like a thick, wild wig."

"I don't even know what half those things are."

"You will by the end of the summer. Bryan and I had a magnificent garden. I wish you could've seen it. We also had a backyard to put it in, which helps. But this'll be a knockout. You've got a good-size deck."

I pace around the living room, carrying the bowl of hamburger, mashing at it with a wooden spoon. "Do you think about Bryan very often?"

"Sure, all the time."

"You rarely mention him."

"Don't I? It's another life, I guess. Kind of like your friend Randy."

"I talk about Randy constantly, so much so that my friends accuse me of not being able to let go."

"Why would you want to let go?" Jeff says. "It's not like you want to forget him."

I stop in the deck doorway.

"Jeff?" I ask.

"Yeah?"

"How would you feel if you had to watch me get sick? I mean, really sick. Even to the death. Like Bryan."

Jeff stops his scrubbing. He glances up at me, then shivers. He dunks the brush into the bucket and studiously shakes it out. "I don't know," he says. "We'll just have to cross that bridge when we get to it."

"Maybe you don't want to go through it again," I suggest.

"Nobody *wants* to go through it again, Zero. But we do."

"You don't have to, Jeff. You don't owe me a thing."

"Hush. Just stop talking like that. It's not an issue now, and hopefully it won't be for some time."

We look at each other.

"You're probably right," I say. "I'm just being overdramatic as usual." I smile.

How strange life would seem without Jeff Lake. Six months now, and we've rarely discussed our relationship. We've never once talked

May 1990

about moving in together. We've just spent our time as it comes, day by day.

Chet Baker starts crooning "I've Never Been in Love Before" from *Guys and Dolls.*

Jeff sings along, singing it to me.

"Liar," I say, laughing.

"What do you mean?"

"The hell you haven't been in love before."

"It's just a song, Zero."

"Yeah, and this is just life."

I return to my hamburger and amble back to the kitchen, grinning.

"Great burgers," says Lance, polishing off his first.

"Thanks. It's what I do to the meat. Plus a little touch of nutmeg."

"I taught him that," says David.

"Help yourself to another one, Lance," says Jeff. "Flatter the cook."

Jeff passes the platter. "Is this your first trip to Canada?"

"This is my first trip *anywhere.*"

"What do you think?"

"It's big. Though I've really only seen the airport, and the skyline from when we were driving in. I want to go up in that space needle though, for sure."

"It's on our list," says David.

"How are things in Little Rock?" I ask. "Or dare I bring that up?"

"Pretty good," says Lance. "People are still reeling from the MacNoo Family Capital Hotel Shoot-out."

"Is *that* what they're calling it?"

"Yeah, and it got ten times more coverage than the release of Nelson Mandela. Y'all wiped him clean off the front page."

"That's disgusting."

"They're still writing about it, too. There's something in the paper at least once a week."

"What do they find to say?"

"Oh, whether people should have the right to bear arms is a

149

favorite debate. Little Rock's image is another. The business community wants us portrayed as a 'sophisticated Southern city,' to attract outside dollars and conventioneers. And when there's a shootout at the classiest hotel, it's just not good P.R. 'Course, other people say that's what gives us character. But what I'm curious about is whatever happened to your mom's boyfriend, that man who kept calling me 'boy'? They never mention him in any of the articles."

"Probably because he owns the newspaper syndicate."

"Did his wife shoot his balls off or what?"

"No. The bullet just went into his thigh. But his testicles ascended from fright and they've yet to fall back into place. Apparently, his voice has become quite high-pitched."

"Now they call him 'Squeaky' "—David laughs—"instead of 'Sparky.' "

"According to my mother, though, the necessary parts still function sufficently."

"You mean," says Lance, "that she's still seeing him? After all that?"

"Of course she's still seeing him. He's her true love."

"What about his wife? Did they put her in jail?"

"Jail? Sparky wouldn't dream of pressing charges, which ticked my mom off more than anything. Hilda's receiving some extra counseling to try to cope better with the situation."

"The D.A.'s been buggin' my grandma," says Lance. "They want her to hand over the weapons so they can make a case. They say innocent people could have been hurt. But Stellrita maintains she gave the weapons to your dad, and he says he sold 'em to his alien friends. Intergalactic weapon sales, he calls it. Free enterprise."

"I'm surprised they haven't charged them both with contempt of court."

"They have," says Lance. "But the governor intervened on their behalf."

"Why'd he do that?"

"He and Stellrita go back a long way. He comes 'round to see her. Asks her advice on things. I guess she got your dad off as part of the deal. She said to tell you hi."

"Well, tell her hi back."

I rest my feet in Jeff's lap.

"Do you think you'll stay in Little Rock, Lance?"

"Sure. I like it. It's my home. Besides, we all can't leave. Some-body's gotta stay. To change things."

David sighs. "I am completely satiated from that delicious din-ner. Thank you, guys."

"Yeah," says Lance, "top-notch." He starts gathering up the dishes.

"Leave 'em, Lance. You don't work here. You're on holiday."

"But I want to do my part. I don't want y'all to get sick of me."

"Nonsense, you're the guest of honor. Save your strength. I'm sure you'll need it." I throw a look at David.

"Can't you think of anything but sex?" David asks me.

"Sure I can. World peace, hunger, human rights, funny things I've heard, sad things, life, death—I can think of a lot of things besides sex."

"I can't," says Jeff, squeezing my toes.

"I was counting on that."

"Neither can I," says Lance, looking at David, but saying to Jeff and me, "You don't know how much I've missed this man."

"Sure we do," says Jeff. "We know all about how absence makes the cock grow harder."

"You two may be excused at any time," I say. "We won't take offense."

"Well," says David, rising, resting his hands on Lance's shoul-ders. "Shall we?"

"I'm all yours."

And the two of them go downstairs.

"Cute pair," says Jeff.

"Aren't they?"

We sit there a minute, taking in the night, then Jeff suggests we smoke a joint. "You in the mood for that?"

"Sure am."

I hop up, go inside, and get one out of my special box.

"You know," I say, standing in the deck doorway, lighting up and toking, "I always told myself that if my T cells got below a hundred, I'd stop my vices. But now that they've taken the plunge, I see no reason to give up a thing."

"Not if you have a taste for it."

THE PRESSURE OF DREAMS

"Why deprive myself of a few simple pleasures?" I puff away, inhaling deeply, then take another hit before handing it to Jeff. "Aw, that feels good."

He tokes a couple of times, then hands it back.

After the smoke is finished, we settle into the lawn loungers and watch the sky: the pattern of jet trails drawing lines against the odd star. Such a good place for dreaming.

"Zero?" calls a jolly voice. "Darling? Knock-knock. C'est moi!"

Jeff and I are in bed, sound asleep, but not for long.

"Is that someone at your door?" Jeff asks me in a grog.

"It can't be," I say. "My friends know never to visit before noon."

Then we hear it again. "Zero, hon? Knock-knock."

"It sounds like Searcy," says Jeff, hiding his head beneath a pillow.

Then, suddenly, I remember. "It *is* Searcy! I forgot all about him coming. Damn!"

"I'll just sleep this one out," Jeff mutters, "if you don't mind."

"I do mind." I kick him playfully. "He wants to meet with us all about this big benefit he's doing. He needs volunteers. You've got ten minutes."

I get up, pull on my bathrobe, and answer the door.

"Hon!" Searcy exclaims, taking in the sight of me. "Don't bother to dress on my account. And I just love your new 'do! Why, you look positively electrocuted!"

"We had a rather late night. I was just about to put on a pot of coffee."

"Honey, you read my mind."

He follows me into the kitchen and sits himself down at the table. "I take it Miss David and his little Miss Friend are late as well?"

"Looks like it. Want to give 'em a shout?"

"If I must."

Searcy heaves himself up, walks back to the door, sticks his head out, and bellows, "David! Get your butt up here!"

"Comin'!" David hollers back. A moment later, he clumps up the stairs with Lance in tow.

"Well, well, well," says Searcy. "Who have we here?"

"This," says David, "is my new Arkansas friend, Lance Howard."

Searcy bows and kisses his hand. "Enchanté, mon cheri."

Lance giggles. "Nice to meet you, too."

"I'm Searcy, by the way. Sit. Zero's making coffee."

"Let's get right at it," says David. "Lance and I have a lot on our agenda today."

"Well," says Searcy, "first of all, you'll be glad to know things are really beginning to shape up. I can't tell you how thankful I am. It's the biggest thing I've had my hand in since Show Babies shut down. In fact, I feel like my old self!" He jiggles with merriment.

"What kind of thing is it?" asks Lance.

"Hasn't your beloved explained it to you?" asks Searcy.

"No, my beloved has not."

"He just got in last night," says David. "We've been occupied with more pressing things."

"Oh, how you titillate my imagination!" Searcy laughs gaily, then returns to the matter at hand. "It's a benefit for this special AIDS hospital clinic we want to get going. A week from Sunday night. Eight o'clock. The auditorium at the 519 Community Centre. Be there or die!"

"Is this the abridged explanation?" asks David, "or the epic?"

"If the young man wants to hear about it, the least I can do is tell him."

"I hope you're making the coffee good and strong," David says to me.

"I am."

Searcy continues, "You see, Lance—I just love that name: 'Lance'—it'll be a grand variety extravaganza. I happen to host a Gong Show at one of our bars. I've chosen half a dozen of the most talented participants to fill the first act: lip-synchers, baton twirlers, fire breathers, you name it. And for the first-act finale we've got the *enormously* gifted Misty Morning doing her fabulous gender strip."

"Gender strip?"

"You know, where you start off as woman and end up as a man. Hard as a rock, I might add, and certain to inspire some hefty donations during intermission, which is the point of the exercise. But it's the second act I'm really excited about. I'll be doing one of the

impersonation medleys I made famous in the great days of Show
Babies."

"Yeah, I've heard about that place from Jesus Las Vegas," says
Lance.

"You know Jesus?" asks Searcy.

"Why, sure! I used to see him perform all the time before he got
famous and left Little Rock."

"So incestuous, our little circle. And regardless of what Jesus
may have told you, *I* was the star of that place. Once. Long ago.
Before the bastards tore it down, taking my career halfway with it. But
never mind. 'Ever onward' is my motto. Now where was I?"

"The second act. Your impersonation medley."

"Oh yes. That will lead to a finale to end all finales! A parade
of fashion and gorgeous wigs. I'll be off to the side dressed as a
majorette, singing 'Beautiful Girls' from *Follies*. In a comic style, of
course. But I'll be backed by the entire Gay Men's Chorus. Imagine!
A hundred strong, virile voices. Can't you just hear it? And guess
what else? Guess who's set to make a star's entrance, inspiring even
more donations?"

"Who?" I ask.

"The Celebrity AIDS Person!"

"What?"

"He'll look just like Carol Channing in her last *Dolly* tour. Lord
knows, he's thin enough. He'll wear a full-length red gown covered
in sequins, a blond wig, and a red-feather headdress on his little
shrunken skull. He'll parade around the stage, then into the audience.
Darlings, we're gonna make a fortune."

"Do you really think he's up to it?" asks David.

"Of course," says Searcy. "He's invincible! And you wouldn't
believe how many more tickets we've sold since adding his name to
the bill."

"But isn't he in the hospice?"

"Hon, the hospice is *not* a jail. He can get out. And it'll be good
for him. Think of all the attention."

"I don't know, Searce. It sounds like a bit much." I set the
coffeepot, mugs, milk, and sugar on the table.

"Of course it's a bit much. But that's theatre!"

"Have you actually seen him lately?" asks David.

"We had dinner just last week."

"He can hardly breathe."

"Oh, he's been like that for years. Now, don't make me paranoid."

"You're the director."

"I certainly am and don't forget it."

Jeff barrels out of the bedroom in his underwear.

"Goodness me," says Searcy. "An almost-naked man!"

"I smelled coffee," says Jeff.

"Um," says Searcy. "I ought to come over here more often in the morning."

"Oh no you don't," I say. "That's usually when I work on my column and I need peace and quiet to do it."

"Absolutely," says Searcy. "You know I wouldn't dream of interrupting your creative flow."

Jeff joins us at the table, pouring himself a mugful.

Searcy stares at Jeff's long, shapely legs. Holds up his hands—thumbs touching and fingers upright—like the quintessential movie director cropping his next shot.

"Have you ever thought about fishnet stockings?" Searcy asks. "Can you walk in heels?"

"What?" says Jeff. "Did I miss something?"

"I just had a vision," says Searcy.

"Not another vision," says David.

"Are you trying to thwart my dramatic imagination?"

"In a word, yes."

"Well, you won't succeed."

"What was the vision?" I ask.

"Yeah," says Jeff. "What was it?"

"To have all the volunteers running the show in drag. But on second thought, I think it'd distract from the actual performance. Still, those legs you've got, honey, are an inspiration!"

Jeff hides them under the table self-consciously.

"What about the rest of the finale?" asks Lance, sipping his coffee.

"Well, after we get through with the Celebrity AIDS Person, I've arranged for some male strippers to model various outfits which have been designed and donated by the fashion industry. These are fun and funny clothes which our friend from City Hall, Councillor Layton, has agreed to auction off."

"The boys or the clothes?" asks David.

"The clothes," says Searcy. "But after each outfit is sold, the boy will take it off and present it to the lucky buyer. Underneath, he'll just have on a cute little G-string."

"What do you mean by fun and funny clothes?" asks Jeff.

"Oh, you know, the latest in hospital drag. A diaper outfit. A tinfoil miniskirt. And lots of jungle wear, oh yes, always a popular item. Then, after the auction, the entire cast will come onstage for an encore of 'Beautiful Girls.' "

"Wow!" says Lance, applauding enthusiastically. "That's gonna be some show."

"Why, thank you, honey," says Searcy.

"You should come down to Little Rock. You'd be a smash!"

"Maybe I'll just do that someday."

"It sounds like a rather gargantuan production," I comment with some reservation.

"I call it 'an entertainment,' " says Searcy. "There's not enough entertainment in this world, in my opinion."

"Well, how are you gonna harness it?"

"By not expecting miracles. The first act is a cinch. I'm not worried about that at all. And in the second, well, the costumes will do ninety percent of the work. And if I can get the Gay Men's Chorus to sway in time to the music, I'll consider it a bonus."

"Are we almost to the point," grumps David, "where you're gonna let us know why we're here?"

"Yes," says Searcy. "We are precisely to that point. Dearest friends, as you might've deduced, I'm gonna need a lot of dependable volunteers to help pull this thing off. I'm gonna need dressers."

"Put me down for that," says Lance.

"You'll have to be at the dress rehearsal next Sunday afternoon."

"No problem."

"And ticket takers."

"I'll take care of that," says Jeff.

"And we need a bartender."

"Snookums wanted to do that," I say.

"Do you think that's wise?"

May 1990

"Why not?"

"He *is* a reformed alcoholic. Perhaps behind the bar isn't the best place for him?"

"He's a very disciplined man, Searcy. He'll be fine. You'd be surprised how many bartenders are reformed alcoholics."

"Well, whatever you say, Zero."

"I'm afraid I won't be able to take an assignment," says David.

"Honestly, I don't know anyone who offers his time as freely as you do, yet you've given me nothing but grief about this particular event. Why?"

"I don't mean to give you grief, but I'm supposed to sit at the AIDS Action Now info table that day. We're gonna set up on the corner of Church and Wellesley every weekend, now that the weather's good."

"A worthy cause," says Searcy, "but no cause warrants missing my show! And besides, the show's at night, not in the afternoon. Why not bring the info table to the 519? AIDS Action Now is one of our sponsors, after all. Think of the hundreds of people that'll be there to pick up brochures."

"That might not be such a bad idea," says David. "Of course, I'll have to speak to the steering committee first. We make all our decisions as a collective."

"Yes. I know. That'd be the end of *my* fast-depleting sanity."

Searcy flips through his notes, then turns to me. "Zero, darling, I've saved you a very special and important job. You'd have to be at all remaining rehearsals, but you're the best person I know for it. Stage manager."

"Sorry, Searce, but I can't. Jeff and I have decided to go out of town next week."

"Out of town?!!"

"Don't worry. We'll be back Saturday. In plenty of time for the show."

"Just my luck! Then may I put you down for"—he glances at his notes—"head usher?"

"Sure."

"Now all I've gotta do's find a stage manager."

"I could stage manage if you can't get anyone else," says Lance.

157

THE PRESSURE OF DREAMS

"I don't know," says Searcy. "David would never forgive me if I cut into your time together like that."

"Lance may do as he wishes," says David.

"I even have experience," Lance says.

"Well," says Searcy, "in that case, why not? You're on!"

I go over to the hospital lab to offer my blood, then stop by the magazine to see Snookums.

I hand him the next two installments of my column.

"But precious," he says, "these aren't due until Tuesday."

"I'll be out of town Tuesday."

"Again? Where are you going this time?"

"Just to California."

"Just?"

"It's a last-minute sort of thing. I have a couple of free tickets, so Jeff and I figured, why not? We're gonna visit my cousin Trebreh *and* see Mary Bull in her show."

"Oh, I wish I were going."

"Come!"

"I can't just pick up and leave. Not now. Not with all the responsibilities I've garnered." Nervously, he pokes at his turban. "I'm growing ever more doubtful about this job, precious."

"I thought you loved it."

"That's what I mean, all I do is work, work, work. Why, I haven't been husband shopping in I don't know how long."

"As long as you're content, what does it matter?"

"You would say that. You, who've had more than your fair share of men. But don't let yourself forget that some of us live the solitary life." Snookums buzzes for his secretary.

"Yes?" calls a voice over the speakerphone.

"Could you come in here a minute, please? Zero's brought his column and I need a couple of photocopies."

"Right away, Mr. Snookums."

The secretary turns out to be Dorothy Evans.

"Hello, Zero," she says in a friendly, businesslike tone.

"Dorothy! What a surprise."

Snookums hands her my work.

"How many copies do you need?" she asks.

"Two."

"Anything else?" She smiles.

"Nothing I can think of."

And out she goes.

"When did you hire her?" I ask in amazement.

"She started last Monday."

"Commuting all the way from St. Catharines?"

"Haven't you heard? She's left her husband. She's living in Scarborough with that sister of hers."

"She's left him? For good?"

"Said she'd finally had enough of the old goat. That he'd been in a bad mood for the last forty-one years and she wasn't putting up with it anymore. I must say, she's extremely efficient."

"I'm sure she is."

"She may even get a quick promotion. To assistant art director." Snookums grins devilishly. "Then, eventually, she could replace my neurotic ex-Jesuit."

"Haven't you settled him down yet?"

"Precious, he's like an ill-fitting shoe. Do you know he showed up at my apartment last Sunday at the crack of dawn. He'd been in the office since Friday night, doing guess what? Redesigning the entire magazine! Poor *City.* I almost didn't recognize it.

"Then, when I got to work Monday morning, I found the typesetter in hysterics. His workstation was covered with the ex-Jesuit's overflowing ashtrays, Styrofoam coffee cups, food containers. And not only that, our entire current issue had been wiped off the computer."

"You mean the neurotic ex-Jesuit used the computer to design? Didn't he realize that when he saved, he'd wipe out what was there?"

"No, precious. He never realizes. That's the problem. Luckily, the typesetter had most of it duped."

"I can't believe you don't just fire him."

"Neither can I. But he has this 'in' with some of the board members. I complain to them, and they just say it's my job to control the employees. I tell you, one of these days it's gonna come down to either him or me."

"Well, it'd better not be you." I see my optimum employment opportunity disappearing before my very eyes.

Snookums shakes his head. "I wonder if some chemical hasn't been let loose on the city. Everybody in town seems to have gone berserk."

"They call it spring fever."

Dorothy returns with the photocopies, which Snookums takes, giving me back the originals.

"By the way, Zero," says Dorothy, "I'm gonna send you a note in the next couple of days."

"Oh? I love getting mail."

"Well, you can look forward to this." Dorothy heads back to her desk.

"Good to see you, Dorothy."

"Good to see you too."

"I suppose I should get going," I say to Snookums. "I've got a million things to do today."

"Don't we all? But have a marvelous time on the coast! And give my love to that precocious Mary Bull."

Late that night, as I'm packing my bag, Jeff is stretched out on my bed, chatting to me. "How'd it go at the lab this morning?"

"Okay, I guess. Actually, it was kind of interesting."

"Really?"

"Yeah. I was sitting next to this guy who was obviously in the advanced stages of AIDS, and we started to visit. He told me he'd had fewer than ten T cells for over two years. That's something to think about, huh?"

"No kidding."

"Then the nurse called him up to the desk to find out what kind of infections he'd had and what medications he was on. He couldn't even remember it all. She was extremely impatient, which made his confusion all the worse, and he started panting and yelling, 'I have AIDS, goddamn it, AIDS!'

"I went up and kind of patted him on the back. He calmed down a bit, reached into his pocket, and handed the nurse a sheet of paper on which all the info was written.

"She read it, looked at him like he was some kind of corpse, then pointed him toward the blood room.

"When he came out, he seemed refreshed, jolly almost. He pulled on his bomber jacket and said to me, 'Good health to you, brother.'

" 'Good health to you too,' I muttered. Then he left.

"If I had a choice, I certainly wouldn't choose to be infected. But as long as I am and as long as the battle rages, well, I must say I've learned a thing or two I never expected."

"The camaraderie of the front lines?" asks Jeff.

I think about that a minute.

"Yes, that's exactly what it is."

"How come I never have these inspirational visits at that lab?" Jeff asks. "Whenever I'm there, it's just me, a bunch of pregnant women, and a few old folks trying to piss into a jar."

"I don't know." I zip up my bag, then undress for bed.

I lie in the crook of Jeff's arm and look around my cozy room. The trees pressing at the window. My cluttered desk. My dresser. "We're going away tomorrow," I say.

"Ca-li-forn-i-a."

"I don't want to think about AIDS or talk about AIDS for the entire week."

"It's a deal."

"Miss Virus is just gonna have to sleep this one out."

"Right on."

I reach for the bedside light and flick it off.

We cuddle up in a tight knot.

"Where're our seats?" asks Jeff.

"In the last cabin."

"We might as well get in the lineup."

We go down the ramp, board, and walk the length of the plane. I grab a copy of *People* magazine as we pass through Business Class.

"Every time I fly," Jeff says, "the seats seem to get smaller and smaller." He crams our bags into the overhead compartment.

"I'll take the window and you can have the aisle. Give those long legs a little breathing room."

THE PRESSURE OF DREAMS

"Thanks." We settle into our seats. "Remember the days when air travel was actually a thrill?"

"I remember the first flight I took. I was ten and flew from Little Rock to Springfield, Missouri. I was so excited I could hardly stand it. Especially taking off and landing. And looking out the window, I just loved that."

The flight attendant passes by, handing out pillows and headphones.

"What's the movie?" Jeff asks her.

"I forget the name," she says pleasantly. "But it's a military thriller."

Jeff groans. "Why can't you ever show something fun? Like *All About Eve*."

The flight attendant smiles. The glaze on her face doesn't crack. "You gentlemen enjoy the flight."

"We'll do our best."

A mother, carrying a child who looks to be two years old, has the seat behind me. The child has been brought on as an 'infant,' therefore will spend the duration of the journey in the mother's lap. The child immediately starts to squirm, entertaining himself by methodically kicking the back of my seat. Kick, kick, kick. Right in the middle of my back.

I turn around and ask the woman, "Would you please get him to stop that?"

"Sorry," she says kindly. "Don't kick the nice man, Eric."

But Eric doesn't stop.

"Maybe you could tie his legs together," I suggest.

"Eric," she says, "stop kicking the nice man!"

A hassled, middle-aged woman comes barreling down the aisle, toting enough carry-on luggage for three passengers. She has the seat behind Jeff.

"Oh god!" she whines, seeing the little boy. "A child! Why does this always happen to me?"

"Don't worry," says the mother. "He'll be as quiet as a mouse."

"Right," says the whiny woman, opening the overhead compartments, looking for a place to stow her bags. All of them are full. She turns this way and that, huffing in frustration, hitting Jeff in the head with a large handbag in the process. "Where am I gonna put all my stuff?" she whines.

"I'll take it," says the flight attendant. "I'll store it in the back."

"Will it be okay?"

"It'll be fine."

"I don't want anyone to steal anything. You'll keep an eye on it, won't you?"

"You may think of me as your guard dog."

"I'll keep my purse with me, though. I never let go of my purse."

"Fine."

The plane rolls away from the gate. We taxi out to the runway. Jeff glances at his watch. "Only five and a half hours to go," he whispers, his breath hot against my ear.

"Are you trying to turn me on?" I ask.

He shrugs innocently.

Eric keeps kicking me, the middle-aged woman keeps whining, and I keep trying to ignore them both by thumbing through *People* and amusing Jeff with my own versions of the headlines.

We take off, glide over the city and the lake, and wait out hour one until the cocktail cart comes our way.

"Something to drink?" the flight attendant finally asks.

"Yes," says Jeff. "A double Caesar."

"Double gin and tonic for me."

Before she can get them poured, the purser announces over the sound system, "Ladies and gentlemen, we'll now be showing a short film, and then, our feature. Would all passengers seated by a window please close their blind."

I look outside. We're flying through a stunning dome of blue. There's not a cloud in the sky. And the geography of the earth below us is breathtaking.

"I can't fly on a day like this with my blind down. Look at that view!"

"Then, don't," says Jeff. "It's not a law."

The whiny woman whines even more loudly, loud enough to hear herself over the soundtrack coming through her headset. "I can't see! The stewardess is in my way."

"I'll be through in a minute, ma'am. Would you like something to drink?"

THE PRESSURE OF DREAMS

"Cof-fee." Whine, whine, whine. "And could you get that man in the row in front of me to shut his window? I can't see."

"Would you please lower your blind, sir?" asks the flight attendant.

"I really don't want to," I say, trying not to sound too irritable. "I took a window seat because I like to look out." Then, for drama's sake, I add, "I'm claustrophobic. It's a medical condition."

"But people can't see the screen," she whispers.

"Sure they can see it. Look. I can see it. Can't you?"

"Yes, but—"

"Besides, what do they expect? This is a plane, not a cinema. The airline can't force me to sit in the dark and watch an asinine war movie. The film is a choice, not a requirement."

"I know," says the flight attendant.

"I like this movie," whines the woman. Her voice is giving me a headache. Little Eric is still kicking me. "I've seen it before," she whines, "and it's good."

"There," I say to the flight attendant. "She's already seen the damn thing."

"Just put the blind down a few inches," the flight attendant says in a conspiratorial tone. Then she adds brightly, "As an effort to get along."

I take a healthy sip off my drink, consider the situation, and wonder if I'm being totally ridiculous.

"All right," I finally say, and pull the blind down exactly two inches.

The flight attendant smiles. Another problem solved. She moves on to the next set of rows.

"I still can't see," whines the woman. "I still can't see at all."

Now I am intent. Committed to enjoy looking out the window every single moment, just to prove my point. My nose is pressed to the plastic. A cramp begins to form in my neck. And somewhere down there the state of Wisconsin is turning into Iowa.

Jeff sips his Caesar, watching me with amusement. He takes my hand, holds it, and leans back in his chair, which really thrills the whiny woman.

"God!" she mutters. "Why don't you just lie down in my lap?"

Jeff shuts his eyes.

May 1990

My drink begins its glorious calming effect, thank god.

A porky man in a business suit gets up to go to the washroom. He's stalled by our row, thanks to the flight attendant and the cocktail cart not far behind us. He sees my hand in Jeff's and snorts. "Where ya goin', boys, San Francisco?"

Jeff's eyes pop open. He looks at the man. "What did you say?"

"Where ya goin'?" the man repeats, imitating a lisp. "Tan Frantithco?"

"Fuck off," says Jeff. Then Jeff says to me, "What an asshole. Can you believe this asshole?" He leans back in his chair again and shuts his eyes, shaking his head.

"Hey," the porky man announces to the rest of the passengers. "We've got a couple of fruits here!"

Oh Christ, I say to myself. I can not believe this is happening.

The passengers all start jumping up, trying to get a good look, as though we've got three heads or something.

"Leave it alone," Jeff angrily says to the man. "Just leave it the hell alone."

"What are you gonna do, fruit? Beat me up?"

"Stewardess?" I call.

Jeff unsnaps his seat belt and stands up to the bastard. Jeff's a head taller. "Get moving," he says more forcefully. "What's between me and my friend is none of your business. I don't like your attitude. I don't like it at all."

"Oh, I'm really shaking in my boots. Faggot's getting tough."

For a moment it looks like Jeff is gonna slug him. But he restrains himself. He laughs at the guy instead.

The plane enters an area of turbulence.

Bing! goes the seat-belt sign. "All passengers please return to your seats and see that your seat belt is securely fastened."

"Hear that?" says Jeff. "Return to your seat. Now."

The porky man, in a fit of rage, grabs Jeff by his collar and starts shaking him.

Jesus! I roll up my copy of *People,* reach over, and start whacking at him to let go.

"And you've probably both got AIDS," raves the man.

"We do," says Jeff pleasantly. He grabs the man's hands and removes them from his collar.

THE PRESSURE OF DREAMS

"Gentlemen, please," says the flight attendant. "No fights at thirty thousand feet. The seat-belt sign is on."

"They're a couple of faggots!" the man raves.

"This airline does not discriminate," the flight attendant says matter-of-factly. "Please sit down."

"They're still fucking faggots," the man mutters, going back to his seat. "I don't like to fly on planes with faggots."

I glance around the cabin. Surely we're not the only ones. So I call out, "Would all gay people on this plane please raise their hands to show this homophobe how many of us there actually are?"

Great. Two hands go up. Mine and Jeff's. Another success story for the struggle of equality and visibility.

But wait a minute.

Here come a couple more, two guys from the back. Thank you, boys. Then another. And another. Then the woman sitting right next to the homophobe. Excellent!

"I'm never taking this airline again," the man cries. "This plane is fucking crawling with faggots. They're probably even faggots in the cockpit."

"Sir, what planet do you come from?"

"Orillia, Ontario, and proud of it! In all my years of flying, I've never been so insulted."

"Neither have I!" I say, throwing my fist in the air. "Vive la différence! Gay liberation now!"

"Put your arm down," whines the woman behind us. "I can't see the movie!"

"Eric," the mother says quietly, "I want you to stop kicking the man's chair!"

The turbulence subsides.

The seat-belt sign goes off.

Lunch comes down the aisle.

By the time they get to us there's only one choice: overcooked strips of beef on a bed of pasta—"Stroganoff," they call it—accompanied by a small cooked half tomato, three mushrooms, a custard cup, and a limp, browning salad with mayonnaise dressing.

"I don't believe I'll have any lunch today," I say to the flight attendant, handing it back. "The journey has just been a little too exciting for me to contemplate food."

"I agree," says Jeff. "We'll just get something when we land. But we would appreciate another round of drinks."

"Oh, goodness. That'll be a while," says the flight attendant. "You see, it's all timed. After we do the dinners we have to do coffee, tea, and liqueurs. We can't really get you another drink until then."

"We'll be waiting. Patiently."

That gets her. She motions to her lackey in the back and mouths, "Double Caesar and double gin and tonic," then points to our row.

The lackey brings them with a big smile. "Here you go."

"Thanks."

"You're most welcome."

"A toast," Jeff proposes. "To a relaxing week."

"Amen."

Jeff pats me on the knee.

"Ladies and gentlemen," says the captain. "We're currently flying over the Grand Canyon, one of the natural wonders of the world. If you look out the right side of the aircraft, you'll see a spectacular view."

Passengers quickly push up the blinds. The cabin fills with light.

"Now I really can't see!" says the whiner, pulling her headphones off her head and letting them dangle around her neck.

Eric, enticed by the muffled sound emanating from the headphones, reaches out and grabs them, pulling with all his might.

"Ow!" screams the whiner. "Goddamn it, he's trying to choke me. This brat's trying to choke me!"

"Eric, let go of the nice lady's headphones!"

"If I have a bruise by the time we land," says the whiner, "I'm suing. Got that? Suing!"

"Eric, honey, if you're gonna try to make it as a child star, you've got to be nicer to strangers."

"Welcome to L.A., Jeff. Land of smog, palm trees, and movie stars. Miles and miles of one-story hell."

Jeff laughs. "Come on. It's a beautiful day. Let's go rent us a car."

* * *

167

THE PRESSURE OF DREAMS

We drive into West Hollywood to the gay guesthouse Trebreh recommended. A good-natured queen, who calls himself "Charlotte," checks us in. He gives us the lowdown, then shows us to our bungalow out back of his house.

"I hope you'll be very comfortable," he says, unlocking the door. "We serve coffee on the patio at nine every morning. Breakfast at nine-thirty. Nothing too fancy. Pastries, muffins. And fruit, of course. Let me know if you need anything."

"Thanks."

"You're *so* welcome." He sashays out.

"I like this place," says Jeff.

"Yeah, it's cute. Cozy." Then I plop down on one of the double beds. "Uh-oh," I say.

"What?"

"This bed is so saggy the springs are poking through. I'll never be able to sleep on this."

"Well, try the other one, Goldilocks."

I do. "Not much better."

Jeff dives down beside me. "Oh, it's not so bad," he says, pulling me into a bear hug. "Not with the right company. And not if we sleep on our sides."

"We'll still roll to the middle."

"That's what a saggy bed's all about." He weaves his legs through mine.

"You're trying to distract me."

"Travel involves a lot of give and take, Zero. Surely you're not gonna be so cranky you can't take it."

"You're getting a hard-on."

"Am I?" He grins.

"Yeah, I feel it through your pants." I grin back. Then I snap open his trousers, unzip his fly. He moans as I take hold of his cock. And I blow him.

His back arches. His legs stretch. He gushes over my tongue and down my throat. I love the taste of him and keep him in my mouth as he softens. He's very sensitive, so I'm careful not to move. He keeps saying my name, running his hands through my hair.

Afterward, I snuggle up beside him and give him a squeeze. "You are one sexy monkey."

May 1990

"So are you."

I give him a kiss, then reach across his chest for the telephone.

"Who you calling?" he asks, somewhat taken aback.

"I'd better check in with Trebreh."

"He's expecting us for dinner, isn't he?"

"That was the plan last time I talked to him. But you never know with him, Jeff, you just never know."

I dial his number. One ring, two rings. "I'm telling you, it reminds me of when we were in high school. Trebreh turned into this god after going through puberty. Boys and girls just flocked after him, wanting to take him out, go for a ride, whatever. I stood on the sides, a skinny nerd type. Trebreh would look at me over the crowd, shrug like we'd see each other at home, right? It wasn't malicious. It's just the way he was."

I hang up the phone.

"Twenty rings. And his machine didn't even come on."

"Maybe he misunderstood our arrival time."

"He knew exactly when we were arriving. He's got our tickets for the show tonight and everything."

"We could go by his apartment and leave him a note. He lives just a few blocks from here, doesn't he?"

"What good's that gonna do? If he's not home, he's not home."

"He probably just ran down to the corner store for something."

"He probably just ran down to Palm Springs!"

"When did you actually talk to him last?"

"A couple of weeks ago. But he sent me a Mailgram two days ago, detailing our entire itinerary. I tell you, Jeff, I just don't get him. I've known him my whole life, and I still don't get him."

"Well, no reason to let it ruin our trip."

"No, it certainly isn't."

Jeff pushes himself up from the bed. Pulls up his pants and stretches. "What do you say we take a walk, stroll down Santa Monica and check out the scene? Maybe get something to eat. I'm starved."

"Sure, but I need to hang some clothes up first."

"Fine. I'll wait for you out on the patio."

*   *   *

169

THE PRESSURE OF DREAMS

Five o'clock. I try Trebreh again. Still no answer. I call the number I have for Mary Bull.

A husky female voice answers. "Yo! Big Ellen's Garage." Loud music plays in the background.

"Is Mary Bull there?" I ask.

"Not at the moment, bud. What can I help you with?"

"What about Big Ellen?"

"Speaking."

"Hi. This is Zero MacNoo."

"Mac-Who?"

"MacNoo!" I say more loudly. "God, it sounds like you're in a disco."

"This is a garage, buddy. Car repair. Hang on a minute. Ginger," she hollers, "turn that thing down. I can't hear the man."

The music stops.

"Now, you say you left a car here?"

"I didn't say anything about a car. I'm Trebreh's cousin."

"Oh," she says. "Right. Mary Bull and Treb mentioned you were coming."

"Well, that's a start, at least."

"So why're you calling me?"

"I can't seem to get ahold of Trebreh."

"That's not unusual."

"His machine's not even on."

"He does that sometimes."

"That's all very well, but it's getting late and he's got our tickets for the show tonight."

"You mean for *Into the Woods?*"

"Yeah. Where's Mary Bull?"

"This is a matinee day. Saturday, you know? She doesn't get home between shows. But tell you what, I'll call down to the Ahmanson and leave her a message. Let her know what's going on. There're two of you, huh?"

"That's right. Me and my friend Jeff."

"Well, you and your friend Jeff just go on and go. Mary Bull'll have something set aside for you at the box office."

"Great. That was easy. Thanks a lot."

May 1990

"We aim to please. You know how to get to the Ahmanson? It's downtown at the Music Center."

"We'll find it. And listen, we thought we'd take Mary Bull out afterward. If she feels like it, and if it's okay with you. Then we could drive her home."

"Sure, fine." Then Big Ellen says to Ginger, "You don't have to pick Mary Bull up tonight. The boys are gonna do it. Maybe we could go over to Mavis and Nell's."

"Sure, Big Ellen, sounds good."

Then back to me: "Zero? You do whatever Mary Bull wants. And hey, you're gonna love the show. Mary Bull's just about the most talented child you're ever likely to see."

"I tend to agree."

Big Ellen chuckles. "We're gonna get along just fine."

"I hope we get a chance to meet."

"Oh, we will. Don't worry. But right now I've gotta get my ass back to work. I got a Datsun engine spread out all over my floor, and a Toyota that won't tell me what's wrong with it. Computer diagnostics. Crap!"

"Talk to you later."

"Crank her back up, Ginger!"

Charlotte gives us directions to the Music Center. We get there in plenty of time for a detailed reading of the program.

Our seats are excellent. Though I've seen *Into the Woods* several times before, as the lights go down and the curtain goes up, I'm covered in goose bumps.

The show begins with a musical montage. Red Ridinghood enters early on, tough and sassy. She visits a baker and his wife to loot some sweets, then heads off to Grandmother's, doing a two-step with a wolf on the way. She endures the ordeal of being eaten and eventually rescued (in one piece). Then comes her solo. Mary Bull sings it beautifully, every syllable perfectly pronounced and the tricky changes in the music handled with ease.

At intermission, Jeff and I snake through the crowd, trying to pick up comments. The Sondheim aficionados are having a field day, but the thick-headed types wish it were simpler. "Too many plots," they complain. They want *Phantom.* Something they can watch with a belly full of food and wine.

After the final curtain, we go backstage. Our names are on a list, so we're admitted at once. The doorman directs us toward Mary Bull's dressing room. The door is partway open. I can see her, sans costume and wig, sitting at the dressing table, removing her makeup.

"Zero! Jeff!" she says, jumping up and joining us out in the hall, giving us both a big hug. "I'm so happy to see you! God, you don't know."

"You did a fantastic job!" I tell her. "I'm definitely gonna come see it again."

"You were just wonderful," says Jeff. "But am I surprised?"

"Oh, thanks, guys. And thanks for the flowers! That was so sweet."

"So," I say, "do you feel like going out? Are you hungry?"

"I'm starved! But I've gotta have a quick shower first. You wouldn't believe how much this show makes you sweat. My costume's like a sauna! Costume designers should have to sing, dance, and act for three hours in everything they make, don't you think?" She giggles. "Just have a seat out here. I'd invite you in, but I share the dressing room with Rapunzel and Cinderella. They're a little more reserved than I am. See you in a sec." She throws us a perky wave, then disappears.

A moment later, Julie Mercer walks by.

I gasp, rise to my feet, and exclaim, "Excuse me, Miss Mercer, but I must say you made a positively radiant witch!"

"Why, thank you," she replies in that famous throaty voice of hers. She extends her hand. "And you are?"

"Zero MacNoo. And this is my friend, Jeff Lake."

"Ah." She smiles knowingly. "Mary Bull's cousin from Canada. I've heard about you."

"Well, actually, we've met before. I'm originally from Little Rock, and you came through town in *Company.* My uncle was in that show. I was about half the age I am now, but—"

"Who's your uncle?"

"Markus MacNoo."

"Really? How is Markus?"

"Great. He's running a bunch of dinner theatres down in Florida."

"Always was such a clever man. I'm envious of that business know-how. Mary Bull's been quite excited about your visit. I hope you enjoyed the show."

"I loved it. And it was the fourth time I've seen it."

"Wonderful," says Julie. "There's nothing I love more than true enthusiasm."

"And I am one enthusiastic fan where you're concerned. Aside from your work in theatre, I've seen your cabaret act. I have your recordings. I just think it's amazing how much you can put into a song."

"Well, I'm sixty-six years old and I've been in the business forty-nine years, so when you tell an old broad something like that, it makes her feel pretty darn good."

"You deserve it. Every bit of it."

"Thank you."

She bows her head and excuses herself.

"How exciting!" I say to Jeff. "To talk to Julie Mercer. To be backstage."

He smiles. "Don't look now," he says, "but here come the two Prince Charmings. In towels."

They giggle madly as they go into their dressing room.

"Do you think all Prince Charmings are that gay?" Jeff asks.

"God, I hope so."

Mary Bull comes out dressed, ready to go, and carrying her flowers.

"Where to?" I ask.

"Gosh, any old place is fine with me. We could just go back to West Hollywood. There'll be lots of places open."

"Sure."

We end up at a little diner, sitting in a booth shaped like a half-moon, which gives all three of us a view of Santa Monica Boulevard. Mainly traffic, hairdos, and fashion on Saturday Night Boys hopping their way from one bar to the next.

"I've gotten old," I say, watching this parade.

"So have I," says Jeff.

The waiter comes, takes our order, then speeds off toward the kitchen.

"Okay, Mary Bull, I want to hear all about your wild success in show business."

"I've extended my contract," she says. "After we close here, we go up to San Francisco."

"Great!"

"Yeah." She smiles. "It's been crazy. I mean, who would've thought a year ago all these things could've happened to me? Like getting this job. I mean, if I hadn't taken the bull by the horns and run off to New York, if Lily hadn't taken me to that audition, where would I be right now? The only other thing I tried out for was *Annie 2*, and that's already closed on the road. After *Into the Woods* shuts down, I don't know what I'll do. Study probably. Hopefully in New York."

"It sounds like you've got some pretty good ideas."

"You're even starting to sound a little bit like an adult," says Jeff.

"Am I? I know I've changed, but I don't feel I've changed that much."

"It's good for you to change."

The waiter brings our drinks, and we sip them.

There's a lull in the conversation. Mary Bull starts fiddling with the saltshaker and finally says, "I talked to Trebreh."

"That bastard," I mutter. "Do you know he was supposed to make us dinner, drive us down to the theatre, and join us for the show?"

"Well, I talked to him," she says again. "Besides, he's seen the show a million times."

"I'm sorry, Mary Bull, I just refuse to excuse his behavior any longer. I haven't got time for it. If that's all I mean to him—"

"It's not. He's been really excited about you guys coming."

"Oh, I'm sure. So excited he left town the minute we arrived, huh?"

"He hasn't left town. And he isn't that bad. A little flighty perhaps—"

"Perhaps?! He hasn't followed through on one thing he said he would do since getting in touch with me last fall!"

"He's done other things."

"Like what?"

May 1990

"Introduced you and me."

"Yes," I admit, "he certainly did."

"Anyway, he wants to take us all to brunch tomorrow. He suggested we meet him about eleven o'clock at Marix's. It's Mexican food. You guys think you can make it?"

"Sure," says Jeff.

"If the suspense doesn't kill us," I add.

Jeff and I are up much too early in the A.M., thanks to the three-hour time change.

We shower, go around the corner to pick up the newspaper, then sit on the patio, waiting for Charlotte to appear with the coffee.

Charlotte stumbles out of his back door about five after nine, carrying a big self-dispensing thermos. "Sleep well?" he croaks.

"Well enough," I say.

Actually, it was torturous. But the Visiting Princess had best not piss off the Queen Bee until she's at least sufficiently awake.

Jeff knows exactly what I'm thinking and quickly changes the subject. "What are all these exotic flowers?" he asks.

"Lord knows," says Charlotte. "I just water them and up they come. Mutants, I call them. Plants do very well in L.A. It's all the carbon monoxide."

Charlotte squirts a cup of coffee for himself, then takes a sip. "Ah!"—great sigh of relief—"now, that almost makes me feel human. So have you boys been to Westwood yet?"

"No. We just got in yesterday afternoon. Remember? We've only been to the Music Center."

"Oh, right!" he exclaims. "You're the ones from Toronto. It's all coming back to me now."

Strange, I think to myself. There're only three bungalows, therefore only three sets of guests. Surely he can remember who's who.

"Perhaps the carbon monoxide does something to the memory banks as well," I suggest.

Charlotte laughs. "Oh, definitely. That is too funny. I'm certain it does! Why, half the time I can't even remember my own name." He pauses. "What did I tell you my name was?"

"Charlotte," we say in unison.

175

"Right. That's right. At least I got that one right. But seriously, boys, you *must* get to Westwood. You can walk through the UCLA campus. It's just beautiful."

"We'll keep that in mind."

"How are you finding your bungalow?"

"Oh, very nice," says Jeff.

"Though the beds are a little—"

"As long as you're happy, I'm happy! So many of our guests can't do anything but complain. I don't know what they think they are, royalty? Well, I don't cater to royalty. I run a simple establishment. If you want royal, you go to the Bel Air Hotel." Charlotte giggles. "But I just love you Canadians. You're so polite. And appreciative!"

"Don't be fooled," I say. "The only thing that makes Canadians agreeable is an inferiority complex."

"Is that so?" asks Charlotte.

"Somewhat," says Jeff. "Living in the American shadow and all."

"Actually," I say, "I don't know what they've got to feel inferior about. Canada is a far more civilized place."

"And that's coming from the mouth of an expatriate," says Jeff. "Zero was an American. Once."

"But you're working on him, right?" asks Charlotte.

"I try," says Jeff. "I understand from people who've known him longer than I have that his manners have improved greatly since he moved north of the Forty-ninth Parallel. They say he's not nearly so much of a loudmouth."

"Too cute," twitters Charlotte, heading back inside.

He pauses on the porch. "Carbon monoxide," he says. "That's our secret out here: good old honest-to-god carbon monoxide!"

We drive by Big Ellen's to pick up Mary Bull. She's sitting on the front steps. "Don't honk," she says, racing toward the car. "My mom had a late night. She and Ginger are still asleep."

She guides us through the streets to the restaurant. We park and go in. The place is packed.

"We have a reservation," Mary Bull tells the host. He's a cute

young thing. Eighteen, maybe. He checks our name on the list, grabs
some menus, and leads us to our table.

"Look at how his jeans fit," I whisper to Jeff.

"Um," is his reply.

"Here we are," says the boy, pulling out our chairs.

"Thanks," says Mary Bull crisply.

"Movie people!" I exclaim. "Look. There's Keanu Reeves."

"Where?" asks Jeff.

"Over there. With the big blond."

"Now, *he's* Canadian."

"I know. He was a spear-carrier at Stratford one of the summers
Randy worked there."

"He sure is cute."

"Don't ogle," says Mary Bull.

"And there's Matthew Modine," I say. "Gosh, I love him."

"He's not gay," Mary Bull tells me.

"But he's so . . . tall! He looks kind of like you, Jeff."

"He doesn't look a thing like me."

"Will you guys please stop? You're gonna make a scene. You
don't want to ruin my reputation before I even get one, do you?"

"Guess who's sitting right behind me?" I whisper. "Pia Zadora."

"You'd never make it in this town," says Mary Bull. "You're
supposed to be blasé about stars. You're not even supposed to notice
them."

"I am blasé," I tell her. "I could care less. It's just being in the
vicinity of so much fame that excites me."

A harried waitress stops by our table to rattle off the specials and
ask if we want a drink.

"Have the strawberry margaritas," advises Mary Bull. "My mom
swears by them. Two strawberry margaritas," she tells the waitress,
"and a Coke with lots of ice."

The waitress nods, jotting it down, then turns on her heels,
running.

"Some chips and salsa?" I call after her.

"And guacamole!" shouts Mary Bull.

"Busy place," says Jeff.

"It's popular," says Mary Bull. "Everybody eats here. Sooner or
later. Though the food's not the greatest."

THE PRESSURE OF DREAMS

"Do you 'do' brunch often?" I ask.

"No," says Mary Bull. "But I come here with my mom. I'm a nobody in L.A. terms. Stage folks don't count in this town unless they happen to be former movie stars or on some hit TV show."

The waitress circles back, depositing chips, salsa, and drinks. "Ready to order?" she asks.

"Actually, we're waiting for a fourth and it looks like he'll be a little late." I glance at my watch: 11:20.

"People just can't slow down here, can they?" says Jeff.

"It's not the kind of place to slow down in," says Mary Bull.

I pop a tortilla chip in my mouth. "Think I should go give him a call?"

"Who?" asks Jeff.

"Trebreh."

"I don't know," says Mary Bull. "I don't know what to think."

"We ought to just order," says Jeff. "The minute the food comes, he'll walk right in."

"Good idea." I flag the waitress.

"Going ahead without him?" she asks.

"Yeah, I believe we will. I'll have the tostada special."

"Two," says Jeff.

"Three," says Mary Bull.

"Agreeable group," the waitress comments.

"What about our guacamole?" Mary Bull asks her.

"Oh, right," the waitress says. "Carlos," she calls, "give me an order of guac for table twenty-three."

Mary Bull looks toward the door, obviously searching for Trebreh. I catch her at it, and she quickly turns her eyes toward Matthew Modine. "He does look kind of like Jeff," she says.

"See?" I tease, pinching Jeff's cheek. "And you're both just too cute."

"Fuck off," he mutters, swatting at me playfully. "You're in some merry mood today."

"Must be all that carbon monoxide." I pick up my margarita and toast. "To your career, Mary Bull. May you work long and hard and land good roles in many musicals to come."

"Hear! Hear!" says Jeff.

"Thanks," she says.

And we drink.

Carlos brings our guacamole. Eagerly, we dig in.

"You don't think the musical is a dying art form?" asks Mary Bull.

"No way," I say. "As long as there's civilization, you can bet there'll be a musical or two."

"It's civilization," says Jeff, "that's the dying art form."

"Jeff, I'm surprised at you. You, who are always so positive about things."

He shrugs, takes another sip off his margarita. "Well, I have my moments."

The waitress appears, plates lined up and down her arm.

"Tostadas," I say. "Now there's something that makes sense."

She sets them on the table and we eat.

Still no sign of Trebreh.

It is not the most delicious tostada I've ever had, nor is it the worst. I feel much better for having eaten it, and I lean back from my clean plate, cradling my margarita. With the last sip, I propose another toast. "To the ever-absent Trebreh."

Mary Bull looks very strange. "I don't feel so good," she says, setting down her fork.

"Is it the food?"

"I don't know."

"You want to go?"

"Yeah, let's go."

Jeff waves for our check. The waitress brings it quickly. Jeff slaps fifty bucks on the table and tells her to keep the change.

"Where to?" I ask.

"Trebreh's," says Mary Bull.

"You think he's there?"

"Well, he's not here."

Jeff and I look at her.

"It's nothing," she says. "I'm just tired of trying to fool every-body. I've had it."

Trebreh lives in a tiny house, set way back from the street, that he's rented since he first came to L.A. almost twenty years ago. We head up the walk.

THE PRESSURE OF DREAMS

"When I was in Arkansas, Mary Bull, the family just couldn't get enough of hearing about you."

"Why?" she asks.

"Curiosity. Never underestimate the power you have at being the newest member of the family. They're all anxious to vie for your soul."

"I'm not even sure I have a soul," she mutters.

She steps up to the door and knocks. The screen rattles in the frame: *bang-bang-bang-bang-bang.* "Trebreh?" she calls. "It's me."

A woman who looks like a miniature Oliver Hardy answers, saying, "Sshh! What are you trying to do, break down the house?"

"Uh-oh," says Mary Bull. "Things must be bad if *you're* here."

"They ain't great," says the woman. "I'm Big Ellen," she says to Jeff and me.

"Zero MacNoo."

"Jeff Lake."

"What's goin' on?" I ask.

"Why don't you come in and see for yourself?"

The minute we step inside, the whole scenario falls perfectly, horribly into place. What stuns me is that it's never once crossed my mind. How could I not have known, not figured it out?

A short hallway leads into one big room. In the center is Trebreh's bed. In the bed is what's left of my cousin.

Treb turns his head slowly toward us. He's very thin, very frail, shaky, and his breathing is labored—hiss, huff, hiss, huff—his lips, dry and caked.

I move toward him. Big Ellen says to Mary Bull and Jeff, "Let's give them some time alone." They go back out to the porch. The screen door again snaps in its frame.

For a moment, I wonder if Trebreh knows me.

"Sit," he says. The sound comes out like a small, spastic explosion.

There's a chair next to the bed.

"Why didn't you tell me?" I ask.

He smiles faintly. "Hoped I'd get better."

I laugh at the absurdity. "Better enough to meet us in a restaurant for brunch?"

"You never know."

"Are you crazy?"

"Probably." He swallows a few times. "But it's not over till it's over."

I reach out and squeeze his hand.

He winces.

I pull back. "Sorry."

"It's okay," he says. "I hurt all over. But please, go ahead."

I take it more gently.

"Zero, I'm so glad to see you."

"I'm glad to see you, too. But why didn't you tell me?"

"I didn't want anyone to know. If the gossip had gotten out, it would have been the end of my career, and I needed the work. Besides, I'm telling you now."

"But I could've come sooner. I could've done so many things."

"That's not what I wanted."

"How long have you been like this?"

"Since last winter."

"And that's why you cut your tour short? Why you came back to L.A. and never made it to Toronto?"

He nods. Smacks his lips. "I was diagnosed over five years ago. I've done pretty well. I've had it all, the whole gamut. I've fought. And now it's time to let it go. The last time I was in the hospital, my specialist said he'd done all he could do and I could either go to a hospice or come home. Of course, I sought several other opinions before accepting that. But I knew. Now, I'm off most of my medication. Except morphine, which makes me fucking crazy, and cocaine, which makes me sane."

"Cocaine?"

"Yeah. When you're constantly tired and weak and nauseous and hurting, it helps a lot. It helps you just to have a conversation."

I trace the veins on his bony hand, outline his knuckles. "Have I told you lately how much I love you?"

He shuts his eyes. A tear rolls down his cheek. "Say it again."

"How much I love you."

I walk out onto the porch. "He's asleep."

"He sleeps a lot," says Big Ellen. She sits on the stoop, her arms around Mary Bull. Jeff sits next to them in a daze.

THE PRESSURE OF DREAMS

"I need to run some errands," Big Ellen tells me. "Can I count on you to hold down the fort for an hour or so?"

"Sure," I say. "I'd like to call my Uncle Markus, if that's all right. He and Trebreh go back a long way. I know my uncle would want to see him."

"But does Trebreh want to see your uncle?"

"I'll be sure and ask him."

"Yes, do. We don't want to bother him with any surprise visitors at this point. Just friends. Real friends. Too many assholes have turned their backs on him. There's a lot of denial in Trebreh's business."

"He's not the first porn star to have AIDS."

"No, and those who've been ill have really stuck together. Trouble is, most of them are already gone. You do realize Trebreh won't last much longer."

"Yes, I realize that."

Big Ellen gives Mary Bull a squeeze, then pushes herself up. "Well," she says, "see you jokers in a while." She saunters toward the street, gets in her van, and drives off.

Jeff sighs, then rises as well. "I think I'll go for a walk, if you don't need me for anything."

"No, please, go ahead."

"I'll probably just go back to Charlotte's, or would you rather I met you back here?"

"Charlotte's is fine."

He hugs me. "Hang in there."

"I will."

I sit down next to Mary Bull. We don't say anything for a few minutes, don't even look at each other.

Finally, I ask, "You knew, didn't you?"

"Yes," she says quietly.

"Even when you were in Toronto?"

"Yes."

"And you didn't let on. Not one bit."

"My dad made me promise not to tell."

"What a loyal daughter."

"I'm sorry." She bursts into tears.

"No, *I'm* sorry. I've been a fool, Mary Bull, a stupid bloody fool."

"But I *should* have told you. I just thought somehow, some way, he'd bounce back again."

"It's okay, honey child. It's over and done with, and this is where we are."

"Do you hate me?" she asks.

"Of course I don't hate you. You silly girl, how could you even think that?"

"I don't know." She falls against me. "It's just so crazy. This has been the worst and the best year of my whole entire life."

"Well, get used to it."

She breaks away to wipe her eyes.

Suddenly, she jumps up.

"Oh my god!" she exclaims. "What time is it?"

"One-thirty."

"Shit! I've got a three o'clock matinee."

She dashes into the house, picks up the phone, and calls for a cab.

"And don't take for-goddamn-ever to get here," she says to the dispatcher. "I've got to be at the Music Center in half an hour!"

"Never made it over to Mavis and Nell's last night. After you told me that Trebreh wasn't answering his phone, I came over to check on him and stayed till morning.

"He shouldn't be left alone," Big Ellen says. "He can hardly pick up a glass of water off the bedside table."

I follow her into the kitchen. She unloads some groceries into the fridge.

"Then let's trade off," I suggest. "You nursed last night; I'll nurse tonight."

"If you're up to it, I could sure use some time to unlax."

"I'm up to it. I just need to go by the guesthouse first and pick up a few things."

She shuts the fridge, folds the grocery bag, and puts it in a drawer.

"Go for it," she says. "The sooner you're back, the sooner I can leave."

* * *

THE PRESSURE OF DREAMS

"Zero!" says Charlotte, "been to Westwood?"

"Not yet."

"What's the matter? You look like you've had a damper on your day."

"My cousin. He's dying."

"Oh god," says Charlotte. "My lover's in the house doing the same thing. Where oh where do we get the strength?"

"I wish I knew."

"Well . . . if you should get a free minute, do remember Westwood."

I open the door to the bungalow, muttering to myself, "What is with that guy's obsession with—"

"Westwood?" asks Jeff. "I don't know, but it sure is something."

We laugh, then I tell him I'm gonna stay the night over at Trebreh's.

"I'll miss you," he says.

"I'll miss you, too. But I want to give Big Ellen a break. She's been nursing him nonstop. Come cuddle up with me a minute."

"No problem."

"What a relief it is to be in your arms."

"What a relief you are."

"Listen, Jeff. I want you to go out and find yourself some fun tonight. I'll be back early in the morning. Let's meet here then, okay?"

"Okay."

Mostly, Trebreh sleeps. A restless sort of sleep. Occasionally, he wakes. To check the clock. To swig a little morphine. To take a sip of water. To get me to give him a line of coke, which makes him rather chatty.

"Remember that time I gave everyone the crabs?" he says. "I bet I've had crabs more than any other human being. One look at my pubes, and the little fuckers jump right on."

"You're not itching now, are you?"

"No." He laughs. "No, I'm not. But I keep thinking about that Sunday dinner. The whole family sitting around the table scratching at themselves—you, me, Hortense, Aunt Edie, Uncle Charles, Norm, Doll—and nobody realizing what it was. It took Stellrita coming in from the kitchen holding one of the pests between her thumb and fingernail, cursin', 'Damn white folks done given me lice! If I've carried 'em home to my peoples, there's gonna be hell to pay!' That was some Kwell party."

"Not to mention the amount of laundry that had to be done."

"It's amazing they never thought to pin it on us."

"Really. We got blamed for everything else."

"And we *had* been doing it in a variety of beds."

"Crabs get on toilet seats, too."

"We had us some fun."

"Two little devils." I pause. "Do you think about our family much?"

"Not much. Do you?"

"When I'm with 'em. Do you think about me?"

"Of course. Need you even ask?"

"Well, you never know. We had quite an affair. At least, it seemed like quite an affair to me."

"To me, too, Zero."

"I know I've done a lot of complaining, but I wouldn't trade you for anything, Trebreh. I've often wondered what my life would've been like had we stayed together."

"L.A.'s not the place for you."

"I was so devastated when you left. I couldn't believe you didn't ask me to go with you."

"You had another year of school."

"I still would've gone."

"Maybe that's why I didn't ask."

"You were my first love, my first lay—"

"And your first cousin."

"Three firsts all rolled into one." I pause. "When I was in Arkansas last February, I got Stellrita to let me spend the night in my old room."

"She's opened up the house?"

"According to her own discretion. And she charges. But you wouldn't believe how little it's changed, aside from twenty years' worth of dust. Anyway, I brought you something I found in my room."

"What?"

THE PRESSURE OF DREAMS

I pull it out of my pocket. It's an old black-and-white Swinger Polaroid that we took of ourselves at Calion. Treb was seventeen; I was fifteen. Two big heads just grinning.

Trebreh holds it up and looks at it. "So young and so fresh," he says.

"We were young and fresh."

He puts it facedown on his chest and sighs.

"I haven't had crabs in years."

With his hands still on the picture, he shuts his eyes and drifts off.

I scan the bookshelves for something to read. I spot an old copy of *Auntie Mame* and take it down. I've read it many times, but I'll read it again. *"It has rained all day. Not that I mind rain . . ."*

On page eighty, as Mame is preparing for the fox hunt, Trebreh opens his eyes.

"What's all the furniture doing on the ceiling?" he asks.

"The furniture's not on the ceiling."

"It's not?"

"No."

"Give me another line of coke," he says impatiently.

I get it and hold it up to his nose with a straw.

"Eight shows a day," he mutters, "and I'm supposed to come at each one. Jesus Christ!"

He takes a few labored breaths.

"One time I was in this porn house, sitting in the audience, watching one of my movies. I was going down on the mailman, getting fucked by the plumber. I wasn't half bad, you know?"

"You're one of the few in the business who can read a line."

"I was jacking off some guy sitting next to me. I had just been diagnosed, and this is where I went to ask myself why sex was so important. Then the guy came all over my hand, which made me forget everything; it always happens."

He fingers the photo, having forgotten he had it in his hand. He looks at it.

"I was thinking about that time we were staying in the Village at my ex-manager's apartment."

"Now, that was a jolly holiday. I don't appreciate that kind of thing, Trebreh. You told me he was in L.A. and had offered you his pad."

"I had duped his keys. Smart, huh?"

"Yeah, real smart. But you weren't the one soaking in the bathtub when he showed up with his wife."

"They liked Christmas in New York. I had forgotten that part. They liked snow."

"I could've been killed."

"But you weren't."

"That man had never even met me. I got out of the tub, wrapped myself in a towel, and explained that I was with you. That really thrilled him. 'Where is Trebreh?' he demanded.

" 'Down doin' his gig.'

" 'Fucking imbecile,' he muttered and started out the door.

" 'Wait, I'll go with you,' I said."

"Fucking ex-manager. I was in the middle of my sixth show. He storms backstage and throws on the fucking houselights. The patrons scattered out of there like rats, poor suckers, stuffing themselves back in their pants. And we were having fun. I was just doin' my job. That was the only time that bastard ever got the best of me. There I was, sitting on the stage in my jockstrap, just crying my eyes out. And the only person left in the audience was you." Trebreh gulps to catch his breath.

"Don't overdo it, hey?"

"What the hell?" he says, motioning for another line.

"Are you sure?"

"Addiction is the least of my worries, Zero. Give it to me."

Then he continues. "You rose from your seat. Walked down the aisle. Up on the stage. Your shoes echoing on the floor. Did you ever think of becoming a tap dancer?"

"Only in my dreams."

He smiles. "Then you reached out and took my hand. It was that simple. You didn't judge me. You could've, you had every right to, but you didn't. You just said—"

" 'We all make mistakes.' "

"Yes."

He glances around. Notices the book in my lap and asks, "What're you reading?"

THE PRESSURE OF DREAMS

"Auntie Mame."

"Roz Russell," he says. "Paramount Pictures. Nineteen fifty-eight. See? I'm not as crazy as you think."

"I don't think you're crazy."

"Shows how much you know."

We both laugh.

He sniffs a couple of times, then asks, "How's your health?"

"I'm working on it."

"You're seropositive?"

"Of course."

"How many T cells?"

"Ninety, last count."

"Are you on anything?"

"Sure." I run down my list of drugs.

Trebreh nods.

"What's doing in Toronto? Funny place for you to end up, isn't it?"

"It just sort of happened. I originally went to visit my friend Randy. Then I met David and there I was. I'm writing a column for a magazine now, a sort of serial. It's by far the best job I've ever had. Plus, I have a new love."

"Still writing plays?"

"Not at the moment. I think I've finally found my niche with my column. There's even talk about publishing the episodes as a book."

"When?"

"As soon as there's a buyer."

"Wouldn't I love to have a copy?"

"I'll send you one."

"I hope it's very soon."

His eyes hold a far-off gaze. I wait for him to come back.

"I'm at peace with myself," he says.

"I know. But then again, you always have been."

"Thanks a lot for the picture."

"You're welcome."

"Feels so good just to have us in my hand."

* * *

May 1990

Big Ellen's arrival the next morning wakes us both. I've been dozing in the chair. My body is cramped; my legs tingle with pins and needles.

Trebreh just groans. "Morphine, Big Ellen, morphine."

"In a minute," she says.

"What time is it?" I ask.

"Nine o'clock," says Trebreh. "At least. If I feel like this, it must be nine."

"Is there coffee?" I ask.

"Should be," says Big Ellen.

I go into the kitchen to put some on.

Big Ellen opens a few windows. "It's a beautiful day. Get a whiff of that air."

"Stinks in here," says Trebreh. "Smells like shit."

"It is a little smelly," Big Ellen concedes. "Ready for me to change you?"

"I'm ready for some morphine."

"You'll get the morphine as soon as I clean you up."

"How'd it go?" Jeff asks when I get back to Charlotte's.

"It's going," I say.

He kisses me. It's meant to be a comforting kiss, a small kiss, but it quickly turns hot.

I pull back.

"Sorry," he says.

"There's nothing to be sorry about."

"I don't want to suffocate you."

"Far from it, Jeff."

"What time does your uncle's plane get in?"

"Three."

"Is he gonna go right over there?"

"Yeah."

"Think you can get some sleep today?"

"If I drug myself."

We look at each other, a look full of longing and love. A look that says: This will be over soon and life will return to some semblance of normalcy if we can just hold on.

189

THE PRESSURE OF DREAMS

I open my medicine bag and swallow a couple of sleeping pills. "So much for our little getaway, huh?"

"Don't worry about it, Zero, don't worry about it at all."

I reach for his hand. Kiss it. "What'll you do all day?"

"I don't know. Maybe I'll check out Westwood."

The death scene begins with a champagne feast that Uncle Markus has had catered. I get over there about five-thirty and find them all drinking, hovering around Trebreh's bed, eating. The picnic basket is a Southerner's dream: fried chicken, milk gravy, mashed potatoes, turnip greens, cornbread, the works. Trebreh greets me with, "Zero, you finally made it."

"Yeah. Looks like quite a banquet."

"My last supper," he says with some amusement.

"So everything's prepared?" I ask.

"The doctor was here earlier," says Big Ellen. "He left us the goods."

"One glorious syringe," says Trebreh. "Most people have to take a gob of Seconal. Luckily, my doctor's a friend, so I get the quick method."

"I was just noticing these champagne flutes," says Uncle Markus. "They belonged to your mother, did they not?"

"They did," says Trebreh. "I have her china as well."

Uncle Markus inspects the crystal before pouring himself another glass. "A lovely pattern," he murmurs. "I remember it well. Before Lydia married, Mother—your grandmother Hortense—had all the wedding gifts spread throughout the entire front rooms. Not so much for people to admire, but so each guest would know exactly what the others had given. Mother presided over Lydia's wedding like a witch."

"She didn't want her to marry my father," says Trebreh.

"But Mother wasn't the one marrying him," says Uncle Markus. "Of course, when Grover came back crazy from Korea, I don't think even *Lydia* really wanted to go through with it, except that she had already agreed to, and she knew how much it would anger Mother."

"It was her way out," says Trebreh. "It breaks my heart to think she ended up back in that house."

"She was always depressed," says Uncle Markus. "Even as a child. She cried all the time. Over anything."

"She was a poet," says Trebreh. "And terribly out of place."

"To hear you tell it," says Mary Bull, "this Hortense woman didn't get along with anybody."

"She got along with me," says my uncle. "I dare say we were even close. As close as she could be to anybody who wasn't a card-playing partner or a drinking buddy."

"Don't be so humble," I interject. "You were her eldest and brightest. Hortense knew if any of her children could take care of themselves, it'd be you."

"You flatter me, Zero." Uncle Markus hands me a fresh bottle of bubbly. "Would you do the honors? You were a pretty good waiter once."

"Of all the jobs I've done, that's the one he remembers."

"Don't be so sensitive," he says. "I remember many things."

"Zero always was such a sensitive thing," teases Treb.

With the base of the bottle against my thigh and the neck almost parallel to the floor, I pull off the wrapping, then ease the cork out with my thumbs, carefully. *Pop!*

"Well done!" says Uncle Markus. "Pour, my boy. Pour!"

"I'm gonna try that method," says Big Ellen, "come next New Year's Eve."

"More for you?" I ask Treb.

"Please. Half a glass," he says. "That's enough. But I'll have some coke if you'd get some ready for me."

"There's a couple of lines right over here," says Big Ellen.

"To Trebreh," says my uncle, "who's lived a most fascinating, full, and charmed life."

"Charmed?" asks Trebreh cynically, between toots.

"Yes," says Uncle Markus. "Charmed. You've worked hard. Had a splendid career, one I have followed with a keen and curious eye. You've spent most of your life in an absolutely gorgeous body. You've had your share of loving. And you've certainly been loved."

"Why, Uncle Markus," says Trebreh. "I've never heard you sing my praises quite so freely."

"Which just goes to show even an old fuddy-duddy like me can change. It started when I broke my hip."

THE PRESSURE OF DREAMS

"And how *is* Miss Jesus Las Vegas?" I ask.

"Couldn't be better. Sends his love. *Pork Chop* is a smashing success. I've got him under contract until the end of the year. I'll lose him eventually, but until I do I intend to work him for all he's worth." Uncle Markus giggles, then takes a sip of champagne. "Superb," he declares. "Absolutely superb!"

"Yeah, it is pretty good," says Big Ellen, gulping hers back. "Pour me another one, will ya?"

"The food's great too," says Mary Bull, devouring another piece of chicken.

"So glad to please," says Uncle Markus.

"What about dessert? You know my dad loves dessert."

"Yes," says Uncle Markus, producing a tin of tarts, holding them up like a prize trophy.

"Stellrita's lemon tarts?" asks Trebreh.

"Stellrita's recipe," says Uncle Markus.

"Let me have one. Quick. And I'll tell you if they're as good as hers." He eats it, savors it. "Almost," he says. "Give me another one."

"You must have ordered all this stuff before you left Florida," says Big Ellen.

"Any law against that?"

"I'm just impressed," she says. "I like a man who knows how to prepare for things."

"I don't make that claim, Big Ellen, but I do know how to call a caterer."

"Another," says Trebreh.

"God," says Big Ellen, "lemon tarts, chicken, greens. That's more than you've eaten in a week."

"Hell, I won't have to live with the indigestion or the gas, and I probably won't be around long enough to throw anything up."

Big Ellen laughs. "That's one way of looking at it."

Trebreh leans back against his pillow.

He sighs, change of mood.

He tells himself the date, the time, then says, "Thirty-seven years old. I guess that's not so bad, huh?"

"No," says Big Ellen. "In many parts of the world it's the average life span."

Trebreh attempts to brush the food crumbs off of his chest, then finishes his champagne. He looks from one of us to the other and says, "Good life, good death. Okay, Big Ellen. I'm ready."

"You don't have to watch this," Big Ellen tells us. "But if you do, you have to swear you never saw a thing."

She ties a tourniquet around Trebreh's slender arm. "Make a fist," she says quietly. From the bedside-table drawer she takes an alcohol swab and a syringe.

"I have to be the one to do it," says Trebreh. "Just help me get the needle in the vein."

Big Ellen taps his arm. "That looks like a pretty good one right there." She dabs it with the swab. "Once you get the needle in, draw it out some to make sure there's blood. That's how you know you've got a vein."

Very shakily, Trebreh pierces his skin. "Draw it out," he says. "I haven't got the strength to pull it."

She does so. "There's your blood. You're all set. Whenever you're ready."

"I'm ready. Thanks for being here, everybody."

Trebreh pushes in the lethal serum. The effect is seemingly painless and almost immediate. Big Ellen removes the syringe, disposes of it, then straightens Trebreh's head on the pillow. She pulls the bed sheet up under his arms. Smooths his hair across his forehead.

"Such an angel," says Uncle Markus. "How I've always loved him."

"Oh god," sobs Mary Bull.

Big Ellen gets up and walks out onto the porch. Mary Bull follows her.

"Nothing like a little fresh air," says Big Ellen.

"Nothing like it," says Mary Bull.

"This crazy life," Uncle Markus cries, shaking his head. "I'm so glad you called me, Zero."

"I'm glad you came."

"Would you give me a minute alone with him?"

"Sure."

Uncle Markus starts to get out of his chair but totters back down.

"You okay?"

"Just hadn't realized how tired I was," he says, making a second attempt. "I hardly slept last night. And I can never sleep on planes. But I'm fine, yes."

"I'll be outside, Uncle Markus."

"Thank you."

I sit on the steps with Big Ellen and Mary Bull.

Numb.

About eleven-thirty, I return to the guesthouse. Jeff is in bed with the television on: what looks like a giant drag queen is going on about washers and dryers. But the sound is muted. "It's in Spanish," he says, sitting up, hugging his knees to his chest. "Everything taken care of?"

"We ushered him out." I sit down next to Jeff. "A doctor friend of his came by and signed the death certificate. Trebreh belonged to something called The Simple Way. They do it all: pick up the body, file the paperwork, take him to the crematorium."

"Smart guy, your cousin."

"Big Ellen cleaned him up. Dressed him in a faded red T-shirt and an old pair of jeans. I just can't believe it. I just can't believe he's really gone."

Jeff snuggles me to him, comforting.

"Did you get out to Westwood?" I ask.

"Yeah. Walked around the campus. Found a practice room and played piano for several hours. I really needed that. Then I took a bus up Hollywood Boulevard and went to a movie at the Chinese Theatre."

"What was it like?"

"The theatre? Impressive. Chinese Deco galore. Grand, spitting clean. There were only about five of us in there watching the show. Have you ever been?"

"Just to see the footprints out front."

"Well, you must go sometime."

He strokes my neck, the back of my head. I shut my eyes. It feels so good.

"I've been thinking about you a lot," he says quietly.

"I know."

I try to smile, to give something back, but I just shrug.

May 1990

"Let's go to sleep," Jeff whispers.
"Wonderful idea."

I wake the next morning with a pleasant, groggy, forgetful feeling. I feel Jeff lying next to me. Hear birds chirping. See the California sun beating against the windowpane and Charlotte's mutant flowers pushing against the glass.

Then the phone rings. Which makes me jump. Bringing me back to some kind of reality.

Jeff sleepily picks up the receiver and hands it to me.

I fumble with it. "Hello?"

"Morning, Zero."

"Hi, Uncle Markus. Get some rest?"

"Indeed. Did you?"

"Yeah. In fact, I'm just waking up."

"Have I called too early?"

"It's okay."

"I've spoken to Big Ellen. She and Mary Bull are over at Trebreh's. I think we should join them. Should I call a cab?"

"No, I'll come for you. In about an hour, okay?"

"About nine, then?"

"Yes, about nine."

I hand the receiver back to Jeff.

He puts it away, then props himself up on his elbow, looking at me.

I notice his mop of hair standing on end.

"You should see yourself," I say.

"Am I too beautiful?" he asks.

"Too," I say.

He tackles me.

I fight back with nothing but affection.

Trebreh is gone. I don't know why, but I expected him to still be there. Laid out on top of the bed. Not the happiest corpse you've ever seen, but considering what he's been through, not half bad.

THE PRESSURE OF DREAMS

Big Ellen and Mary Bull sit at the kitchen table, eating donuts and drinking coffee.

"When did they come for him?" I ask.

" 'Bout half hour ago," Big Ellen says.

I've got to get out of there. I offer no explanation. I just walk out the door and back to the rent-a-car.

Uncle Markus follows me.

I get in behind the wheel and put the key in the ignition.

Uncle Markus eases himself into the passenger's side, saying nothing, which I appreciate.

I pull out of the parking place and roll down my window. I speed up the street, the warm air blowing against my face.

At Sunset, I turn right.

The traffic is maddening. I turn up into the hills and drive a good ways, eventually reaching a stop sign at Mulholland Drive.

"Didn't Hockney paint this?"

"Yes," says Uncle Markus. " 'Mulholland Drive: the road to the studio.' They have it in the County Museum. We should go see it."

I turn right on the road.

We snake along, the city below us. Eventually, we go over a freeway and end up in a residential section. I keep taking whatever turn seems to lead uphill. Then we come to a dead end with a small parking area and a vista of the reservoir, the mountains, and the Hollywood sign.

"Park," says Uncle Markus, "I wish to pay homage."

"To what? The sign?"

"Yes. To a culture where one gigantic word has the power to engender so many dreams."

I get out of the car and sit on the hood. Lie back, arms spread, and look at the sky.

Uncle Markus gingerly takes a seat beside me.

Several times he begins to speak, but doesn't. I'm glad. Then, finally, he emits a great sigh and bursts out with, "When I was a young man, I did everything I could to divert my sexuality. I was ashamed. I wasn't always. But I became ashamed by something that happened when I was teaching at a college in Louisiana. It was my first job. I fell in love with one of my drama students. A boy of nineteen from Gulfport. We thought nothing could come between us.

May 1990

"We did little to hide our affection. Not that we ran around holding hands, we were discreet, mind you. Yet anyone with a lick of sense could certainly tell the state we were in.

"It started in October and ended in March. One day, the boy failed to show up for class. I called his dormitory, wondering if he was sick. His roommate told me he had quit school and gone home. I was simply stunned. I could barely hang up the receiver. Why hadn't he told me. Why?

"I had a woman friend who worked in the registrar's office. She looked up his parents' name, actually his mother's, and gave me her phone number. I called.

"His mother was very brisk, rude really. She said Bobby wasn't there and hung up.

"I called her right back. 'Please,' I said. 'I just want to know where he is.'

" 'Stop calling here!' she said more forcefully, and again, hung up.

"A few days later, I learned from my friend in the registrar's office that the dean had become aware of our affair and expelled the boy.

"I was furious, though I did my best not to let it show. I called the boy's mother again. I had to know where he was.

" 'Bobby shot himself,' she said bluntly. 'Now please stop calling here.'

"Shot himself. That moment seeded a bitterness in me that took years to get over. I'm still not entirely free of it. Even now, when tragic things happen, it all comes back as though it were yesterday.

"At the end of the term, my contract wasn't renewed, no surprise, and I moved to New York that summer. I met scads of homosexuals there. They all seemed so light and gay, so totally void of seriousness, so completely unconcerned with what life was capable of doing to us beyond the microcosm of a few select bars. Of course, I was wrong. But I was too young to understand that gaiety is the greatest mask of sorrow.

"So I drank a lot. I sat in those bars and watched the beautiful and the hideous come and go. I watched them with equal contempt. I practiced hating. For Bobby. I wished everyone would lose the thing they most loved. It became a curse, a prayer. I didn't get over it until

THE PRESSURE OF DREAMS

Jack came into my life. Yet, every time I see someone die in this hideous, horrible plague, I have the sickest feeling that it's my wish coming true."

"Uncle Markus, for godsake, you didn't invent AIDS."

"I'd go through that call to Bobby's mother a hundred times over if I could just stop some of the suffering."

"Well, you can't. Not like that. You can only be there. You know," I say, "someday it's gonna happen to me."

"Don't say that, Zero."

"It's true. I keep getting worse, not better."

"You just hold on. You hold on, my boy. You never know what might happen."

I want to tell him I've got a pretty good idea, but I don't.

I just pause and take a deep breath.

My first instinct is to return to Toronto early, but Jeff convinces me to ride out the week.

We go to the beach. Walk, relax. Take in a few museums before Uncle Markus goes home to Florida. And help Big Ellen clean out Trebreh's.

We see *Into the Woods* two more times. Once with Uncle Markus, who's tickled pink with Mary Bull's performance, and again with Big Ellen and Ginger.

Friday morning, we're off to scatter Trebreh's ashes. Big Ellen swings by Charlotte's to pick us up. Ginger comes along as well. Mary Bull, though, has declined, afraid we might not be back in time for her seven o'clock call. And Lord knows, the show must go on.

We drive for several hours to the Anza-Borrego Desert. It's just past its bloom, with new growth on the cacti and sweeps of faded flowers gathered in the sand.

"Your cousin spent a lot of time here," says Big Ellen. "Really had a thing for this place."

She pulls off the road three-quarters of the way up a mountain. "He used to climb this sucker. Right up to the top. You can see the coast on one side and the desert valley on the other. This is the place we'll do it."

"All the way to the top?" asks Ginger.

"No, honey. Just up the trail a ways."

With the box of the ashes under her arm, Big Ellen climbs out of the van.

"God, Big Ellen, you should have told me we was gonna be hiking. I would've brung my boots."

"Don't need no boots, honey. Sneakers are fine. Just stay on the path."

"How far up did you say we were going?" I didn't realize how out of shape I was.

"Not that far. Geez, what a bunch of babies." Big Ellen stops and looks at us. "Hell, I guess this spot's as good as any."

With no ceremony whatsoever, she opens the box, then the plastic bag inside of it.

"I've never been one to bandy words," she says, "so here goes."

She dumps the ashes into a neat little pile on the ground.

"Is that all there is to it?" asks Ginger.

"Yep. Mother Nature will take it from here. Well. No sense hanging around." She shrugs, then heads back down the trail at a fast pace, the empty box swinging at her side.

Ginger hops along behind her. "Wait up, Big Ellen. What are you running, a race?"

"I've done what I came to do and I'm ready to go home."

Jeff and I are still standing by the ashes. "Do it," he says.

I pull a Baggie out of my pocket and grab a handful. Just in case.

We get back to Toronto at seven-thirty Saturday evening, both full of a sluggish melancholy, having slept through most of the flight. We go through Immigration, get our bags, then head outside to flag a car.

"You wanna come over?" I ask Jeff, as the driver pulls onto the expressway. "You're more than welcome."

"Sure, but I want to go home first. Get unpacked. Get myself reoriented."

I take his hand. "But I'll see you later?"

"You'll see me later."

We spend the remainder of the ride in silence, watching the lake, the traffic, and our city.

THE PRESSURE OF DREAMS

* * *

David and Lance have left flowers on my table and a note that says, "Welcome home."

I set my bags down, grab a joint, light it, then sort through the pile of mail that's gathered in my absence. I set most of it aside. What I look at is a change-of-address card from Alan in Vancouver. Along the bottom, where you're not supposed to write a personal message, he's scribbled, "New address, new life. Still no word about the movie. How are you?"

How am I? I ask myself, walking out on the deck, thinking about it. I take a seat in my rocking chair and puff on the joint.

What comes to mind is the smell of an old cedar chest. How good it feels to finish something. An old jazz standard that makes me weep, and at the same time fills me with joy. The people I've met, quite by accident, who've changed my life forever.

Alan, I could say I'm a void. A simple filter. But basically, I just have the blues.

"Where are you?" calls Jeff, coming into the apartment. I can hear him kicking off his shoes.

"In the bedroom."

"Nice place to find you. Feeling better?"

"Some."

He takes off his T-shirt, steps out of his jeans; pulls off his socks, and then his underwear.

"You are some beautiful sight."

"Thanks." He crawls beneath the covers.

We twine around each other like snakes.

I don't know where we get the energy, but we end up in the longest, most passionate lovemaking session of our entire career.

We collapse in a sweaty, sticky heap and sleep without dreams.

When I wake the next day, it's early in the afternoon. Jeff is still out cold, so I grab my clothes and creep out quietly.

After a quick coffee, a bath, and a bite to eat, I leave him a note that says, "There's some business I need to attend to. Be back in plenty of time for Searcy's show. XO. Z."

200

*   *   *

Searcy is in the auditorium of the 519, high atop a ladder, helping some technicians focus lights.

"Zero," he says, "you're just in time. Hon, we need all the help we can get."

"Sorry, Searce, but I can't stay. I just stopped by to see if I could borrow your car."

"My car?"

"If you don't mind."

"I don't mind." He reaches into the pocket of his pantaloons and tosses me the keys. "But don't forget, I need you here by six."

"I'll be here. Where're you parked?"

"Up Church by Isabella."

"Thanks a lot, Searce. I appreciate it."

"No problem, hon. No problem at all."

I drive down to St. Catharine's, about an hour and a half south of Toronto, and take the freeway exit Dorothy described in the note she sent.

The exit takes me along an access road. A few miles later, I come to the cemetery gates. I stop at the office and ask the caretaker for directions.

He's eating an egg-salad sandwich and talks to me as he chews. "Who you looking for?"

"Randall Evans."

"You mean 'Scandal Evans.' " He laughs mightily, spraying me with bits of sandwich, which I carefully pick off. "Yeah, go around the second bend, take the first left, and you'll find him under a clump of oaks."

"Thanks." I start to walk out.

"Wait a minute." He bangs on the donation box. "It's customary. Helps maintain the place."

"What about my shirt?" I ask, as I toss in a loonie, then head back to the car.

There's a big monument with the Evans name. I park and get out.

THE PRESSURE OF DREAMS

I search through the family members for my friend.

Randy's marker is nothing special, just a simple concrete slab two feet high and a couple of inches thick. "Randall Evans," it says, "1950–1989." Then, in extremely tiny type, way down at the bottom, is his epitaph: "If there were options in the air, my legs were right up there with 'em."

I have to laugh. Imagine all that angst over this silly little phrase. The things we think are so important.

"It *is* important," says the five-inch Randy, stepping out from behind the stone. "Can you believe I was stupid enough not to specify a type-point-size? You can never trust the living, Zero. Especially when they outlive you."

"Well, at least it's there."

"Yeah, at least."

The sight of him makes me smile. "I've been thinking about you," I say.

"I know."

"You're looking good."

"At five inches? Give me a fucking break! Why don't you set me on top of my marker so I can see you better? But don't grip too hard. I'm delicate and I'd hate for you to squash me."

"Don't worry," I say, picking him up, "I won't squash you."

He sits with his legs crossed, so distinguished, and lights a tiny cigarette.

"You've started smoking again?"

"Sure. It can't hurt me now."

"I guess not." I pause for a moment. "So what's it like, the afterlife?"

"Oh, more of the same. I had breakfast with a bunch of the Toronto boys this morning."

"Really, who?"

"Tim, the three Bills, Tom, Dan, the four Michaels, Carlos, René. They all asked about you."

"Me? Why would they ask about me?"

"I don't know. Maybe because they knew we were friends."

"You don't mean to say my time's up?"

"I don't have that kind of information, Zero." He puffs on the cigarette. "But it's nothing to worry about."

May 1990

"Easy for you to say."

"Believe me, when the time comes you'll be ready."

"Will I?"

"Yes. You will." He stubs out the cigarette. "You really wouldn't believe how integral it all is. This world, that. Life, death."

"If that's true, then what should we do, those of us still living, to stay in touch with those already gone?"

Slyly, Randy smiles. With his index finger he points to one side of his head and says, "Memory." Then he points to the other side and says, "Imagination."

Of course, I say to myself, repeating the words silently, and smiling.

"That's all I can say." He shrugs. "But I think it started for me when you gave some of my ashes to that old mammy of yours."

"To Stellrita?"

"Yeah. She's one of my links. As are you. But then again, you're almost the same person."

"Wait a minute, Randy, this is getting a little confounded. What do you mean we're almost the same person?"

"Memory and imagination," he repeats.

He starts to disappear, like a cartoon character slowly being erased.

"Wait!" I call.

Too late. He's become more and more transparent.

Damn, I curse. I at least wanted to take him back to town to see Searcy's show.

And the moment that thought passes through my mind, I hear his voice clearly whisper, "I'll be there."

Searcy sits in his makeshift dressing room, panty hose pulled up over his big belly and a D-cup brassiere strapped onto his chest.

"Some beauty," I say, tossing him his keys.

"Don't harass me, Zero. I'm nervous enough as it is."

"You? Nervous? I don't believe it."

"We just ran the first act and things did not go well."

"No?"

"Too much dead time between numbers. The queens catfighting

over the order of appearance. And that goddamn Misty Morning refused to rehearse his routine. Said it would spoil him for tonight. So unprofessional. It'll be his own damn fault when the spotlight can't keep up with him. This is my last show, Zero. I swear it!"

"You say that at every dress rehearsal."

"Well, I mean it this time!" He picks up his powder puff and swats at his cheeks.

"I filled your car up with gas."

"You didn't have to do that."

"I drove all the way to St. Catharine's and back, so I thought it only fair."

"What were you doing in St. Catharine's?"

"Checking out Randy's marker."

"Oh? And how was it?"

"Nothing special." I glance over my shoulder to make sure no one can hear me. "Searcy," I confide. "I know this is gonna sound weird, but Randy was there."

"There? Impossible! He was cremated. You know he's not there."

"I don't mean his remains. I mean this five-inch version of him."

"A five-inch version?"

"I've seen it several times in my head, but this was the first time in person. Searcy, we had such a talk."

"I'm sure you did. And I'm so glad you decided to share this with me. Why, the next time I see a Lilliputian, you'll be the first one I call."

"I'm not making this up."

"Five inches, indeed!" Searcy reaches for his satchel, fishes out a bottle of pills, and palms me two tranquilizers. "Take ye, eat ye. That is my sole advice."

"I don't need these!" I hand them back.

"No? Then maybe I do." Searcy swallows them without water. He picks up his mascara and starts touching up his lashes.

"I think you could benefit from some counseling, Zero."

"I've dealt with this just fine, thank you very much."

"That, hon, is a matter of opinion."

"Oh, really? I'd say I've dealt with it so well I deserve a medal."

"Who doesn't?"

"Okay, fine. Since you don't believe me, you force me to show you my trump card, a Polaroid I took at the cemetery." I pull it from my pocket and hand it to him. "See? That's Randy's marker and there's the five-inch Randy sitting right on top of it."

Searcy examines it closely, then hands it back. "That is *not* Randall. That's one of those Pee-wee Herman gumby dolls."

"It is not. It's him!"

"Why are you doing this to me, Zero? Why, on today of all days? I just haven't got time for it!"

"Well, I'm sorry to have disturbed you," I snap. "I thought you might be interested. He was your friend, too."

"I am interested. I'm fascinated. Nothing thrills me more than the occult. But at the moment, I'm on the verge of a nervous breakdown! Tell you what, tomorrow I'll come over to your place and bring my Ouija board. Or we can have a séance. Whatever you like—"

Lance dashes into the dressing room. "Searcy, come quick. Something's happened to the Celebrity AIDS Person."

Searcy slams down his mascara. "What now?!" He rises from the dressing table, not bothering to throw on his kimono, and follows Lance.

In another makeshift dressing room, the Celebrity AIDS Person is laid out on the floor. He's in full costume: beaded red dress and blond wig, with red feather plumes slightly askew.

Searcy feels for a pulse. Nothing. He bangs on the Celebrity's chest. Nothing. He tries artificial respiration. Nothing.

"Well, isn't that just great?" says Searcy. "The son of a bitch has gone and died on us."

"Oh god!" says Lance. "What are we gonna do?"

An evil smile crosses Searcy's face. "Get a phone book and look under *T* for taxidermist."

"Are you serious?" asks Lance. "Is he serious?"

"I have built the entire finale around his entrance. You could wheel him out, Lance. We could just say he's resting. Set the donation bucket in his lap—"

"You can't put a dead man onstage!" says Lance, aghast.

"You're right," says Searcy, "it's been done a thousand times."

"Listen, I think I saw my doctor," I say. "I'll go get him."

THE PRESSURE OF DREAMS

"Yes," says Searcy. "He's one of the volunteers. As is that hairless hunk, Garth. Let one of them deal with this. I've got enough to do!"

Grandly, Searcy walks out.

I find my doctor and lead him to the dressing room. He bends down to examine the Celebrity AIDS Person and says to me in a quiet aside, "I got your test results back, Zero. You'd better come see me first thing next week."

Slowly, I walk home. Not wanting to think. Not wanting to do anything.

Jeff sits at the kitchen table in his underwear, looking like he just crawled out of bed. But the newspaper has been read and discarded, there is a touch of cold coffee in the bottom of his cup, and he is sketching. "Hey there," he says.

"Hi. What are you drawing?"

"Plans for your garden. Tomorrow's the day I get to work on it."

"Really?" I glance at the sketch. "Looks great. I'll help you."

"I thought you weren't the gardening type."

"I've changed."

He grins.

I wander over to the stereo, squat down, and look through my records. I pull out an old Julie Mercer and set it spinning on "It's Only a Paper Moon."

No one ever sings the intro, but Julie does. I stand in the middle of the room, listening to the lyrics.

"Dance with me," I say to Jeff.

He sets his pencil aside, eyes sparkling, and pushes himself up from the table.

As we move to the beat of the refrain, I rest my head against his shoulder, running my hands up and down the soft of his back. "You feel so good," I whisper. "So warm and so alive."

"Lucky thing." He laughs.

"I just can't hold you tight enough."

"I'm not going anywhere, Zero."

"I'm counting on that."
"And I'm counting on you."
"My sweetheart—"
"Dance."

Doug Wilson

Peter McGehee's first novel, *Boys Like Us*, was published in February 1991 by HarperCollins in Canada and St. Martin's Press in the U.S.A. He was the author of two collections of stories, *Beyond Happiness* (Stubblejumper Press) and *The I.Q. Zoo* (Coteau Press). He wrote the music and lyrics for, and performed in, the musical revues *The Quinlan Sisters* and *The Fabulous Sirs*, both of which toured extensively. His short stories appeared in a wide range of North American periodicals and anthologies.

Originally from Arkansas, Peter lived in Dallas, San Francisco, Saskatoon, New York, and, most recently, Toronto. He died peacefully at home, September 13, 1991, from complications resulting from AIDS.